S

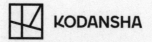

S

(Es)

Koji Suzuki

Translation
Greg Gencorello

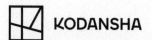 KODANSHA

S: Es

A VERTICAL Book

English language version produced by Kodansha USA Publishing, LLC, 2024.

Originally published in Japan as *Esu* by KADOKAWA CORPORATION, Tokyo, 2012, and reissued in paperback in 2013.

Previously issued in English in hardcover in 2017.

ISBN 978-1-64729-403-8

Printed in the United States of America

First Paperback Edition

www.kodansha.us

 KODANSHA

Table of Contents

Prologue

The room was a little over 200 square feet in size. There was a desk set against one of the walls, and on top were a black rectangular object that looked to be a chestnut red bean jelly, a cup of green tea with steam coming out of it, and a notebook.

Pulling out the chair, Kashiwada sat down and closed his eyes.

The notebook was one thing, but he didn't feel like reaching for the jelly or the tea at all. Sweet things weren't his favorite, and he wasn't in the habit of drinking green tea. To be one of those people who can be satisfied with drinking tea and eating snacks in their final moments on earth—that was the last thing he wanted.

Facing his imminent death, he needed to clear his mind. This ordeal was something he'd gone through once before. *I'm like an ant falling into a pit trap...but I'm not scared. I just feel empty.*

Wait a minute. What's giving the room this unusual mood?

His nose twitched as he sniffed the room, and when he opened his eyes, it suddenly hit him.

It's the color.

What dominated the room was this nice, soft color rising from the floor around his feet. As he felt the softness of the carpet through the soles of his shoes, it seemed like his vision was being enveloped by a purple veil. He wanted to know why the color of the carpet was purple, if there was a reason.

Maybe the color purple was associated with the underworld, on the other side of the Sanzu River or the Styx. When this room was

9

designed and built, and the carpet color was chosen, the builder's intention must have been involved somehow. Why was purple chosen? What did the color stand for?

Kashiwada's pet theory was that symbols were important, always.

On his right side, a Buddhist painting of the bodhisattva Kannon was hanging on the wall, with an altar placed in front. He clicked his tongue when he saw the Amida Buddha figure enshrined on the altar, but the sound didn't reach the head prison guard, the prosecutor, or the prison chaplain.

Kannon, Amida Buddha...those were also symbols, no doubt.

The notebook on the desk was all blank inside, and he was free to write anything he wanted. Maybe he could draw a picture, or write something down, he supposed.

He snapped off the lead of his sharpened pencil and licked it with the tip of his tongue, as if he were breathing life into it. He licked the pencil to make it round, and after it had absorbed his saliva and softened enough, he put it to the paper.

He started drawing a curve, moving his hand slowly from top to bottom.

It looked like a snake wriggling, but also like a hangman's rope that had come undone.

When they'd asked him whether he had any last words, he'd lowered his head to show his intent, and so they'd given him this notebook. What he wrote in it was a large letter "S."

It was nothing but a little act of mischief. He wanted to ask every person there if they could understand what the symbol meant.

The head prison guard Sahara peeked in at Kashiwada's notebook, and almost at the same time, looked down at his wristwatch.

Guess it's about time, huh?

Still gripping the pencil, Kashiwada had already stopped moving. In Sahara's eyes, the figure written in the notebook looked like the letter "S" for sure, but it was so big that it seemed weird somehow.

Or maybe Kashiwada had tried to draw some meaningful figure, but he'd just stopped drawing before finishing it...

Sahara tried to ignore his curiosity about what Kashiwada really wanted to say. If the last words he wanted to leave in this world before dying were just one letter, he must have put a number of meanings into the shape. He must have boiled all his thoughts down into an abstraction.

Wanting to know more about it stressed him out. If he could get rid of his curiosity, his mind could be at peace.

After Kashiwada's arrest and the commencement of the court trial, tests had been conducted repeatedly by more than ten psychiatrists and clinical psychologists. Even having spent almost ten years on him, on studying his mental condition from various angles, they'd never been able to reach a unified judgment.

Ironically, it seemed like the harder they had questioned him to get at his motive for the crime, the deeper the truth had gotten lost in the darkness. As if reflecting this, all the newspaper headlines had run the same set phrase.

"The darkness of his mind only grows deeper..."

Even now, his motive for the crime remained unsolved. At the very least, no one in the judiciary believed he had done it to satisfy his selfish sexual urges. They'd needed to be able to explain his motive in words that everybody could understand, or else he'd be declared innocent on the grounds of mental illness. If the court couldn't judge him to have been responsible for his actions and deliver a death sentence, the people wouldn't have accepted it. There would have been a storm of public criticism directed at the authorities, and so the doctors had needed to take that situation into account in concluding their evaluation. It had been clear as day that a death sentence would be handed down if they could just get him to be deemed accountable.

That was how much Seiji Kashiwada was despised by the masses. Over the span of one year and three months, he'd kidnapped four girls and killed them, cutting off a piece of their bodies.

S

Sahara had two daughters of his own, and seeing the crime scene photos had made him even more determined to close this case as soon as possible.

If the victims' families were here, they would no doubt be feeling a murderous hatred for him. Sahara could understand that emotion and accept it. But as he had no connection to those victims, his feeling toward Kashiwada wasn't hatred. It was awe...or maybe more like a fear, that Kashiwada could have the outward appearance of a human being yet have a demon lurking inside him. Sahara knew that when people wanted to eradicate the object of their fears, they tended to do things like stab their enemy repeatedly or smash the body up into little pieces. That's why he admonished himself. *Stay cool. The best thing is to do your job calmly, with a clear head.*

When the sentence was carried out, it would mean the end of an existence that went beyond understanding, and a bottomless abyss would be no more.

"Well, it's almost time," Sahara whispered in Kashiwada's ear, urging him to stand up.

Three prison guards approached Kashiwada from behind. They placed his hands behind his back, handcuffed him, and covered his eyes with a white cloth.

With his hands restrained and his vision gone, there was nothing Kashiwada could do except focus all of his nerves on what he heard.

He sensed that the airflow had changed ever so subtly. They thought they were being considerate to the condemned when they quietly opened the accordion curtain in front of him, trying as best they could to avoid making any sound. Theirs was a contemptible, shallow sense of concern. Even if both of his eyes were covered by the white cloth, for instance, as long as he still had use of his other sensory organs, he could easily tell exactly what was going on.

He was being pushed from behind, and with each step forward that he took, his reality was being reflected in his retinas. In that world, he could see little purple spots flickering.

Prologue

His footing didn't feel any different, so he knew that the carpet had been laid out in the same thickness on the floor leading to the hanging chamber. A purple corridor was leading him to the middle of this place of execution.

Finally, he arrived at the center of the room. Dead center. The flooring beneath his feet lacked the firmness of a solid foundation.

He could sense that a number of people were in motion. A few of them were descending the stairs from the execution space on the first basement level to the room beneath the hanging chamber on the second basement level. They were going down there to watch him die. *So,* he thought, *you want to see a person hanging from the ceiling like a piñata? Goddamn, that's vulgar. It'd feel good to scatter my urine and feces over these guys' heads. That'd make one hell of a parting gift.*

Then, the door on the left opened. At the same time that the security chief gave the signal, one of the guards crept up from behind, tied up his legs, and placed a rope around his neck.

The process was quick, and afterward he sensed that the three prison guards were quietly taking their leave.

Beneath where he was standing was an endless hell. The floorboard—a three-foot square—had a mechanism where a hydraulic system would cause the door to open. It was about a ten-foot fall. There wouldn't even be any time to suffer before his consciousness was gone. He simply wouldn't feel anything at all.

He told himself to maintain his concentration, to prepare for death, which would be visiting him in but a few seconds.

Once they pushed the red switch on the wall in the next room and turned on the electricity, the floorboard would open and his body would fall. In that one moment lay his only chance. He'd already done this brilliantly once before. He couldn't afford to forget that he was in the same situation now. The will that you emitted in the moment of death was so very powerful. He knew that from his own experience. *Narrow down your target, concentrate your mind, and just pray like hell.*

S

He felt that he was being gazed at from one spot in the room, by something that wasn't human. Diagonally upward from him, there was an observer present. It wasn't a person. It wasn't a living eye that was watching him, but a machine. It had to be a security camera, he thought. Executions were always recorded by a video camera. That was because they wanted to keep a record so that if any problems occurred, they could deal with them right away.

Where is it? Where's the camera? Is it in the corner of the wall on the right, or on the left... Find it. The interface is right there. Focus on it!

The moment his eyes focused on it, the floorboard gave way with a crashing sound and his body fell. He was released from gravity... though it lasted less than a second, he felt like he'd keep on falling forever.

Seiji Kashiwada's body fell ten feet, and then the winch turned on and slowed his descent. Once his body stopped two feet from the ground, the recoil caused it to bounce up and down several times. When his body started to spin with his neck as the pivot, the curtain opened, and the medical officer and a prison guard came in and took hold of his body, which was still swinging.

For Honjo—the prison guard—it required more muscle than usual. Kashiwada must have come in at about 150 pounds. And yet his still-dying body had an unnatural weight. Some enigmatic force was at work on the body, pulling it downward. A body wasn't supposed to swing like this—it was impossible. Honjo had never needed so much strength to hold a body before.

When the spinning stopped, somehow the blindfold came off, and Kashiwada's eyes were revealed. His pupils turned upward, moving slowly as if they were focusing on one spot on the ceiling.

Honjo unconsciously followed Kashiwada's line of sight. There was a camera installed on the wall next to the stairs.

Kashiwada's eyes were fixed on the camera as if they were engaged in a staring contest with the lens.

Prologue

His hands were cuffed behind his back and his feet were tied with rope. The disablement of his hands and feet made the death-throe spasms look so odd. It was not unlike the movements of a measuring worm trying to climb up the trunk of a tree.

Though his consciousness was gone, his body continued to move by reflex. The area around his crotch was wet and turning black, and for about a minute after that, the air kept leaking from his lungs.

In the hanging-chamber basement, where silence reigned, the lone sound of the air escaping his lungs echoed ominously. This breath was coming from something that had once been alive, yet it lacked any warmth, resembling more the whooshing of a machine.

Soon the sound of his breathing trailed off, the tips of his fingers moved only subtly, and all biological reactions stopped as far as they could see.

Condemned prisoner Seiji Kashiwada, convicted for committing a series of kidnappings and murders of young girls, was executed on May 19th at 10:04 a.m., and his death was confirmed.

Everyone there, having watched this demonic soul die, was immersed in deep sentiment, each in their own.

Only the eye of the camera sitting there on the wall kept on watching. Void of all feeling, retaining perfect objectivity, it continued recording the cells in Kashiwada's body as they passed on from this world.

CHAPTER ONE   *A Distant Memory*

1

Akane Maruyama glanced around at the women seated in the OBGYN waiting room at the general hospital, and gave a sigh. She thought this was a cruel place.

Some of the women here may have been happy to know they were pregnant, but there also had to be women who wished that the positive marker on their pregnancy test had been wrong. Others might have come here for reasons that had nothing to do with pregnancy, because of a gynecologic disease they had.

Regardless of the department, hospital waiting rooms were places for people in more or less the same situation to gather, though of course some patients would be in more serious conditions than others. But with obstetrics and gynecology, the gap was too great. While one woman knew the healthy joy of being blessed with a child, the woman beside her was suffering from hardship.

Akane had been examined by a gynecologist before. One time when she was a high school student, her menstruation had stopped, and she had been taken to see the gynecologist by the facility director.

While she'd been sitting waiting for her name to be called, her unease had gradually grown and developed into something closer to fear.

Compared to the unease she'd experienced as a high school student waiting to be examined, Akane now felt she was blessed.

She'd missed her period and was experiencing nausea akin to

morning sickness, and when she'd checked her pregnancy test it had been positive.

There was no doubt that she was pregnant. She needed this examination in order to give definite shape to an uncertain future and to allow her to rearrange her work plans.

A present concern was that she was supposed to lead the mountain climbing class to be held during summer vacation. The school was scheduled to go on break at the end of next month. Now that she was pregnant, it would be impossible for her to lead them, and she'd be forced to have one of her senior teachers take her place. *They'll all hate that for sure. Who can I hand this pain of a job off to? Well, I guess it's the principal's job to bell the cat.*

When Akane wondered whom to tell first about the results of today's exam, the principal and his bald head came to mind. *What am I thinking?* she asked herself, and banished his face from her thoughts straightaway.

The first person should be the father of the baby growing inside her, Takanori Ando.

Takanori had said he'd accompany her to the hospital, but something urgent came up at work and he simply couldn't get away from the office in the end. Right now, this very moment, he was probably waiting for the news with his cell phone in one hand.

First, she'd get in touch with Takanori, and then she'd have to submit their marriage registration right away, then inform the school of her situation, and then get her future plans in order... That's what she needed to do once she knew for certain she was pregnant.

This summer would be hectic, with all kinds of things going on. The scenes of her future self that flickered in her mind were terribly noisy, as if somebody were tramping loudly in her head. Meanwhile, the waiting room in the hospital where she currently found herself was so quiet.

The waiting room and exam rooms were partitioned by a wall, on the other side of which was a narrow interior corridor where three exam rooms were lined up. Once her name was called, she would enter the corridor and take a seat, and that meant she would be seen next.

When the woman next to her dropped the bookmark from the book she was reading, Akane bent to pick it up. At that moment, her ears caught an odd sound.

She couldn't figure out what it was at first. It sounded like drumming that was leaking from an iPod, but soon she knew that it had nothing to do with music. It was an inorganic sound, like something was being polished. *What could it be? Is somebody polishing a wall with sandpaper?*

The source of the sound was right behind her, and Akane turned around unconsciously.

Despite it being an OBGYN waiting room, she saw a boy sitting there who looked to be about ten years old.

The sandpaper sound was coming from him as he scratched a sheet of paper with a pencil.

The boy was putting all his force into his fingers, and the strain was traveling through his wrist to his upper arm, elbow, and shoulder, causing his back to quiver. The harder he drew, the more it looked like his soul was slipping out from his back; his presence was so unbelievably thin that it was almost terrifying.

He had his B5-size sketchbook spread out and was drawing a picture with the pencil, his head shaking as he carried on intently.

Twisting her body into an uncomfortable pose, Akane tried to peek at the sketchbook.

With a single glance the pattern was burned into her retinas. It felt as if a long and slender creature had forced its way into her eyes.

Taken aback, Akane stared at the boy's face. At the same time, he noticed someone's eyes were on him, and his fingers, which had been crawling on the sketchbook, halted. Retaining his posture, the boy raised his hands slightly higher and then twisted to show her his picture, placing it right in front of her face as if to say, *You wanna see? Here, I'll show you.*

It was an abstract picture, far removed from realism. It reminded

Akane immediately of the drawing exercise that her counselor had conducted. Just before graduating from elementary school, she'd been told to draw a picture. That was why it registered right away.

In her elementary school days, she'd experienced something so terrifying that it was too much to remember. After she'd become unable to go to school, she was immediately taken against her will to see a counselor, who instructed her to draw a picture. The themes she was given were "house," "tree," and "animal."

She easily drew a house and a tree but couldn't come up with any animals she might draw. She drew an alien as a last resort, at which point the counselor labeled her as suffering from schizophrenia.

The boy's picture wasn't unlike the one that Akane had attempted. The incongruity between its primitiveness and its sophistication threatened to destroy the entire composition, perfectly depicting what was in his mind.

There was a swirling sun floating above an apple tree, and two triangular houses which were interspersed in a vacant field. The peaceful scenery of the grassy field was flat and had no depth. That was why it came across as primitive; the composition lacked any sense of perspective. The houses and tree were drawn well, but there were no people. Instead, there was a snake wriggling around the root of the apple tree, forming an S shape.

As the snake occupied most of the space in the center of his picture, it must have been the thing he wanted to draw most.

It looked as though the snake had swallowed something large, much larger than itself, and was unable to move. Seeing how bloated its belly was, Akane imagined that the snake surely must have swallowed something other than a living creature. It didn't have the slightest warmth or roundness, or any kind of suppleness to it, and the corners of the thing in its belly were so sharp that they almost tore through the skin from inside and popped out. In this flat picture, the snake's distended belly alone had a certain grotesque realness.

Whatever was inside its stomach, it seemed to be a rectangular object. Its considerable weight was working inside the snake's belly and pressing its whole body against the ground, leaving the snake cruelly immobilized.

Akane held her breath without thinking. She couldn't help dwelling on the intention channelled into the picture.

It had to have something to do with his background.

He was a patient at this hospital, that much was certain. Since he was wearing a hat in early summer weather—warm enough to make one perspire—she assumed that he was undergoing chemotherapy.

Most of all, she wanted to know what the snake had swallowed. Given the shape, it could have been a brick or perhaps a concrete block, but the boy's intention must have been otherwise. He'd put something in the snake's belly that normal people would never be able to imagine, and had given it real meaning.

The snake...had reached out intentionally to this thing and put it in its stomach, rendering itself immobile.

Akane was gripped by an ominous feeling. What if the snake symbolized her own future? What then?

By showing her his picture, it seemed like the boy was making a mockery of her.

Feeling nauseated all of a sudden, she held her mouth with the back of her hand and moved her eyes right and left in search of a restroom.

She saw the sign for one hanging from the ceiling just a few dozen feet ahead. To her it felt so far away, the contents of her stomach seemingly on the verge of bursting out.

When she tried to stand up, she heard the boy's muffled laughter coming from right behind her. It overlapped with her own name, Akane Maruyama, being called out.

"Ms. Akane Maruyama, Ms. Akane Maruyama, please wait outside Exam Room 3."

Not knowing what she should do first, Akane remained seated in the waiting room chair, unable to move.

When he stood in the open-air corridor and opened the door, a foul smell poured out of the room. Although it was an odor that he was used to smelling, it spoiled the pleasant mood he'd been in that morning.

Takanori Ando turned his head back outside and took a single deep breath before stepping into the entryway and removing his shoes.

The whole time that this studio apartment—located in a prime section in the heart of Tokyo—was being used as a production office, the smells of the industry had been seeping into the place. The room was full of videotapes, cameras, and editing and digital-info devices that were scattered about... The smells they gave off had blended with those of the cigarettes that the company president Yoneda smoked, along with the coffee and tea that had been spilled on the carpet, producing a distinctive odor that filled the room. Yoneda, who was both president and producer, had quit smoking one week before, but the cigarette smell showed no signs of going away.

Sitting with his legs crossed in the middle of the cramped room, Yoneda beckoned with his hand.

"What kept ya?" he asked. "Well, anyway, come and sit."

Takanori sat down in front of him.

Whenever he wanted to discuss some new project, Yoneda always sat cross-legged on the carpet, shaking his knees. It was a peculiar motion: he violently shook his knee joints up and down, quite unlike the slight jiggling people sometimes did. The way he was shaking now was different than usual, perhaps as a side effect of having given up smoking.

Takanori could anticipate what Yoneda was going to say.

Honestly, I want to get your thoughts on this.

Trying not to look at Yoneda's shaking, which was gradually growing more pronounced, Takanori turned his eyes to the calendar on the wall. The note for that day's date read *tai-an*, meaning it was an auspicious day. Something flashed in his mind when he saw this, and at precisely that moment, his cell phone rang. On the display was Akane's name.

"Excuse me, I have to take this."

Takanori stood up with his phone in hand and stepped outside from the entryway. With the office being so small, he had to do so if he wanted to have any privacy.

As he rushed out the door, Takanori pressed the answer button and put the phone to his ear.

This time, too, he could guess what she was going to say. Based on the changes that were happening to Akane's body, and the positive on her pregnancy test, the result was already obvious.

"How'd it go?" Takanori asked, eager to hear what the doctor had said.

"'You're with child,' apparently."

Coming from the mouth of a twenty-four-year-old woman, the old-fashioned expression seemed to carry a special sort of nuance.

Phew.

That was his honest and heartfelt reaction.

"We should file the marriage paperwork right away," he said. "I gotta get a copy of my family register."

"Me too."

Just then, Takanori felt a sudden urge to meet her and talk, like he couldn't wait. He wanted to hold her close and to feel the tiny heartbeat of the child they had conceived.

"Where are you now?" he asked.

Akane was about to head to her job. She had only taken the morning off and had classes to teach in the afternoon.

Takanori for his part was keeping Yoneda waiting, having stepped away before he could hear about the new project.

"Let's talk about it tonight. Take our time."

It looked as though the two of them wouldn't get off work until after seven that evening. After making sure that she would pack some things and spend the night at his apartment, Takanori hung up.

When he stepped back inside, he was reminded once again of the foul odor. Despite all the effort he'd made to adjust to it, after stepping out and inhaling the fresh air he found himself right back where he'd started. Each time he went in and out, the vile smell would greet him anew.

"Your errand done?"

Yoneda was still in exactly the same pose, siting with his legs crossed on the carpet. Judging by the plastic tea bottle placed in front of his knees, he must have made a round-trip to the refrigerator. Knowing Yoneda, he'd probably crawled there without even getting up. Takanori could picture it.

"I guess you could say I found the motivation to work."

"Glad to hear it."

Takanori sat down facing Yoneda, who then tossed over a USB stick.

"Then this one's all yours."

Picking up the USB stick—which looked just like any other—Takanori asked, "What's on this?"

"There's a brief video."

"What kind?"

Takanori could at least surmise that some kind of video was saved on it. He was a director specializing in video processing.

"You remember about a month ago, when that weird short film was uploaded to a certain video site?"

"A weird film uploaded to a video site? There's tons of those."

"I mean that live video of the suicide."

"Oh, yeah, *that* one."

Takanori knew about it. It was around the middle of May. After announcing his intentions, a man in his forties hanged himself, broadcasting the whole scene live from his computer camera. There had been a number of similar cases overseas, but this was the first such instance in Japan, and it had caused quite a stir online.

Takanori had only heard the gossip surrounding it—he hadn't seen the actual footage. Yet even those whispers about it had seemed to vanish so quickly. As for what had transpired afterwards, he knew none of the details.

"What happened with that?"

"Right after the live broadcast, the video feed was cut off."

Whenever a video got uploaded that was contrary to public order or morality, it was typically deleted by the site administrator. A live feed showing a suicide by hanging was so graphic that it could give viewers a violent shock.

"That makes sense."

"In cases like this, what do you think usually happens next?"

"Someone's bound to have dubbed the video, so even if it gets deleted, there'll be copies popping up online one after another. It's like a whack-a-mole game that goes on and on."

"But that's not what happened here. The only recording of it that exists is that one, on there."

Yoneda's manner of speech was so exaggerated that Takanori reflexively tossed the USB stick onto the carpet. "Why do we even have this in the first place... If this were a real suicide video, the cops would've gotten involved already."

"Huh? You mean you really don't know?"

To be sure, Takanori had heard about a suicide being broadcast live on a video site about a month earlier. Then again, the buzz hadn't lasted very long and had fizzled out almost immediately.

"Was the video a fake?"

"Once people started talking about it online, a certain amount of information got into the hands of the police, but they couldn't even identify the guy's address or name. Obviously, not even the body was found...and it still hasn't been."

"So, it was a fake after all. The cops must've thought so, and that's why they let it go. They're busy enough without wasting their time looking into some dumb farce, right?"

Even without professional equipment, it was very easy to manipulate a video. With the steady stream of shock vids being uploaded to the internet these days, once it was revealed to be a hoax made by a fanatic, a live suicide broadcast would be forgotten right away.

And yet, if that was so, what was Yoneda driving at by bringing it up?

Takanori picked up the USB stick once more and asked, "What do you want me to do with this?"

"I want to use it for a special summer program."

Whenever Yoneda said that Studio Oz—the CG production company of which he was president—was going to do a "special summer program," it could only mean the two-hour slot on KTS TV, a key network channel based in Tokyo.

"What're you talking about? That's impossible. There's no way we can play footage that was deleted from a video site on a commercial TV station."

"Scratch that. I meant to say, I want you to find out whether we can use it for the summer program."

"Mr. Yoneda, have you watched it already?"

"I have," the president replied, grimacing.

"So, you think we can use it?"

"Like you said, not as-is. But if you work some editing magic on the original here, we can make a convincing CG film that could be mistaken for a real suicide by hanging. If we change the face, we'll be able to get around the problem of portrait rights. More than that, though, I'm curious about the background behind how this was made, you know? Who created it, and for what reason? We might even be able to add that story into the film as a segment."

For a smaller production company such as Studio Oz, a two-hour slot for a special program was a mouthwatering prospect. Naturally it was their wish to be a part of that somehow. Even a minor involvement in the CG process would aid their precarious financial situation.

As long as the company was certain to receive compensation—even a pittance—Takanori would be compelled to contribute to improving its finances.

"Understood. Anyway, I'll take a look."

Takanori picked up the USB stick and put it in the inner pocket of his bag.

3

The distance between the Studio Oz office and Takanori's apartment was walkable. If he opted not to walk, his only alternative was to go by taxi, and his choice depended on his mood.

He decided he would walk and enjoy the early summer weather, getting some sunlight while casually surveying the street scenery. When he stepped out onto the sidewalk, he heard the chirp of a car horn, and turning toward the sound, he saw an empty taxi slowing down. From the way the driver approached, he seemed eager to pick up a customer.

Takanori involuntarily raised his hand and stopped the taxi. Why, when he'd already decided to walk, he wondered.

Oh well, it'll save me some time.

He got in the back seat and gave the name of his condominium, which everyone knew.

"Wow. You live there, sir?"

Takanori quietly clicked his tongue. *Not this again.* Every time he got into a taxi and provided his destination, he was invariably asked this same question. If he answered yes, there were always follow-up questions, with the driver wanting to know if he was rich and what he did for a living. Since Takanori tended to wear more casual attire like T-shirts and jeans, his appearance hardly gave off an aura of affluence.

"No, I'm just visiting a friend," he evaded, hoping to cut off the conversation.

People got nosy whenever they spotted an incompatibility. They often overreacted when something seemed to be out of place but didn't bat an eye if they could immediately tell you were well off.

Takanori was often taken to be younger than his actual age of twenty-eight. It was a sign that he didn't look very mature, and it wasn't something to be pleased about. He had an air of good breeding, and something about him seemed naïve, which only belied his desire to be a real adult male.

That was why he wanted to tell the taxi driver that he was going to be a father next year...

He had a serious romantic partner, who was now pregnant; this was a happy accident that he welcomed with all his heart. Taking on the role of husband and father would allow him a proper sense of responsibility, and it seemed he would be climbing his first step toward true adulthood.

He felt no hesitation about marrying Akane or about living together with her openly. Her pregnancy was a major incentive for him to take a step towards marriage, which he had been putting off.

The only problem was that he didn't know how his parents would receive a so-called marriage of necessity. But foreseeing that they probably wouldn't oppose it, Takanori could afford to take in their reaction from a position of safety.

Thus far, his parents had never sought to stop him from doing anything he wished, leaving him free to make his own choices in all things. They always respected his free will to the point where he had to wonder why. From around the time he was a high school student deciding on his future path, he was made to feel that his household was different from others, and his doubts only multiplied.

His parents' attitude was the exact opposite of a lack of affection—he felt that he had been cherished to an excessive degree. Takanori had never doubted that in the least. Yet their attitude in dealing with him seemed reserved somehow. At times, he really sensed a certain nuance in their manner, as though they were treating him gingerly.

That was how it was during his first year in high school, when he had to select the humanities or the sciences track. Although his grades were reasonably good, always falling within the passing range, his parents never pushed him too hard to enter medical school. His mother's parents had owned a private general hospital, and his father, a former lecturer at a university medical institution, had succeeded them and currently served as director. While it was obvious that Takanori's parents wanted an heir to the business, his mother seemed to anticipate his feelings and even gave him her resigned reassurance.

"Uh-uh…if you don't want to be a doctor, that's fine."

And so Takanori had entered an arts college, where he'd studied drawing and video processing, and upon graduating he'd joined a small production company to pursue the path of a film director.

While he'd freely chosen whatever he wished to be, as for whether that pattern applied to his sister, four years his junior, the answer was no. She'd always been prodded to attend medical school and was currently enrolled in one. Takanori was mystified about the origins of this difference. It wasn't as though they'd abandoned him, nor had they given up on him because he wasn't intelligent enough. And yet…

"We're here," said the driver.

Takanori raised his head and saw the familiar vehicle drop-off area. The high-rise condominium, among the most famous in all of Tokyo, boasted a magnificent entrance like a grand hotel's. It wasn't anywhere he could afford to live on his salary. From among the several properties that his parents owned, he'd simply chosen the one here due to its proximity to his workplace.

After paying the fare and exiting the taxi, he passed through the auto-locking entryway and took the elevator up to the twelfth floor. The unit he lived in, No. 1214, faced westward.

It was a 700-square-feet one bedroom, too luxurious for a person living alone. Even after they got married and their child was born, he figured, they could live there for a little while. If they wanted, it would even be possible to convert the space into a two-bedroom unit.

His parents did own larger condominium units in central Tokyo, but this place was to his liking. The evening view from his spacious balcony at day's end brought comfort to him.

There was still plenty of time for the sun to come in through the west-facing windows.

Wanting to finish up his work while it was still bright out, Takanori turned on the desktop in one corner of his living room and set his coffee maker.

Though there was no need to wrap up the work Yoneda had requested of him before it got dark, Takanori just had a vague fear about watching the video alone after nightfall. Perhaps he should have conducted the analysis at Studio Oz, but the office was so cramped and had frequent visitors, and he'd have gotten distracted.

Takanori removed the USB stick with its creepy vibe from the inside pocket of his bag and set it atop his table.

Apparently, what was saved on this totally ordinary little plastic vessel was a video of a suicide. The fact that he had just been informed of Akane's pregnancy made a dark premonition come over him. A life newly conceived, and another one cut short by the deceased's own hand...having the two of them mingle together so near him gave Takanori an unpleasant feeling.

What he needed to do first was to determine whether or not this live-streamed video of an unidentified man in his forties hanging himself was authentic. Judging from the fact that the body in question had never been discovered, he supposed it must have been some nasty prank.

These days, even a novice with a modest bit of equipment could easily craft a video that could be confused with the real thing.

Hoping it really was a prank, Takanori brought the coffee that he'd put beside his computer to his lips and started playing the video on his monitor.

What appeared on screen was a studio apartment. Compared to Takanori's place, it was a small unit of a considerably lower grade, with the wallpaper peeling away in spots and an overall shabby impression.

At first, all he saw was a shot of the room. He got a brief glimpse of the hallway outside through the front door, but then it closed and the camera turned back to the interior; then, for a moment, the outdoor scenery flashed by. Not a single person had appeared.

This didn't seem to have been recorded by a computer camera. Someone was walking around the room and filming with a handheld video cam, which made the images shaky. As Takanori watched, he started to feel queasy like he was getting seasick.

The man put the camera down on the desk, and it seemed that he was connecting some cords. One of the buttons of his shirt wasn't fastened, so part of his body from his chest to his belly was peeking out from the gap. A mole stood out on his pallid, unhealthy skin; strands of hair that had grown unusually long, as if it had fed on some dark nourishment, nestled on it. His chest was so close to the lens that even his moles and blotches were visible.

At last the man adjusted the focus of the lens and gradually stepped away, showing his back to the camera. Then he turned and faced it, and as he continued to step backwards, the sections of his body below his hips and above his chest came into view.

When the man's chin became visible, for some reason he walked forward and tried to adjust the lens again. The mole from before was captured vividly in the center of the monitor, as though that were the point.

Overcome by an oppressive feeling, Takanori arched his upper body backward and turned his face away from the monitor. It felt so real that it seemed to exude the man's body odor, and the video professional instinctively shouted out in his mind.

This can't be fake.

He was certain. The unmistakable, raw presence of a human being came across through the computer screen.

The man turned around, facing away, and stepped back from the video camera he'd placed on the desk. His shirt was short, revealing a horizontal strip of skin in the gap between it and his cotton pants, with the waistband of his underwear running parallel underneath. The long sleeves of his shirt were rolled up to around his elbows, and he was opening and closing the palms of his rugged hands.

His back still turned to the camera, the man raised one leg onto a chair in the middle of the room, then stood his whole body on it. At this point, the monitor showed his back, his hips, and his legs from thigh to heel. Since his cotton pants were also rolled up, his Achilles' tendons were exposed.

A subtle wobble traveling upward from his heels seemed to climb from his buttocks to his back. It was a round rotating chair, and he appeared to be struggling to balance himself on it.

The man put his arms up in the air. Though it was unclear what he was doing since his body was out of view from the shoulders up, Takanori already knew that this was a suicide film and assumed the man was putting a rope around his neck.

The man's struggle was palpable from his shaking body parts. Then Takanori suddenly noticed something—he didn't hear the chair making any creaking sounds, though it surely had to be.

Usually in these cases, people wanted to utter something like a last will and testament in front of the camera. Had this man no final words as he prepared to leave this world behind? Every last sound had been erased from the video.

In total silence, the man's arms dropped down around his hips. He seemed to have finished putting the rope around his neck. If so, all that remained to do was to kick out the chair and fall.

Using his toes skillfully, almost like a ballerina, he rotated the chair to the left and stopped when his body was facing the camera.

Though not as intensely as before, he was weakly closing and opening both his hands, so Takanori couldn't help focusing on them. The man wasn't holding anything.

Then, abruptly, the chair was kicked out to the front, and the man's body fell across the center of the monitor—first his legs, then his thighs, hips, belly, chest, shoulders, neck, face, and head disappearing downward. After a pause, his body fell again, from the direction of the ceiling, starting with his toes, then his knees, hips, belly, and chest, and was momentarily pulled up in recoil. After that it stopped about a foot off the floor and began to spin rightward.

The man's body from his chest up was still hidden from view, and so from start to finish, his face remained unclear.

For a few minutes the body slowly turned left and right, but besides that there were no changes. It was just hanging loosely from the ceiling.

As Takanori scrutinized the video, trying not to miss anything, he saw the man's hands and toes twitching. Every time the body swerved from left to right, a black stain forming around its crotch gradually spread.

Time seemed to flow very slowly around the body as it hung from the ceiling, the face still invisible. If any meaning could be given to this phenomenon, the only interpretation Takanori could think of was that it recorded the process by which vital reactions ceased. Death was a transitory phenomenon, not an instantaneous change. If the sound had been streaming, he might have noticed the breaths escaping from the man's throat getting lower and the intervals getting longer. No air was being inhaled; it would simply keep leaking. Soon it would die down, and the heart would stop beating.

Takanori could imagine the changes occurring in the man's body. Thinking about how it no longer breathed, he felt a pain in his own chest—he'd been holding his breath, in fact. He couldn't turn away from the display even for a second, as if the scruff of his neck was being pressed from behind and his eyes were being sucked into the screen.

He didn't fail to notice something rising ever so slightly. It was oozing out from the gap of the man's shirt—a mist wafting toward the ceiling, like steam. Was it coming from his incontinent urine, or was it an optical illusion? A pale pink cloud, shrouding the body, gradually rose from the feet and was now coalescing around the neck. Takanori couldn't see because it was off screen, but the cloud seemed

S

to be rising yet higher after enveloping the man's face.

Watching, Takanori began to believe in the soul's existence. Beset by a mixture of awe, amazement, and solemnity, he didn't even notice that the video had ended.

He stood up from the chair as if he'd been flipped out of it. Then, approaching the balcony door, he opened the shutters and drank in the outside air.

Cold sweat had broken out over his whole body, and his T-shirt was drenched.

4

When Akane got off the bus, she saw the school gate about a hundred yards up ahead. Although a year had passed since she'd become a teacher, this distance still felt long to her. The closer she got to the gate, the gloomier she felt. *When will I get used to it?* she wondered, detesting her own timidity.

Going out into the world had made her acutely aware that your achievements in high school and college and your capabilities as a teacher were completely different things. And yet her former teachers and her senior instructors had told her the same thing at every turn.

"You're going to make a great teacher, Akane."

Reality, however, wasn't as forgiving. She found herself being toyed with by bratty young girls some seventeen years old, and she couldn't quite understand what they were thinking. With each passing day, she lost more of her confidence and didn't know how she could get it back.

On a typical morning, the road leading from the bus stop to the school gate was full of female students making their way to school in small groups. Whenever they greeted her, Akane tried her best to muster a cheerful smile, but if she failed to conceal the slightest unease or irritation, the girls would openly start whispering in front of her. *Miss Maruyama's kind of weird today,* they'd say. Encountered individually, they were always the picture of the honest, adorable student. Yet the moment they formed a group, they had a power far beyond their numbers. That was also what made a girls' high school so frightening.

If this were the morning, and I ran into a pack of those girls around here on their way to school, they'd know in an instant I was pregnant. With a nervous gaze, Akane scanned the area.

Not a soul could be seen on the street.

Good thing it's ten minutes to noon, she thought, breathing a sigh of relief. At this time of day, no students or teachers would be on the road from the bus stop to the school gate. It was because she'd been absent from her morning lessons to visit the hospital for her exam that she was arriving this late.

There was usually one more obstacle on the way to the school gate from the bus stop, but it wasn't in sight now.

Every morning, this person would overtake Akane with a leisurely stride and torment any girl who wasn't following school regulations. She was Miss Yoshiko Ohashi, also known as "Hardass." She would say things like *Your hair's tied the wrong way,* or *Your sock color is inappropriate...*always pointing out such little things, with almost amazing powers of observation, that the students would shrink away and try to flee from Hardass's gaze.

Why can't she let these violations go and try to be more cheerful in the morning, Akane would think. *It's the beginning of the day. Both sides would feel a lot better if she did.* She couldn't understand why Miss Ohashi became such a slave to her job the moment she got off the bus, when she wasn't even on the premises yet.

If Akane didn't keep her wits about her, then despite being a teacher, she could become a target too. Overlooking a student's breach of the school rules could bring down Hardass's wrath upon her.

"What are you doing? If you find any students breaking the rules, you need to scold them."

When a veteran teacher gave you such advice, the only thing you could do was to say yes and lower your head. But unable to be strict with the offenders, Akane could only shrink in fear, stuck in a dilemma.

In the small community that was the school, the power structure was obvious. At the bottom was Akane, forced to accept her lowly position, looked down upon by the students, while feared Hardass was at the top...

Today, in her unusual situation, Akane grew more and more depressed as she walked. She didn't know how she ought to inform the school that she was pregnant.

She had finally made it to her second year as a teacher. Fortunately, she wasn't in charge of any class, but she was an assistant homeroom teacher and an assistant advisor for a club, and also had to lead the mountain climbing class, for instance; it was obvious that certain changes in school duties would be forced on the other teachers. The baby was due around the end of next February, and Akane would need to take a total of four months' maternity leave, for two months before and after that date. That worked out to a leave of absence lasting from winter vacation that year until the new school term began next April. The school would have to take Akane's delivery date into consideration in planning the yearly schedule. Thus, she needed to report her pregnancy sooner or later.

The problems were the order and the timing of the things she had to do. She couldn't afford to screw up when to tell the school about these matters.

We're getting married soon, so maybe afterwards I should tell them about my marriage and pregnancy at the same time? No, no, not at the same time—I should tell them first that I got married, and a little while later let them know about my pregnancy...

The teachers are all adults, so they'll understand without my telling them everything, but with the students, it isn't going to be so easy. At least one girl will count the days from when I got married to my delivery date and realize I became pregnant before I got married. And as soon as she's figured it out, she'll tell everybody in the school, bragging like she's some genius for putting it all together.

"Hey, c'mere, c'mere. You do know, right?"

It wouldn't take even half a day before everybody knew the truth.

Akane decided to say nothing for today. She'd already told the head teacher that she hadn't been feeling well and had visited a clinic, but she thought it best to pretend she'd caught a cold and to hold off on reporting the exam results. In any case, it would be reckless for her to say anything before talking things over with Takanori that night and clarifying their future plans.

She'd put these matters aside for now...

Having decided how she should behave that day, Akane stepped inside the school.

The info you obtain through your five senses alter as you move: the wind caressing your face, the sound of car motors passing by, or the sight of a train running on overhead tracks in the distance enter your awareness through your tactile, auditory, and visual senses. The small change that beset her at that moment related to her sense of smell, but she didn't notice it right away.

Akane felt as if she'd crossed beyond an invisible boundary. A metallic sound echoed in her ears, and her field of vision became mushy and distorted. It was too early in the year for cicadas. There'd been no rain for a few days, but the moisture in the eighty-five-degree air clung viscously to her neck.

Unable to remain standing, she suddenly sank down right where she was, holding up her body with both hands on the ground.

She'd felt nauseated when she was waiting in the hospital, but that was from her pregnancy. This time, that wasn't the only cause. It was more remote: a horrifying experience she'd gone through more than a decade ago. The smell had awoken her memory.

Akane searched for its source, moving only her eyes. Immediately beside her was a freshly dug flowerbed. The surface had been tilled, and new flowers had been planted. The smell of soil that greeted her nostrils nearly made her choke. A worm crawling out from one of the bulges of soil added a special accent to the scent.

Even when Akane closed her eyes, the worm—stretching itself toward the sky—crawled on her retinas. Her heart was beating fast and hard, and her field of vision was growing narrower and narrower. Recalling the snake that the boy in the hospital waiting room had drawn, she felt a cold sweat dripping from her forehead.

She put her hands to her mouth and endured the nausea welling up from the back of her throat.

The long shadow of her body on the ground overlapped with a larger one coming from behind her.

"Are you all right?"

Reacting to the male voice, Akane turned around. Hands covered in a pair of muddy rubber gloves hung down in front of her. One was holding a scoop shovel, and the other a bundle of seedlings.

Still stooping, Akane raised just her eyes. The man's face appeared before her, blacked out and featureless due to the sun behind him.

When you're about to faint, it feels as if the world is shutting down. A lace curtain rolled down from the roof to the first floor of the school building that Akane knew so well, rapidly shrinking her vision.

As her consciousness was enveloped in darkness, a sequence of images long sealed away in a distant memory surfaced instead. She had experienced something similar once before. She could watch objectively at her own body collapsing. Although the man was there, trying to catch her, she couldn't make out his face because it was blurred out by the darkness.

"You're all right. You're gonna be okay."

Back then, too, a man had whispered those words to her. The memory was coming back to her in patches, and the more she tried to push it away, the nearer it drew to her in response.

She'd collapsed on the slope of a mountain. She could see damp humus peeking through the weeds.

The man worrying about her now was working for the school as a gardener, and somewhere in her heart she knew that he posed no threat to her. But with her consciousness fading, behind the gardener's face she saw the shadowy visage of the man she'd encountered over ten years earlier. His dark, expressionless face was coming toward her with a vividness that seemed quite real.

She couldn't allow herself to trust this voice telling her that she was all right. The man who'd uttered the same words so very long ago had tried to kill her.

"No...please stop," she whispered impotently.

Akane pushed away his rubber-gloved hands and sank onto the ground.

5

Takanori descended to the underground bicycle parking area and took out his bike, which he hadn't used for some time. A month ago he'd gotten into some trouble after hitting a pedestrian, and ever since then he'd lost the desire to ride it. He was about to travel to and from the Studio Oz office, though, and going by bicycle was the best way. He guessed that Akane would be arriving after seven, which meant that he needed to wrap this business up and return to the apartment before then. Going to the office wouldn't even take him five minutes on a bike.

Traveling light—without a bag or anything else, just the USB stick stuffed into his jeans pocket—Takanori pedaled his bicycle and ascended a slope. Each time his wheels jumped on a small gap, little fragments of the images stuck in his mind leapt up. Even a cursory viewing would have revealed the video as being exceedingly unnatural. To say nothing of its eeriness, any number of questions squirmed inside his head.

The man's body exuded the reek of flesh, and that simply couldn't be faked using CG or any other contrivance. This was a real video—there was no doubt. Yet the way his body had moved after kicking out the chair was unnatural in the extreme.

Once he kicked it out, his body should have fallen only a foot or so. And yet it had seemed to fall right through the floor and to come crashing through the ceiling, dropping from above a moment later. There was no way that a body could fall through the floor one second and then pass through the ceiling the next. What was more, the man had stopped his fall at a position where he couldn't be seen from the neck up as if he'd arranged it that way.

Takanori could sense that the man had intended to conceal his face. It could be identified for only the briefest of moments: after the fall, when the body passed straight down through the center of the screen. Yet the eyes had been covered with a white cloth, obscuring the overall features.

Takanori had studied the video very closely, playing it frame-by-frame as the man's face passed straight down the screen from top to bottom. Watching it repeatedly, he'd been seized by an unpleasant sensation. He felt like he'd met the man somewhere—not just seen him in a video or a photo, but in person.

The man's body was real, but his movement was fake... Who in the world had made this freak of a video, and for what purpose? But first and foremost, Takanori's doubts took on a more realistic cast. Even if he analyzed and processed this live suicide video, it could never be used for television.

Working in CG once used to be a more creative job. The technology's real purpose was to craft images that couldn't exist in the real world, to broaden the scope of what could be depicted in TV commercials or animated films. No matter how Takanori processed this creepy suicide video, it could never be used in a two-hour program. If anything, it might be usable for a short scene in a horror movie. Or perhaps Studio Oz was trying to get involved in making horror movies now? He supposed it was possible, but he'd never heard even a whisper of it at the studio.

He was pedaling his bike on the slope now because he was dying to know Yoneda's real intention in handing him the USB stick.

Locking his bike in front of the shrubbery, Takanori passed through the auto-lock entrance into the lobby. It was his second time visiting the office that day. He took the elevator up to the fourth floor, walked along the outside corridor, and opened the door without knocking, as usual. It would have been unlocked when he rang the intercom.

Yoneda was so blinkered that once he started working, he hated to stop what he was doing for even a moment. If there was time to knock, just come in—or so went his logic.

Takanori didn't have a particularly sharp nose, but he could easily discern at least this much: a new scent flowed in the entrance now that hadn't been present a few hours earlier when he left the office, an alluring aroma clearly distinct from the foul smell of cigarettes and mold and scattered shoes.

The simplest explanation was that there had been a visitor right before him, but no woman ever visited Studio Oz before to leave a scent so full of pheromones, and he couldn't figure it out for the life of him. The only woman on staff was Kanako Nishijima, and she had no affinity whatsoever with cosmetics or even skin lotions.

There were no women's shoes, and even if there had been a visitor, it was obvious that she was already gone.

Yoneda was sitting with his legs crossed in the center of the room, and there were cards arranged on the carpet. Takanori had never seen him playing cards before.

"My, my, solitaire?"

Takanori sat down with his legs crossed, facing his boss.

"No, dummy," replied Yoneda. "Can't you tell? These're tarot cards."

Takanori found that even more unusual. Yoneda hated fortune telling. "Does it really work?"

Having always been lectured by the same man about the stupidity of such practices, Takanori looked down at the tarot cards with disdain. Meanwhile, Yoneda seemed not to care and was quite absorbed in flipping the cards.

This was a method for beginners, using only the major arcana cards. Yoneda shuffled them, picked a few with the picture side facing down, and placed them on the carpet.

With tarot fortunes, you needed to read a story into the pictures on the lined-up cards. First you had to think about what you wanted to know, and after picturing it in detail in your mind, you flipped the cards over, and then intuited the meaning from the drawings. There was no single, absolute interpretation with tarot, and the story changed depending on the sensibility and whim of the person seeking to divine the meaning.

"What do you want to learn?" asked Takanori.

"Well, it *is* tarot... Romance, of course."

He's not the least bit romantic and hates fortune telling... Now he's playing tarot for luck in love!

After feeling dumbstruck, Takanori laughed out loud.

"I don't think you're playing with a full deck. This hot and muggy weather must be getting to you," he said.

"You wanna laugh? Go ahead. I wanna get it on with a hot woman one more time. Something wrong with that?"

Yoneda didn't mind the ridicule at all—he just kept trying to read the meaning from the cards he'd lined up. It seemed that he couldn't set up the story in the way he wanted, though. "This isn't what I want," he complained, shuffling the cards again when he was halfway through.

Then he looked up at Takanori, who was still laughing.

"Your turn, then," Yoneda said reproachfully. "*You* do it."

Takanori had never once tried tarot.

"I don't know how."

"Just pick three cards and place them in the form of a triangle. The meaning is gonna be different depending on where you place them vertically, so be careful about that."

Major arcana cards could be arranged in various ways, and each one was called a spread. Though unsure whether Yoneda's directions conformed to the official rules, Takanori followed them, shuffling the cards well, picking three, and placing them in a triangle. Since the cards were still upside down, it was unclear what kind of pictures they hid.

Takanori raised his head and waited for the next instructions. Yoneda took turns looking at a booklet called *Tarot for Beginners* and at the cards as he spoke.

"You gotta picture what you want to know in your mind. The past, the future, it doesn't matter. Even something to do with the job you're working on, like how you're gonna do with it. Now, once you can picture it vividly, start from the top of the triangle and flip one card at a time, counterclockwise. Got it?"

Takanori still couldn't picture what he wanted to know but flipped the card at the top. It revealed a crowned woman covered in a white veil and sitting in a chair.

"Wow, the High Priestess. But it's in the inverted position," confirmed Yoneda. He opened the book and started reading out the drawing's significance. "She's the highest among all the women in the priesthood. The pages of the book she's holding in her hands are opened up to the viewer, which means she's offering us knowledge and learning. The meaning when it's in the normal position is 'knowledge, learning, wisdom.' In the inverted position, it means 'cruelty, hysteria, selfishness,' et cetera. All right, flip another one."

Takanori flipped the card on the bottom left. It featured a drawing of a man who was hanging upside down, with one leg tied to a bar that had been placed between two trees.

Yoneda began to interpret this immediately. "The card's called 'The Hanged Man.' Also known as 'The Condemned.' The man is hanging upside down, with his left leg tied to a tree that's shaped like a *torii* gate. Beneath his head is a deep valley, but even though he's in an extremely difficult situation, he has a defiant smile on his face. It's as if he willingly accepted this condition. This punishment is a form of initiation, and once he's endured it, he can reach even greater spiritual heights, or so it's implied. In the normal position, it means 'self-sacrifice, ordeal, perseverance.' In the inverted position, it means 'meaningless sacrifice, a surrender to desires,' and such."

As Takanori listened to Yoneda's explanation, his consciousness became more and more drawn to the image.

In the normal position, "The Hanged Man" was hanging upside down, but because the card was in the inverted position from Takanori's perspective, the man was not hanging, but appeared instead to be standing with one leg bent. His pose looked exactly like the man in the video immediately before he'd kicked out the chair and hanged himself. Unconsciously, a sound escaped from Takanori's lips.

"Huh."

Seeing Takanori's expression change abruptly, Yoneda nudged his elbow, looking pleased with himself. "Ha ha. You've got something on your mind, haven't you?"

Admiring how insensitive Yoneda could be, Takanori stared hard at his face.

Takanori was here to find out just why he needed to analyze the video of a live hanging. His boss had ordered him to.

Have you forgotten? he wanted to complain, but held his tongue. From his side the drawing looked like a person preparing to hang himself, but he realized that from his boss's perspective the man was doing a handstand with his leg bent. Perhaps Yoneda didn't associate the image with the suicide hanging.

"Okay, down to the last card. Time to face your past."

My past...

Only after hearing this did Takanori realize that he hadn't decided what it was he wanted to know.

The past... I've been trying to learn about my past?

Now he understood. Trying to recall his past was often vexing to him. When he turned the pages of his life, which spanned twenty-eight years up to that point, one part was always blotted out in black. No matter how hard he tried, it wouldn't come to him, and just tracing the threads of his memory got painful.

Was this one page of his past—shrouded in dark clouds—being revealed?

Takanori flipped the last remaining card.

Looking at the drawing, Yoneda frowned.

"Now you've done it. That's 'Death.' An extremely bad omen. Let's see... Drawn on the card is an image of Death holding a scythe in its hand, reaping the souls of mankind. Death is a skeleton without any flesh, and no identifiable gender, so it could be associated with androgyny. Its pointed foot is piercing the ground, and with this leg as a pivot the body is rotating. This spiral motion is none other than the Dance of Death. In this normal position, it means 'destruction, the end, an omen of death.' In the inverted position, it means 'rebirth after death.'"

From where Takanori sat, the card was in the inverted position.

"Rebirth after death"—the words began to coil around the folds of his brain. They overlapped parts of the black memory that was inserted in the pages of his past. An image of sinking slowly into a dark abyss rose in his mind, and as it did the veins of his temples began pulsing intensely. He felt like he was suffocating, as if there were a lump in his throat.

Unable to stand the sensation, Takanori reached out to the cards and mixed them up violently as if to destroy the story that was forming.

"Give me a break."

Seeing Takanori exploding with irritation, Yoneda sipped his green tea and pouted.

"Not much use in complaining about what your fortune said, y'know."

With one knee bent up, Takanori took out the USB stick from his pocket and tossed it on top of the shuffled cards.

"I didn't come back to find out my fortune. I'm here because I wanted to know what this is all about."

"Same thing. It's all the same."

Takanori had no idea what that meant and asked, "What are you talking about? What's the same?"

"I mean the one who brought the USB and the one who brought the tarot cards is the same person."

At that moment, Takanori felt like he could see Yoneda's very skull through his scalp and patchy, balding hair. What Takanori had ended up cultivating in the film department at his fine arts college was not so much facility with the latest video technology but rather the traditional ability to draw. In fact, his skills as a painter helped him more than anything in his current occupation. In trying to render a figure on a canvas, you needed to see into the bone structure that made up the human body. Without that ability, making realistic CG images was impossible. With video technology, once you landed a job you could learn naturally little by little, but drawing well required a lengthy apprenticeship.

Just as Takanori was about to probe into Yoneda's skull, the scent from a little while ago came back to his nostrils. That alluring aroma, specific to women, had lingered at the entrance...

He came to realize that "the same person" Yoneda mentioned was the woman who had visited the office a little while ago.

"So, who is it? The woman, I mean," Takanori asked.

"Her name is Kiyomi Sakata."

Through industry rumors, Takanori more or less knew who she was, even though he'd never met her. A former actress turned fortune-teller. She had to be close to fifty years old but still possessed a miraculous youth—truly a woman of indeterminate age. She composed her own screenplays and made TV programs and movies as a producer. And she also had many followers, not only actors and TV personalities, but even musicians. Her influence reached to every corner of show business...

That was about everything that Takanori knew about Kiyomi Sakata.

So the video I'm trying to analyze was brought to us by Kiyomi Sakata.

Takanori ruminated on that fact.

6

It was a 35-mm film, a relic from a bygone era. She'd never seen one before and knew of them only thanks to Takanori. But that was what this was, running on a projector and clanking as if it were about to fall apart any minute.

Akane was looking at both the images and the device projecting them. The scene couldn't exist in the real world.

Film is nothing more than thin plastic subjected to photo processing, so she had to wonder where this much light was coming from. The unnatural profusion formed bands and was emanating from everywhere. It was so lifelike that she felt she could almost touch it, each individual band seemingly asserting its existence.

A thorn of light very nearly speared Akane's cheek but retreated at the last moment. Then a picture scroll of a life began to unfold before her.

She saw a young woman passing through a school gate, a female teacher conducting a language lesson in the classroom, a college student studying to be a Japanese teacher in a department of education, a girl going to junior high and high school from the facility... All of them were Akane.

The life she'd led until now was being projected on the screen in reverse. The more scratches that appeared in these black and white images, the younger Akane was getting. When it got to the age that she was in her last year of elementary school, the screen went black for several seconds. Then the face of someone dear to her appeared, someone now gone. Next, Akane was a baby again, cradled and nursing at her mother's breast. Finally, after going through a tunnel, she stopped moving inside a small sphere.

Within the sphere were the echoes of a slow heartbeat. When a clanking noise took the place of the heartbeat, the images and the device disappeared, leaving her surrounded in darkness.

But Akane felt no anxiety—she felt endless joy and warmth, and gratitude welled up inside her. She'd gone back into her mother's womb.

Then, at the peak of her happiness, she woke up.

She didn't know where she was. As she grew more aware of herself, trying to figure out where this was, her fear that she might be dead receded.

At first, her entire body seemed to be covered by a white veil. A new world coated in a sticky white film surrounded her. She felt like she was at the center of the world, and it wasn't a bad feeling. Not only wasn't it bad, it was tickling and elating.

She didn't even want to blink to miss this moment, so she kept her eyes open. The soft, floating sensation withdrew, and a hard, flat, rectangular surface gradually started to rise up. This thing above her looked like a rectangular lid. Its four corners were connected to white walls stretching deep down, the bottom of which disappeared beneath her, beyond her field of vision.

Now it feels like I'm lying down on a bed in a small room.

A fluorescent light in the center of the ceiling bathed the room in white. This light was of a different kind than the ones in her illusion—it was unsteady, and fragile.

Akane moved only her eyes to ascertain the circumstances around her.

Suddenly, the scent of soil climbed to the surface of her consciousness and nearly made her choke, only to be replaced by the medicinal smell of alcohol-based sterilizers.

Recalling what had happened to her, she presumed that she was in a hospital room.

Now everything came back to her. She remembered stepping through the school gate, and then she'd smelled the soil, lost consciousness, and collapsed. Right next to her, there'd been a man who looked like a gardener or a guard. He must have called the ambulance. If so, she guessed that this had to be the emergency ward in a hospital not far from the school.

"You're awake now."

She heard a voice near her ears and sensed somebody standing up. A young woman dressed in white walked toward her, crossed her field of vision on her left side, and called a doctor using the intercom.

The doctor who came into the room right afterwards looked even younger than the nurse. He peered into Akane's face, smiled, and began talking very rapidly. She couldn't understand very well what he was saying thanks to the special medical terms and his fast pace. What was more, a metallic sound echoed deep inside her ears at times and interfered with her hearing.

...Stabilization of cardiopulmonary functions, degree of impairment of consciousness, oxygen saturation level, vitals...

The words she could catch were breaking up, and it was hard to grasp the whole context. That said, she couldn't ask him to repeat himself, and she simply sighed.

"There's no need to worry. Your consciousness is only minimally impaired."

That wasn't what she was hoping to hear. She wanted to know how long she'd been unconscious.

Since she'd been brought in by ambulance, allowed to rest in the treatment room, and given basic tests, at least several hours must have passed. But as far as the worst-case scenario, she had no idea. Passing out and going unconscious, then waking up and regaining consciousness... It felt like a momentary blink, but that moment could conceivably have lasted a whole year.

"What's today's date?" Akane asked fearfully.

They were the first words she'd uttered after waking up.

"It's June 18th, 2:50 p.m. You've been unconscious for two hours and fifty minutes."

Realizing that only two hours and fifty minutes had elapsed since noon when she collapsed, Akane sighed with relief. Having any more blank periods cutting into the film of her life would be unbearable.

As Akane followed the exchanges between the doctor and the nurse, she began to grasp her condition.

No evidence of any alcohol or drug use...

Naturally. She wasn't accustomed to drinking alcohol, nor had she taken any medications for the past two or three years.

...Cardiopulmonary functions stable...no sign of infectious disease or external injury...cranial CT scan came back fine, brain center functioning normally...

The doctor rattling away at high speed and the nurse, who spoke in a placid tone in contrast, together conveyed that none of the tests performed thus far had revealed the true reason Akane had lost consciousness.

For her part, Akane couldn't tell whether that was a good thing or a bad thing. Even if the indices they used to evaluate her health were all favorable, as long as they couldn't pinpoint why she'd been unconscious, the same thing could happen again at some later date.

While her intellect struggled to make sense of her physiological state, the surface of her skin detected an anomaly. From her head to her neck on her right side, she felt a current of air recurring at a certain rhythm.

Someone was there on the right in her blind spot. There seemed to be another person in this small room besides herself, the doctor, and the nurse. Had the person been standing not three feet behind her this whole time, perfectly still and with bated breath? Perhaps it was another nurse preparing an intravenous drip or trying to take her blood pressure. But Akane couldn't tell the person's gender. Was it a man or a woman behind her? Her ability to sniff that out just from the ambience wasn't functioning properly.

She raised her head and turned it right.

A woman wearing a kimono was sitting on a stool in the corner and staring at Akane. It was an old-fashioned kimono that looked out of place in an E.R. She had a folding fan in her hand and was waving it gracefully.

What Akane had felt on her skin was the wind coming from the fan.

Even after meeting Akane's gaze, the woman showed no change in expression. She didn't even move an eyebrow and kept fanning herself at the same speed.

The doctor and nurse carried on, too, ignoring the woman's presence.

"Forgive me, I'd just like to confirm something. Are you pregnant?"

When the doctor asked her this, Akane's head was still turned around. His words reached her brain, but she couldn't bring herself to respond. With both eyes open wide, she observed the woman's handsome face.

She had crow's feet—appropriate for her age—and her skin was so white it seemed almost transparent. Her fingers were slender and elegant, but the cuticles of her nails were peeling.

Mom, why are you here?

She almost wondered it out loud. Bringing the back of her hand to her mouth, she swallowed the words along with her breath and frantically sealed them in her heart.

Akane's mind was nearly thrown into chaos. When she struggled to think of a logical reason for her mother's presence, there was a buzzing in her brain as if her blood vessels were short-circuiting.

They brought me here by ambulance, so maybe it's to be expected that the school would've called my immediate family. But they couldn't have known how to get in touch with my mom. Even if they did, there's absolutely no way they could've made contact.

When Akane looked in front of her again, the doctor's face was extremely close to hers. He seriously wanted to know if she was pregnant.

"If your loss of consciousness was caused by eclampsia, which can occur in early pregnancy, it's a bit of a problem. Your blood pressure is normal, so I doubt that's what happened, but we need to check just to be sure..."

Akane realized her predicament as she looked back and forth at the doctor and the woman behind her.

Right in front of her mother, Akane was going to have to tell the doctor about getting pregnant out of wedlock.

Her mother considerately maintained a neutral expression, waiting for Akane to answer, but her cool gaze seemed to be saying, "You *are* pregnant, aren't you?"

For Akane, her mother was an eternal mystery.

Akane had been three years old when her mother died. She'd departed this world at the age of twenty-four, the very same age that Akane was now. Whether her mother had died from illness or from an accident, Akane had never been told. She didn't even know who her real father was, and her memory was even vague about whether a funeral had been held for her mother.

Sometimes, roughly once a year, Akane's mother would appear to her like this as a hallucination that only she could see.

But what felt even stranger was that her mother—who had died young—appeared to have aged appropriately in her illusory form.

If she were still alive, she would be forty-five this year. Though she remained as beautiful as she was during her lifetime, the luster of her skin had faded in keeping with her age.

Mom, you got old...

Her mother hid her face with her fan as if she could hear Akane's silent mutter.

7

Takanori never sat down on the train, not even when seats were free. He always stood leaning against the doors and stared at the scenery outside.

At night during the rainy season, the inbound train on the Keihin Express had empty seats, but as usual Takanori was standing with his cheek nearly pressed against the glass. His own reflected face, melting into the scenery of the city as it passed by on the other side, looked like a ghost's.

Three hours earlier, when he had been heading to Kawasaki on the outbound train, he'd spotted a cluster of tombstones beneath the elevated track on his left in the direction he was traveling. They hadn't been on any temple grounds, but rather had been lined up closely together in rows in a small space that cut through a residential area. Originally, such a cul-de-sac could only have been used as a parking space, but it had been turned into a graveyard. Seeing tombstones directly under you when you opened your apartment window made for a bizarre view, he'd thought, and he couldn't help but stare.

This time, he couldn't find any graves in the scenery outside the window he was leaning on. With the track as a dividing line, the view on his side had a completely different character than the townscape on the other side, with the sloped road that passed through the residential district disappearing into the darkness over the hill.

It felt like almost a whole day, but when he looked at his watch, obviously, he'd only learned three hours ago of Akane's hospitalization.

For him, the day felt very long. He'd gone to the studio in the morning and received the call from her that she was pregnant. Then, President Yoneda had given him the USB stick containing the video of the suicide scene. Takanori's doubts had grown deeper and deeper as he analyzed it in his home office, and he'd had to go back to the studio. While Yoneda was telling him about Kiyomi Sakata, Takanori received another call: Akane had passed out in the schoolyard and been taken to the hospital by ambulance. He rushed to Fujimi Hospital in Kawasaki on the Keihin Express, and after confirming Akane's condition, was now going back on the same line.

He'd been traveling back and forth all day.

On the stool beside her, he'd held her hand the whole time, right up until visiting hours were over. Her thin fingers had felt so cold— she'd intertwined them with his, showing how much she needed him.

Even after being transferred from the emergency ward treatment room to a four-bed room in the general ward, Akane had sometimes raised her head and looked at the wall, her expression suggesting that her mind was elsewhere. He'd followed her line of sight and gazed in the same direction, but there'd been nothing to see.

It was past eight now; it would soon be lights out. Takanori thought of Akane's loneliness, what with her being left alone in a hospital room at night. Since he knew about her upbringing, he could imagine how she'd be tormented by anxiety.

The thought that he could no longer allow her to be alone was bubbling up inside him. He was the only person she could depend on. No matter what the results of her exam, once she was released from the hospital, he wanted to file the marriage registration right away and start living together.

For now, her blood pressure and kidney function were both normal, and there were no signs of eclampsia. All the numbers from her blood test and urine analysis were fine, too. She was not at risk of seizure, either, and her head CT scan hadn't discovered any abnormalities. They were waiting for more detailed test results, and if nothing was out of the ordinary, she'd probably be discharged the next day.

That means I'll have to do this same trip to Kawasaki again and help with her release.

Suddenly feeling tired, Takanori redirected his gaze to the train interior and searched for an empty seat. There were several, but for some reason, he just staggered over to the doors on the opposite side without sitting down. The train came to a stop at Aomono-Yokocho station, and the doors that were now across from him opened. He'd moved to this side in advance in order not to block the way for people who'd be boarding.

Just as he'd thought, a drunkard got on and grabbed the spot where Takanori had been, and once there the man sneezed twice, magnificently. The stench of alcohol mixed with sweat wafted from his body, and the foul odor filled the car.

Guess I was right to move from that side to this one.

Lifting his face, Takanori returned to looking at the scenery outside. There was a long, narrow gap between the wall on the platform and the roof, and in that slim space he spotted the windows of an old-looking apartment building. Though he couldn't tell how many floors it had, he saw six balconies lined in a single row with an elevator in between.

He was struck by a powerful sense of déjà vu.

I've seen this place before…I'm sure of it.

Takanori could predict exactly what was going to happen next. Of the units that were visible from the gap at that moment, only the two on either end had their lights on, but the ones in the third apartment from the right were about to come on.

…Three, two, one..

He began counting down, and just when he reached "zero" in his head, light leaked through the window of the unit he was looking at. The scene he'd foretold now presented itself before his eyes. As he continued to look, the light from the apartment window got blocked out, gradually, before being restored to its original state. *Maybe the blinds were shut, and then opened again?* Yet a curtain would have opened and closed from side to side while this had occurred up and down, like a shutter falling and rising. To Takanori it seemed like blinking.

Even more than the light turning on as he'd predicted, what truly surprised him was his sense that an enormous eyeball floating in the darkness had blinked.

He couldn't avert his gaze from the window. The third apartment from the right made him uneasy, as if it had imparted some sort of sign. These past few moments, he'd been able to foresee the immediate future, which only braced him against what was to come.

On his back, he perceived a subtle change in the mood inside the train. The vile odor was no different than before, but he'd gotten used to it and no longer minded it as much. Despite his fatigue, his senses seemed to be growing sharper. The jumble of other passengers' conversations stood out to him clearly and reached him on a conscious level. He could distinguish the sounds of each and every car running along the Keihin No. 1 route and picture the crow that had cawed and the dog that had howled.

The skin of his neck told him that the temperature inside the train car had risen. *It's definitely gotten even muggier in here.* When he turned to look behind him, the reason became clear. The doors had been left open, allowing hot air to flow in from outside.

Takanori now noticed that they'd been held for too long at the station. If this were a local making every stop, it might need to remain at the platform for a while, waiting for a connecting train to arrive, but this was an express.

A few seated passengers half-rose and looked around, their heads tilted in confusion. Everyone seemed to have begun wondering why the train was being held for such an unusually long time.

Following the movements around him and scanning the interior, Takanori's eyes came to rest on the sub-headline in an ad for a weekly magazine.

Rapid Rise in Suicides Over Last Several Months, Cause Unknown

To be sure, he'd seen and heard about quite a few suicides in the news recently. And tucked inside his pocket was the USB stick with the suicide video.

Intrigued, Takanori began to approach the ad poster, and just then an announcement came over the loudspeaker.

"Ladies and gentlemen, due to a fatal accident ahead of us at Shinagawa station, this train is now out of service. We sincerely apologize for any inconvenience."

Gasps and tongue clicks escaped from the passengers' lips.

Suddenly, an image of four limbs scattered on the tracks arose in the back of Takanori's mind. The person's abdomen had been cut in half, and steam was rising from the viscera that had spilled out. It was so vivid, he felt as if he were actually seeing it.

Takanori scratched his neck as if to scrape away the imagery and moved back to where he'd stood before.

When it came to such accidents, you needed to be ready to wait a rather long time. The sensible thing to do was to get off the train and hail a taxi. It would necessitate extra travel costs, but staying inside a rank, sweltering car with no idea how long the cleanup might take was sheer agony.

As he prepared to step onto the platform, Takanori looked up again at the apartments peeking through the rectangular gap.

When did the light go out?

The third apartment unit from the right was covered in darkness.

8

The hands of the clock said it was past 11 p.m. This long day would be over in another hour. Having bathed, Takanori was about to throw the jeans he'd taken off into the washing machine when he recalled that the USB stick was still in its pocket.

Yikes, that was close.

Yoneda had told him that this was now the only memory stick on which the images were saved. If it were lost or damaged, the rare video would be no more. Takanori couldn't quite remember if he'd saved his data when he played the video that afternoon.

He removed the USB stick and turned toward the desk where his computer sat.

Everyone on the Studio Oz staff liked to take their work home with them. A home computer customized for personal use made the work go more smoothly than the machines at the office.

Takanori was no exception. That was why he'd left the office in the afternoon and returned to his apartment. He'd made a round-trip between the office and home twice that day. The second time, it had been to ask Yoneda why they were analyzing the video.

Yet the president hadn't given a straight answer, and the conversation had gotten nowhere. As for what Kiyomi Sakata's intent had been in delivering the USB stick, not even Yoneda knew for certain. The plan to process the scene and use it in a special television feature had long since vanished into thin air.

In other words, he had come to share Takanori's doubts.

"Sakata's usually pretty blunt, but the way she talked this time was weird, like she was trying to hide something, y'know?" Yoneda had said, tilting his head.

Withholding the most crucial bits, namely which parts of the video she needed them to analyze, and how, and to what end, she just seemed to want to know how viewers might feel after watching it and if they might find anything strange about it—that was Yoneda's impression. Moreover, he'd sensed trepidation and unease from her speech and in her mannerisms. Now, in Takanori's view, the president could be a bit obtuse. He wasn't the type to pick up on every psychological subtlety lurking behind somebody's outward behavior. Had Sakata been so shaken that even Yoneda could discern her mental state? It seemed to contradict the image Takanori had of her as a strong woman, based on the rumors he'd heard—it somehow just felt unlike her.

Whatever the reason, Yoneda figured that having Kiyomi Sakata in his debt couldn't be a bad thing. Takanori could picture the president promising to assist in any way possible, thumping his chest with pride, sure that obtaining the woman's gratitude would net more jobs down the road.

"So there ya go. Anyway, take care of this one for me. If you notice anything, anything at all, let me know, okay?"

Yoneda's attitude suggested that he had some ulterior motive, as though he regarded the USB stick as a nuisance and was looking to get it off his own hands and into Takanori's.

Takanori did owe the man a favor. Before coming to Studio Oz, Takanori had performed a wide variety of tasks, from computer graphics to animation, at a general production company that handled a great many commercials. The job had been worthwhile in its own way, but ironically enough, as he mastered it, he became increasingly subsumed into the commercials division. Having hoped to polish his skills in a more comprehensive manner and eventually to put them to use in filmmaking, he wanted to avoid being trapped in a specialist job away from a broader field of possibilities.

At just that time, Yoneda, the head of a subcontracting production company, invited Takanori to join him.

Having recognized Takanori's talent, and enticing him with dreams of creating a film production company together, Yoneda promised him carte blanche when it came to producing short films.

Takanori jumped at the offer and quit his job at the major production company, and two years had passed since his move to Studio Oz.

In an industry where people offered the impossible by way of an introduction, Yoneda actually kept his promise. Studio Oz spent what little money it possessed to start producing short films using CG and entrusted Takanori to direct a work. "The Green Wall" was screened at a regional film festival and won a prize; after being released on DVD, it gained a fairly high reputation among enthusiasts. On top of that, it generated enough revenue for the studio to recoup the production costs, and so with his first creation, Takanori managed to exceed expectations. All of it was thanks to the opportunities Yoneda had given him.

Considering all that, he couldn't complain about the chore Yoneda was thrusting onto him.

Takanori turned on his computer and displayed the video on the USB stick.

As he suspected, he hadn't saved it on his hard drive. First he executed a command to read it into his Docs.

He'd intended to turn off the power once he was done but held off, thinking he should watch it again before going to bed. It wasn't a pleasant video; if he wanted to get a good night's rest, the best thing to do was to go to sleep right away. But if he resisted the temptation and went to bed, he might dwell on it even more...

Takanori decided to set a time limit for himself. Often, while video processing on his computer, daylight would break. He gave himself ten minutes, certain that he could check the video again in that much time.

Yet as soon as he played it, the monitor captivated him and the time limit he'd set vanished. It was thanks to the gravitational pull of his experience from earlier in the day.

What first appeared onscreen was the studio apartment where the man had hanged himself. The man walked around the room, video camera in hand, the lens gliding over the dingy wallpaper and balcony doorframe, the table, and then the chair. The entryway door was open, and after part of the common corridor was captured on camera, the viewpoint turned back to the unit's interior.

Takanori paused the video there. He had this feeling that while the door was still open, the number of the unit across the hall had shown. Scrolling up from the center of the facing unit's door, he captured a rectangular shape that looked to be a number plate and gradually enlarged it. The numerals written on the plate were now magnified.

311.

Directly in front of the unit where the suicide had taken place was "Room 311."

Next, the camera shook as it moved in an arc, and after going over the walls, it focused on the balcony doorframe before finally coming to rest atop the table.

Takanori paused the video once again, rewound it, and played it back frame-by-frame. He'd already honed in on his target. The specific scene that so aroused his interest was definitely in that segment. Though it had lasted but a brief moment, there was no way he could miss it.

When the camera focus cut across the glass door that led to the balcony, a view of the outside scenery appeared onscreen. The condominium unit opened to a jumbled cityscape. Though Takanori couldn't tell which town, train tracks stretched from left to right.

He stopped the video at that scene and scrolled until he located his target, which he then enlarged.

There was a train station out there roughly parallel to the building but lower down. The upper section of the platform was covered by a roof, and the sides were enclosed by soundproof walls, but a thin rectangular gap provided a partial view of a train stopped there.

Takanori enlarged the image further. There was a digital display above the red train car indicating the destination. He could just barely zoom in enough for it to be legible.

Haneda Airport, Express.

If it was bound for Haneda Airport, he could immediately name the line. It was the outbound track of the Keihin Express.

After leaving Shinagawa, a special express headed for Haneda on the Keihin line would either stop at Kamata or proceed directly to its final destination. A regular express would stop at Aomono-Yokocho, Tachiaigawa, Heiwajima, and Kamata.

Just as he was about to return the video to its original size, Takanori paused it again. He saw an area in front of the platform where a cluster of rectangular objects stood. Shifting and enlarging the focus point revealed the objects to be tombstones. They were squeezed into a space beneath the eaves of several houses, forming a graveyard on a tiny plot of land.

Takanori gulped and just continued staring at the monitor.

Get a grip, he told himself. His mental screen flashed back to what he'd seen on his return trip from the hospital only a while ago.

When the outbound train on the Keihin Express had stopped at Aomono-Yokocho, he'd looked up through the gap between the roof and the wall of the platform to espy six apartment units lined up in a row.

Something clicked in his head.

Takanori looked away from the screen and drew a simple sketch on a piece of scratch paper he had handy. Next, he began assigning numbers to the row of six apartment units, starting from the right side with apartments 1, 2, and 3, and continuing from the left with 7, 8, and 9 for the units across the hallway. If he took the space for the elevator in the middle into account, Room 11 would be across

Room 3. Across the way from the unit where the man had hanged himself was Room 311. That meant the one Takanori was looking at now was No. 303. In other words, it had to be the third unit from the right.

The one that had drawn his attention so powerfully and slowly blinked at him, invitingly...

It was possible that the floor he'd seen wasn't the third floor. Judging from the position of the outbound express's destination display, however, the part near the top of the balcony door would be visible from an inbound train. If you could see there from here, you could also see here from there.

On the train, Takanori had been compelled to act in anticipation of an event as if some precognition had taken effect. If he was still in its grip, the convergence couldn't be a coincidence.

Did someone really commit suicide in this unknown studio apartment? If so, who was he? Casting aside the questions he should be asking, Takanori cowered at the invisible force filling the air around him.

He was being guided by somebody. Was this some clever trap, or was he just being made to watch some meaningless video? He couldn't tell. All he could say for certain was that the genesis of this film had something to do with him.

The veins in his temples stood out. He could feel his pulse throbbing all over his head.

The hands of the wristwatch he'd put beside his computer indicated that it was almost midnight. The long day was nearly at an end.

Today's events were merely a prologue compared to the nightmare that was about to unfold—somehow, Takanori understood this.

CHAPTER TWO   *Guided*

1

Up ahead and over the hill was Takanori's condominium, where he was waiting. When Akane got close and looked up, she slowed her gait, overpowered by the sight of the super high-rise. Just then, the figure of a man on the opposite sidewalk entered her field of vision, and she instinctively came to a halt.

On her left stretched the display window of a brand-name store. Akane approached the glass so that her cheeks were practically touching it. It wasn't because she was interested in the fancy handbags, but an instant reaction; she didn't want this person to see how leery she was.

She had a terrible memory from her past of being followed by the shadowy figure of an unknown man, so this sort of thing especially made her shudder.

She knew that it was all in her mind. Similar things had happened to her many times before. Sure that she was being followed, she'd halt and observe the man's behavior, and most of the time it would end with her feeling relieved because it had just been her imagination. Once, strolling in Shibuya, her eyes met a passerby's who then made a U-turn and started following her. In that case, he obviously meant to chat her up for a date. When she made eye contact with a man and her instincts kicked in and she thought, *Oh, he's coming over to me*, she was never wrong about it. After following her for a while and checking her out thoroughly, they almost always called out to her in a cheerful voice, which deflated her fear.

Thinking that this was probably another such instance, Akane pretended to look at the bags and kept a watchful eye on the man's reflection in the display window.

He was standing on the sidewalk on the other side of the street with his back turned to her and a cell phone pressed to his ear. It felt a little strange to her that he'd chosen to stand there when he could easily have talked and walked at the same time.

What even made me notice that man? She tried to figure out why she'd unconsciously acted as she had.

She'd made the first move by abruptly stopping in front of the display window, and the man had reacted by coming to a halt and nonchalantly taking out his cell phone... That was how it had played out.

Maybe my nerves are just overactive. Could be an after-effect from when I fainted at the school gate two days ago. Not knowing why she'd collapsed made her more anxious than was probably necessary.

With her back still turned to the man, Akane kept watching his reflection in the window. It looked as though he might be in his thirties. He was slim, tall, and finely dressed. He had on a casual summer necktie and was wearing a short-sleeved white jacket over his shirt. She could find nothing suspicious about his appearance.

Twisting his body slightly, the man looked at Akane before casting down his eyes and kicking pebbles with the tip of his toes. Something about it seemed contrived to her. Then again, she wasn't getting the sense that he wanted to pick her up.

Akane wanted to hurry over to the apartment where Takanori was waiting, but she was prevented from moving. It irritated her not to be able to go to him when he was only a stone's throw away and surely waiting for her to come home.

As the days were longest this time of the year, there was still plenty of light outside even though it was almost past 6 p.m. Lit by his cell phone's backlight, the area around the man's nose had a pale glow in the window.

Akane took that as her cue to start walking.

There's no way I'm going to let something silly like this ruin my first evening after moving in with Takanori.

All she had to do was to take some action to confirm there was nothing to worry about, and then she could laugh at herself for being so foolish.

The display window continued until it reached an elevated promenade, reflecting the scenery diagonally behind her on the right.

When she'd walked a mere couple of dozen feet, the man began in the same direction as if he'd timed his movement.

What? Akane yelped in her mind. *So I wasn't imagining things...*

She and the man were moving in concert.

Just before the display window ended, Akane opened her cell phone and placed her hand mirror on the display, creating an impromptu rearview mirror. To any passersby, she would simply appear to be using her cell phone while walking.

Maintaining a certain distance but in lockstep, the man followed on the right-hand side behind her. Even so, she couldn't afford to stop moving. *Don't do anything unnatural or he'll catch on*, her instincts warned.

After passing under the promenade and ascending the stone steps, she would arrive at the lobby of the condo where Takanori was waiting. If she could just make it through the lobby's self-locking door, the man would naturally break off his pursuit. But then, he'd find out where she lived. On the very first day after she'd moved out of her cheap apartment in Tsurumi and into this midtown condo, her address would be in the hands of some mysterious man.

Mustering all her concentration, Akane struggled to think of the best course of action. She did not know for certain that the man was following her, but she was seized with dread and a mental alarm was flashing on and off.

She made a split-second decision to forgo the lobby and continued up the hill instead. She hooked a right at the T-shaped intersection at the end of the street, and with hurried steps, went inside a glass-fronted coffee shop.

For the entire time that she stood in line at the register, Akane's mind remained focused on the sidewalk outside. She began counting, and exactly ten seconds later the man appeared along the sidewalk.

He didn't turn his head to look inside the shop. Then again, if he'd seen her enter, he wouldn't need to check.

Akane considered leaving the shop and going back the way she'd come, but she had the feeling that the man would be out there somewhere watching for her. If he were waiting for her to exit and started following her again, there might be nowhere for her to go.

Despite walking in such muggy weather, she was thirsting for something hot to drink.

She ordered a cup of hot milk and took a seat with her drink in hand. Her eyes were fixed on the entrance. If he came in, once again, she'd be stuck with nowhere to go.

Am I just being paranoid?

She still couldn't be sure. Though in all likelihood she was overthinking it, she couldn't summon the courage to settle the matter. It felt as if the solid ground was crumbling away from her view of the world. Ever since she'd passed out at the school gate at noon the day before yesterday, delusions had invaded her reality. She wondered if it was being twisted and truth and illusion had become tangled up inside her.

Whenever a customer went in or out, the tepid air of the rainy season flowed in. Yet Akane was trembling. She couldn't help being wracked by anxiety.

She wanted to connect with Takanori right then and there. If she could hear his voice, she could shove away this illusion, solid reality would return, and she'd have the courage to act with resolve.

She took her cell phone out of her bag to call him.

When she brought up his number in her registry and was about to press the call button, she noticed a small difference on her phone's display. There was an icon flickering at the top. A small light was flashing, its rhythm synched with the alarm going off in her mind.

Having never seen it before, Akane wondered what the flashing meant.

As she looked on, though, it gradually dawned on her. Somebody was trying to identify her location by GPS...

Who? And why?

Akane tried to come up with a logical explanation. Perhaps Takanori was worried she might have passed out somewhere with nobody else around her. But she shook her head. She shouldn't be deceiving myself with such a convenient explanation. Takanori wasn't that kind of person. He'd be loath to do anything like track someone in secret—it wasn't in his character.

Was the nightmare she'd pushed away to the bottom of her memory rising up again? If so, the GPS flashing was a sign.

Wanting only to hear his voice, Akane pressed his number.

Waiting for him to pick up, she kept her eyes locked on the scenery outside the window, not even blinking. As the dusk thickened, men and women continued to pass by without ado.

From a blind spot on the left side of the window she was looking through—the man stared at her.

Come out, little girl. Let's play hide and seek, like we used to.

She felt like she could hear the man whispering from somewhere.

2

Takanori went to the balcony, seeking only to shake off his drowsiness. Yet he found himself captivated by the view from the west-facing room and ended up staying longer than he had intended.

The west horizon was covered by thin clouds and painted a brilliant vermillion by the setting sun.

Takanori liked the moderate height there on the twelfth floor of the forty-floor skyscraper. Going higher up diminished the sense of reality of the bird's-eye view.

S

When you soared even higher, you had the illusion that the world had lost a dimension. On an airplane that was about to land, if you got close to the window and looked down at the scenery near the runway, the golf courses and houses that colored the hillsides sometimes looked like the board of "The Game of Life." The world stretching beneath was fictional, and you were gazing down on a two-dimensional flatness from your three-dimensional perch. That feeling—resembling a sense of superiority—faded little by little as the plane descended and the scenery was fleshed out, its reality returning in full when the wheels touched the tarmac.

The view from the twelfth floor wasn't so precarious. The panorama overflowed with everyday life and felt stable. That was precisely because the height was fixed. During a plane's takeoff and landing, the dramatic rise and drop coupled with the acceleration made reality recede...

Toying with such thoughts, Takanori was reminded of the apartment in Shinagawa that he'd visited that afternoon. The view from each landing of that seven-story building was branded in his mind.

Analyzing the video recorded on the USB stick, he'd managed to identify approximately where it had been shot.

It was a unit in an apartment building not far from Aomono-Yokocho station on the Keihin Express line.

To confirm his conjecture, he'd had no choice but to go there himself.

After getting off at Aomono-Yokocho, he hadn't gone directly to the site. Feeling hungry, and needing a little time to gather his composure, he'd decided to slurp down noodles at a ramen shop near the station while running a mental simulation of what he might soon encounter. He needed to steel himself in case he ran into something unexpected. You tended to forget yourself and make mistakes when you were caught flatfooted. Simply by thinking ahead, you could at least stay calm amidst a certain amount of trouble.

Assuming that the man hanged himself in Room 303 in a building near Aomono-Yokocho station, the question was: when did it happen? According to Yoneda, the live video of the suicide had leaked online about a month ago.

If it was real, it meant that more than a month had passed.

Takanori foresaw two possible outcomes—he dared contemplate the worst-case scenario, which was proceeding to his destination unwarily and ending up as the first person to discover a dead body. Unlike in a solitary house in the countryside, with a studio apartment near a train station, there was little chance that a suicide victim's corpse would be left for over a month, but it behooved him to be thoroughly prepared.

Completing his mental simulation, Takanori mustered his courage and left the shop.

He had a rough idea of where he was going and how far away it was. Just after climbing a hill, he located the building that looked like his target. Its name: the Shinagawa View Heights. An old, seven-story apartment building constructed at least thirty years ago. Takanori could guess the size of each individual unit from outside.

In between the janitor's room and the elevator hall was a space where the mail slots and coin laundry machines were located, and after entering, Takanori checked the numbers written on the mail plates one by one.

The unit number he was looking for was 303. He'd imagined that the slot would be clogged shut, packed full of parcels and newspapers, but what he actually saw was quite different.

The slot marked 303 had been neatly maintained, and when he peered in through the gap, there were two pieces of mail on the bottom. After quickly scanning his surroundings, he pulled the slot's handle, and the little door opened easily for him. He took out the mail items and checked the addressee. The same person's name was on both of them.

"Mr. Hiroyuki Niimura."

There was a strong chance that the resident in Room 303 was this Hiroyuki Niimura. Takanori committed the name firmly to memory.

Returning the sealed mail, he proceeded to the hallway and glanced around. It was a little past one o'clock on a weekday afternoon, and not a single person was in sight. There were no signs of any rooms being used as offices, either, and the entire place was quiet. From beyond the janitor's door came the only noise, that of a sink being scoured with a brush.

Instead of taking the elevator, Takanori went back outside and used the emergency stairwell to check the view from each floor.

His first, unassuming step on the edge of an iron stair produced a surprisingly loud sound and made him lift his foot up by reflex. Despite his shoe's rubber sole, a hard clang reverberated through the alley, which was densely packed with stores.

When he finally made it to the third-floor landing and looked down toward the station, the same view as in the video on the USB stretched out below him. At roughly the oblique angle he'd seen from the unit where the man had killed himself, Takanori's line of sight passed through the gap between the roof and the wall and rested on the Aomono-Yokocho station platform.

Just in case, he climbed to the top to compare the views at different elevations, and upon returning to the third floor, he stood at the hallway entrance.

It stretched straight ahead, and there were units on both sides just as he'd imagined.

Six on the right with the elevator in between them, and seven on the left—a total of thirteen units facing each other. The afternoon sun shone in through a window fitted into the wall down at the end, but the area retained a gloomy ambience. Perhaps it was the grubby walls and the oppressively low ceiling, or the dark brown doors lined up at equal intervals...

Glancing around as he walked, Takanori came to stand in front of Room 303 without even noticing.

The time was 1:22 p.m. A typical office worker would be out at that hour. Maybe some total stranger was about to come rushing out of one of the doors right then.

Guided

Takanori's every nerve was focused on his sense of smell. He sniffed the air for any rotten odor seeping through the gap in the door, but all he detected were the ordinary scents of everyday life.

Taking a few steps back, he stared at the door and squinted as if to see through to the other side.

The electricity meter was moving slowly. It seemed like someone was living there and maintaining the apartment. Takanori pressed his ear against the door, hoping to figure out whether the current resident, Hiroyuki Niimura, was home or not. There was no sound, nor any sign of a human presence. He reached for the doorknob but pulled his hand back in spite of himself. The mere thought that the door might not be locked from inside, that it might open to reveal an unanticipated sight, sapped his courage.

He couldn't just keep on standing there in front of the door. He might be mistaken for a suspicious person. Desperate for a breath of fresh air, he made for the emergency exit.

The landing felt like it was floating in midair. Leaning his body against the handrail, he tried to process everything that had happened up to that point.

If Hiroyuki Niimura had been the person in the video and was still alive, that meant the video had been forged and uploaded for some reason. Yet the rawness emanating from the video had an impact that only a real human body could impart. The wrinkles on the skin from the rope eating into the neck, the way the clothes had filled with air and been lifted up when the body dropped, were perfect displays of physical resistance. If that was CG, its creator was unimaginably gifted. Even compared to Takanori himself, the winner was obvious, hands down.

The other possibility was that somebody had committed suicide more than a month earlier and that Hiroyuki Niimura started living here after the unit had been renovated. That would make Room 303 a unit with a sordid history—the site of a recent suicide, with the rent dropping to less than half the market price. Still, even if it were dirt cheap, who'd want to live in a place right after some guy killed himself there?

Takanori's intuition ruled out both hypotheses. There had to be a third possibility, one that he couldn't even imagine, but he had too little info to discern any path to the truth and couldn't even get a rough sense of the right direction.

He did manage to get two things out of this—he'd located the apartment where the suicide video was filmed, and it seemed the name of the person living there was Hiroyuki Niimura. Satisfied with these achievements, Takanori left Aomono-Yokocho.

Once the vermillion tint faded from the view of the town from his balcony and darkness was about to take its place, Takanori went inside and closed the door.

He'd turned on the air conditioner before stepping out, so the apartment was now cool and dry.

First, he stood in front of the home phone in the corner of his living room and checked the incoming call history. When he went out on the balcony and closed the door, he couldn't hear the phone ring. It felt a little late for Akane not to have come home yet. Thinking she might have left a message, he checked the machine, but the call log was still empty.

Takanori turned on his computer and moved the cursor to Documents. Now that he'd gone to the site and observed the view in person, he thought he might be able to discover something new. Meaning to examine it quickly before Akane came home, he called up the video he'd saved.

With his mind on the time, he couldn't bring himself to concentrate on the screen, so he just allowed it to play. But he noticed a slight difference and stopped the video.

When last he saw it, as soon as the hanging man kicked out the chair, the body broke through the ceiling, dropped down the center of the screen, and halted its vertical movement with the body hidden from the chest up.

Before, the man's toes were inside the frame, with ample room left.

But now…his toes were closer to the bottom, which meant that the body had shifted downward a little more than in Takanori's previous viewing.

His eyes moved up as he thought this. Part of the body from the chest up—specifically, the rope eating into the man's neck—was now visible. Last time, the rope itself had been outside of the frame.

Maybe I'm just imagining things, Takanori muttered to himself with a weak laugh. It was somewhat funny to think that the man's body, recorded on video camera, was getting dragged down. Gravitational theory, effective in three-dimensional space, working on a two-dimensional digital space was ludicrous in the extreme.

Takanori was quite aware that not everything he saw was true. Perceptions only became settled in the mind as notions after being processed by consciousness. In other words, there was practically no way to distinguish between dream and reality. That he might be "just imagining things" was a valid interpretation here.

His habit of trying to think through things as logically as possible yielded a certain question: *If the video truly did change, when did it happen?*

What he needed to do was to categorize all the events into those that he could prove and those that he could not, to analyze them objectively.

After 11 p.m. the day before yesterday—that was when he'd copied the video on the USB stick to his computer. The video split into two versions at that point, one being the original saved on the USB stick, and the other being the copy saved on his computer. It occurred to him to compare the two versions side by side.

He hadn't had an opportunity to watch the video on the USB stick again after copying it onto his computer, but now, for the first time in two days, he launched it on his monitor and compared the scenes in question.

As before, the man kicked out the chair and fell, and after appearing to pass through the floor, he crashed through the ceiling and fell from above, only to stop at a position where he was hidden from the chest up. At that moment, his toes were suspended with plenty of room from the bottom of the frame.

So I wasn't just imagining it.

The video on the USB stick was the same as before; the change appeared only in the copy on his computer. The man's body in the copy was gradually shifting downward.

When Takanori tried to check the video once more from the beginning, his cell phone rang. The screen showed Akane's name.

She sounded different than usual. Her voice was anxious and subdued, hinting that she was scared by something around her.

At first, Takanori couldn't understand what she was saying.

Someone was tailing her. Monitoring her. Coming after her.

She spoke in bits and pieces, but based on what she was describing, that seemed to be the situation. He knew quite well that Akane was cautious to a fault, and the only words that came to him were the ones that he'd told himself.

She was just imagining things.

3

Usually she would be inclined to have a leisurely soak in the bathtub, but for some reason that didn't appeal to her now.

While she was showering, Akane realized why. She believed the hot water pouring down on her would wash away her paranoia.

The man hadn't been real...or rather he had been, but not intending her any harm, he'd simply been passing by.

Takanori had come down to the coffee shop to get her and resolved the whole thing.

He'd affirmed that having searched the area high and low, there had been no sign of any strange man. Afterwards, he'd explained that the GPS tracking app was something he'd secretly installed on her phone out of concern that she might fall unconscious again in some unknown place.

"You're just tired. Your nerves are so sensitive that you were reading some special significance into this tiny thing that seemed a little off."

Akane was only too eager to accept this theory, that the man who'd seemed intent on hurting her had been nothing more than a phantom born of her paranoia.

Pelted by the hot water, her delusion was rinsed away, leaving behind an empty space that she tried to fill with more cheerful and pleasant thoughts. She began humming a tune.

Having Takanori near her transformed her moments of anxiety into relief. She'd gotten acquainted with the most perfect man she could imagine, fallen in love with him, and become pregnant with his child, and now that she was about to be married to him, the future looked dazzlingly bright. Their child would be born early next year, and their life as a family of three would begin, releasing her forever from her solitary condition. She'd be able to enjoy a stable life and security. As for whether to quit her teaching job, she could think about that after starting to raise their child. If possible, she actually wanted to keep her job while also being a mother. Encouragingly, Takanori seemed to agree with her.

For Akane, he was truly her "knight on a white horse."

Her mother had been unmarried when she gave birth and had died when Akane was three years old. Not knowing who her father was, Akane had become a child with no family, all alone in the world. She'd entered a foster home named Fureai, or "Contact," founded right around that time, and there she had spent the next fifteen years. After she'd turned eighteen, there had been a party to celebrate all the children who were about to be independent, and that was where she had met Takanori for the first time.

When any children were about to leave the facility and strike out on their own, the director rented out a hall belonging to the Japan Mutual Aid Association of Public School Teachers and held a party to send them off—a modest little gathering, really. Akane had been among the first generation of children to enter the facility, right after it was established, and some of them planned to start working, while others were to enter college. Akane had just passed her college entrance exam, so she was also celebrating her admission.

She didn't remember how their conversation began, but she could still remember what Takanori said to her.

"I came because I wanted to see for myself what my father's efforts accomplished."

That was when she learned that Takanori was the first son of a family that owned one of the top general hospitals in Tokyo.

Fureai had been founded by Takanori's father—Mitsuo Ando—at his own expense, as part of the facilities affiliated with the hospital. Its sole purpose was to make a contribution to society, with no regard for profits.

Prior to then, at that type of facility, an "orphanage," children like Akane without any parents were actually a minority. The vast majority either had parents who couldn't raise them for whatever reason or had run away from home to escape abusive ones. Akane, who had no memories of ill treatment, might have been more fortunate than the other children in that respect.

Just before she entered elementary school, an abuse case at another foster home came to light, after which all such facilities became a focus of public attention. While she'd been too young to grasp the nature of the case, Akane remembered how subtle changes had appeared in everyone's behavior at the facility, starting from the director down to the childcare workers and the supervisors. At the time, she couldn't explain the change very well, but after becoming a high school student, she was finally able to find the perfect expression.

They handled us with kid gloves.

The changes that came to Fureai in the wake of the abuse case were welcome ones. Compared to other facilities, their educational policy had already been far superior, but subsequently it improved even further.

Fureai was also a spectacular experimental facility for its founder, Mitsuo Ando. He'd gathered underprivileged children and invested an abundance of capital. Enough staff were hired to provide almost every child with his or her own childcare worker and supervisor, ensuring that the kids were raised with affection and given a high-quality education. And he did all of this out of a desire to see how much those children, once they'd grown up, would contribute to society, his curiosity focused entirely on that point.

The best way to use his sizeable but not limitless funds was to invest them in nurturing more talented human beings who would be a force for good in the future.

It wasn't that he wanted to give his money away to unfortunate children out of mercy; rather, a certain feeling had sprouted inside him to raise these children with affection and give them opportunities, to make them want to give back to society. From one facility, he would raise twenty or thirty children who would then go out into the world and find themselves in a position to foster others' growth—thus amplifying the social good in a sort of geometrical progression.

And so, having always been made to hear about his father's great ambition, Takanori had come to the party—not as a guest or as his father's proxy, but of his own will, out of a desire to see for himself the fruits of his father's labor.

When Akane told him that she'd be majoring in education at a national university, receiving scholarship money to pursue her goal of becoming a teacher, Takanori looked thrilled for her, and his eyes twinkled.

"I'm glad I came here. It's convinced me that my father's project isn't some self-satisfied philanthropic whim, it's really contributing to society. Please become a great teacher and instill noble ideals in your students."

Akane could never forget the purehearted look he had in his eyes when he encouraged her thus.

Takanori was so different from the stereotype of a pampered millionaire's son. Furthermore, despite having grown up in a doctor's family, he was learning to draw at an art college, and after graduation he was to work at a big production company. It'd been obvious that he was free from the bonds so distinctive of wealthy households.

Thanks to her firsthand experience of his father's educational ideals, Akane understood how this might be. Having felt the benevolence the founding family had bestowed at every turn and fully received its benefits, she could infer what Takanori's home environment had been like. She'd never met a better man than Takanori, and she wasn't exaggerating.

But it wasn't as though, having grown up in a different world, he was just a different breed. When they first met, she felt an affinity with him for some reason, as if the gears in their hearts had clicked together.

Based on what she heard later, Takanori had the same impression, and from the moment they met they gravitated towards each other.

After she finished showering, Akane stood on the bathmat and caressed her skin with her towel. She dried her back, her hips, and her backside, then moved to the front side, and then placed her palms on her belly. It wasn't showing any signs of sticking out yet. In fact, it was perfectly flat. When she thought about how a new life was forming and growing in there, an indescribable happiness welled up in her.

Yet as this happiness heightened, so did a proportionate sense of unease. It just felt too good to be true. As ungrateful as it sounded, she might have preferred it if he came from a poorer, more ordinary family at least.

She'd received a scholarship and worked hard at a part-time job to make ends meet and become a teacher after graduating college. The Ando family's wealth defied the imagination of someone with her economic sensibilities.

Takanori's father, who'd taught forensic medicine at a university hospital, had taken over his deceased father-in-law's position and expanded it even further. Takanori's paternal and maternal grandfathers had both been doctors, and now his younger sister was attending medical school, so he was certainly pedigreed.

Such a household environment was the envy of the average person, but to Akane it felt somewhat threatening.

Prejudices toward those who'd been raised in foster care, though not as bad as it once was, still ran deep. Takanori told her that she didn't need to feel like she was inferior, that she should be proud of having worked so hard to make a life for herself despite her background as an orphan. He wasn't just saying it—his sincerity came through in his attitude. Though she knew she had nothing at all to fear, she still worried about how his parents would react.

After all, they might think that her getting pregnant out of wedlock was a strategy to ensure that Takanori would marry her.

"Don't worry. My parents have already consented to it."

He'd already made it clear to them that he ultimately intended to marry Akane. And so, even though she'd gotten pregnant out of wedlock, Takanori assured her that she had absolutely nothing to worry about. Still, growing up in a bubble free from any hardship had made him so innocent, and she had to wonder if he'd given himself over to baseless optimism.

It's precisely when you're at your happiest that you can't let yourself get carried away—you've got to watch out.

As Akane wrapped the bath towel around her and admonished herself, she recalled that her pajamas were still in her suitcase. She'd packed it full of everyday items, mainly her garments, and brought it over from her apartment in Tsurumi. She was sure the suitcase was leaning against the living room table with her pajamas still inside.

Akane went out to the living room and scanned the area.

The light of a desk lamp streamed out from the bedroom door, which was slightly ajar. Perhaps Takanori was lying on bed and reading a book.

The suitcase was right where she expected. She walked to it, and just as she was about to lean over, she noticed the light flickering on the computer monitor on the table. The power seemed to have been left on.

It was not the suitcase but the monitor that attracted her now.

The instant Akane saw the image, she got startled and stood up straight. Her instincts told her not to look, yet they failed to hold her back, and she found herself being irresistibly pulled closer to it by a mixture of curiosity and fear.

It showed a man with a rope around his neck. The body was moving downward at a deliberate pace. Even though she hadn't seen the original footage, she felt with her very skin the oddness of the transition taking place onscreen.

When the man's body fit precisely in the frame, its falling motion stopped, at which point the body began to rotate slowly.

She wondered whether it was a scene from some movie or television show, or perhaps a CG image that Takanori had been working on, but the rawness she sensed from the video wasn't anything like an entertainment film. If that's what it was, it could only be a horror movie.

What she saw now was the man's entire body with nothing left out of the shot. His face was visible but both his eyes were covered, obscuring his expression as he turned his back to the screen.

…What is this?

Little by little, she came to understand what the video was showing. The man had just placed a rope around his neck and hanged himself. Both of his arms were dangling, and his toes were convulsing. He had ceased breathing, and his heart would soon stop beating. She couldn't tell if he was still conscious.

The black stain spreading around his crotch was the only sign that he'd been alive.

His body was rotating slowly, and its front side was about to face her once again.

Right before his body came face to face with Akane—as if he had timed it—his blindfold fell away, revealing his dead face to her.

His eyeballs were slowly rolling back, with his pupils touching the edge of his eyelids, and saliva was dripping from his mouth down to his chin.

The moment Akane saw his face, she gasped aloud and felt a lump in her throat. Not because the image was unnatural and creepy—she knew his face. Instinctively, she covered her eyes with her hands, but it was too late. A memory that had been sealed in the nether reaches of her consciousness came rising up like a deep-sea fish hooked on a lure, broke through the surface and leapt into the air—springing to the top of her mind, the recollection oppressed her with staggering force.

The grassy mountain slope, the feel of the damp earth, the smell of soil striking her nose...

Her strength failing from the waist down, Akane fell to her knees on the carpet and began to lose consciousness.

No...got to...stay awake.

She tried desperately. Were she to pass out again, an ambulance would be called and she would be taken to a hospital. But she wanted to stay there in the room. The siren would extinguish her happiness, its sound nothing but a sinister omen.

Akane spread her arms on top of the table, just barely supporting her upper body.

With her cheek against the table, and her eyes open a sliver, she could still see the man's face.

When she was twelve years old, she was dragged around and nearly killed by him.

4

Takanori was lying on bed, thinking.

What sort of interpretation was there?

When he heard Akane's humming mixed with the sound of the shower, he grew even more serious. He wanted to rid her of her anxiety, give her peace. To do that, he needed to find a well-grounded reason. Yet he simply couldn't come up with a convincing explanation.

Who besides me could've installed a GPS tracking app on her cell phone, and in secret?

Akane's unease was so intense it was painful to watch, and in the belief that the first thing to do was to calm her down, a lie had slipped from his mouth. He'd come up with a more plausible reason after buying some time and calm, but nothing occurred to him. The worst part was that if she really had been tracked by GPS, what she'd said about being followed by a stranger was also true.

Then he realized that the showering sound had died down at some point. It seemed like she'd finished.

Takanori thought he should consult somebody versed in GPS tracking systems for cell phones. Minakami—his coworker and a director at Studio Oz—knew quite a lot about these things. As Takanori pictured his face and bald spot, he heard the echo of a muffled thud from the living room.

He assumed that her suitcase had fallen over.

It had been very heavy when they brought it over from her old apartment in Tsurumi the other day, so much so that Akane couldn't even move it an inch on her own. The surprising part hadn't been the weight itself but the fact that almost all her clothes had fit. That one suitcase represented just how frugal and reserved her life had been.

Back when she was living at Fureai, the essentials, like clothes, shoes, and bags, had been provided for free. "Free" meant that personal preferences weren't reflected very much, and everything had been plain. Even after Akane started living on her own, the habits she cultivated over many years didn't go away, and her buying desires remained limited to the bare necessities.

That was one of the things that had endeared her to him.

Perhaps due to his home environment, his acquaintances and friends thus far all hailed from wealthy backgrounds. They lived in mansions, rode in luxury cars, and wore high-class brands. Back when he was in college, a former girlfriend who was studying piano used to boast about how her mother had gone to Paris and purchased an entire shelf of new top-brand items in a store. No matter how beautiful and talented the girls were, the relationships had never lasted long because he'd grown tired of their pampered, self-indulgent lifestyles.

Akane was so different from all the various types of women whom Takanori had met. With clothes that fit in a single suitcase, she'd sailed out into the world and maintained her simple beauty. She was very cautious, and somewhat timid, too, but her personality had a core. She was quite resolute, in fact.

That said, it was easy for Takanori to understand Akane's fear— it was almost palpable. She was concerned about his parents' reaction to the fact that she'd gotten pregnant. As understanding as they were, she was afraid that at the last moment, his parents might ruin things. Precisely because she felt happy, she couldn't help but keep an eye on the pitfall that lay but one step away, and this cautiousness made her exhaust herself to no purpose.

No matter how many times he explained that his parents would never say no to them, Akane seemed unconvinced.

Since his childhood, Takanori had enjoyed tremendous freedom. He'd been able to decide everything on his own. Most notably, despite having grown up in a family of doctors who ran a general hospital, he hadn't been forced to enter medical school and was able to attend an art college. With the way they'd treated him, there was no way they'd veto the woman of his choice. The only issue was, he himself didn't know why his parents were always so delicate with him; perhaps that was why he failed to convince Akane.

Really, why?

When he looked deep inside, there was certainly some mysterious part of him that he couldn't identify. Akane had a similar kind of darkness in her, too, and he sometimes thought *that* might be the source of the sound: at the party celebrating the first Fureai generation leaving the nest, Takanori had taken one look at her and heard their gears click. She seemed to have felt the same way, and it stunned him when she described her first impression of him using precisely the same expression—*I heard our gears click.* Their metaphors matching felt like more than a coincidence.

They'd sniffed out a kindred scent in each other, but as to exactly what it was, he was still feeling things out.

Takanori put the book he'd been reading down on the night table and dimmed the light.

As the room grew darker, the silence became more noticeable. That was when he first realized he was hearing too little. After that thud came from the living room, there'd been no trace of any human movement in the apartment.

A bad feeling came over him suddenly, and he leapt out of bed and into the living room.

The first thing he saw was Akane with her fingers latched onto the edges of the table and clinging on to support herself.

At first glance, he thought she'd had another attack like when she'd collapsed at the school gate, but her symptoms appeared to be different.

Just as he ran over to her, Akane fell into his arms. Lifting her up, he carried her over to the nearby sofa and laid her down. She looked to be in a state of shock but was fully conscious. She was blinking repeatedly, and her pupils moved about at a bewildering speed. The area from her neck to her chin was covered in cold sweat, and her pulse was racing.

Takanori ran to the kitchen, grabbed a glass of water, and made her drink some.

"Are you okay?" he asked. "Should I call an ambulance?"

Akane shook her head no with a desperate look.

"Please, don't. I'm all right," she said.

With her face still turned away, she pointed to the computer on top of the table.

Takanori noticed the light flickering on his desktop monitor. He could have sworn he'd turned off his computer a while ago, after leaving Akane to herself in the bathroom, and yet it had restarted somehow.

She had to be pointing to the computer as the source of her shock.

Takanori went around the sofa, stood in front of the monitor, and looked at the screen.

The man who'd hanged himself was exposing his whole body, filling up the screen. When Takanori had viewed it in the evening, the toes had been higher in the frame, but now the man's body had shifted down. Not only that—with the blindfold gone his face was showing, slightly cocked to the side and looking right at the screen.

When Takanori realized that the video saved on his computer was changing little by little, he suspected that this might end up happening. Faced with such an obvious difference, however, he was surprised that he was strong enough not to be panicking, but he knew why. With Akane in a psychologically weakened state, he had no choice but to be strong. If they both caved in, they'd fall into a bottomless mire.

Takanori continued staring hard at the dead man's face. It felt familiar, but he couldn't recall from where. If they'd met, it hadn't been in the last few years. It would have been much longer ago.

"Kashiwada... The man... That's Kashiwada," Akane groaned.

Takanori was startled to hear that.

"Oh, yeah, I remember him," he said.

It was only natural that he recognized the man's face.

Kashiwada, a prisoner on death row for the abduction and murder of several girls, had caused a huge sensation about ten years ago. Around the time he was arrested, not a day had gone by without his face appearing in newspapers and on television. It made sense that Takanori knew his face, but unsettlingly, he couldn't shake the impression that he hadn't just seen but *met* the man. Takanori had been a high school student at the time of the incident. Back then, too, seeing Kashiwada's face on television, Takanori had felt like he'd met the man somewhere before.

Kashiwada had committed his first crime in June 2003. In the year and three months until his arrest the following September, he had abducted four girls around the age of ten and taken them around before killing them.

Once apprehended, he underwent countless psychiatric evaluations, his mental state when he'd committed the crimes and ability to stand trial becoming an issue. The evaluation varied depending on the doctor, but it was determined that the subject's condition fell within the bounds of sexual perversion or a personality disorder, and the prosecution proceeded to indict him.

Throughout the psychological exams and trial, Kashiwada mostly remained silent. His taciturn defiance suggested that he was schizophrenic, but if a man who had abducted and brutally murdered four young girls were found not guilty by reason of insanity, the prosecutor's office would have utterly lost face. Supported by public opinion, which condemned the man as an enemy of society, the prosecution strenuously argued that Kashiwada was to be held responsible and ultimately convinced the court to find him guilty and sentence him to death.

Having followed the story in the papers and on TV news programs, Takanori knew that Kashiwada had received the death penalty. But then what happened? He couldn't recall whether the sentence had been carried out.

An internet search would immediately provide him with info on the sentencing.

Takanori was kneeling beside the sofa and holding Akane close. He rose to his feet and was about to walk over to his computer, but she refused to let go of his hand. She seemed abnormally scared. Why would seeing a video of a serial killer of young girls hanging himself make her this frightened? Takanori didn't understand.

Peering into her face, he asked her with his eyes... *Is there some special reason?*

Noticing his gaze, Akane read his mind and began telling him in spurts the source of her fear.

"I...I think maybe...I was almost killed...by this man."

Her tone made it seem as though she wasn't talking about her own experience. Indeed, when a distant memory sealed away in the depths of your consciousness surfaces out of the blue, you can feel like a stranger to it all. Akane was looking somewhere far away as if she were talking about some other girl's terrifying experience.

"It can't be..."

Takanori suddenly remembered. Kashiwada had been arrested just before he could kill a fifth girl he'd been taking around with him. After the police had received a report from some neighbors, she'd been discovered just in the nick of time, and with Kashiwada caught red-handed, she'd escaped becoming his next victim.

The girl who was going to be his fifth victim...was Akane?

"Was it you? Were you the fifth girl?" he asked, speaking slowly and carefully.

"I don't really remember," Akane eked out from the back of her throat. "My memory is all spotty. After the case, the teachers at Fureai were extra careful in how they treated me. They got rid of related newspaper articles and images at the facility. Everyone was told not to talk about it around me. So, I think I probably tried to forget about it because they were all so worried for me. But I couldn't forget his face. I saw it from up close. My face held down on soft grass, the moist soil, the smell..."

Even those fragments were raw enough to summon a memory that had been rubbed into every cell of her body. Nauseated, she put both hands to her mouth, and her throat clogged up.

When humans experience something utterly terrifying, in order to retain our sanity, we force the memory down into the realm of the unconscious, or so they say. Akane's mind had tried to push an unbearable reality into oblivion.

She swallowed her saliva and somehow endured the nausea.

"It's all right," Takanori calmed her. "He's gone now."

Taking her clinging hand into both of his own, Takanori whispered into her ear, then embraced her skinny body.

As he held her tight, her intermittent spasms gradually subsided and gave way to a constant, soft trembling.

S

It may have been a creepy video, but the fact that this live-streamed footage of a suicide hanging existed was some kind of hint that the death sentence had been carried out. If he could just confirm it and let Akane know, she would surely find some relief.

Takanori shook free of her hand, got up, and went to his computer. An online search for the "Kashiwada Case" turned up numerous hits. There were even several links including the phrase "Death row prisoner Kashiwada executed."

There it is. The sentence was definitely carried out.

Feeling more confident now, Takanori clicked on one.

"On May 19th at 10:04 a.m., Seiji Kashiwada, convicted of abducting and murdering several young girls, was executed at the Tokyo Detention Center..."

What surprised Takanori was the date and time of the execution. May 19th at 10:04 a.m., approximately a month ago.

The date and time had been carved into his memory. Right after they'd consummated the deed that had started the life growing in her womb, the clock beside the pillow had displayed the exact same hour and minute.

Holding his head as it threatened to descend into confusion, Takanori recalled the scene at the hot spring inn where he and Akane had stayed about a month ago.

5

About a month ago...

When Akane told him that she had Monday off from work in exchange for attending an athletic meet the following Saturday, he suggested that they go for a drive. After a long stretch of hard work, Akane was in the mood for a leisurely soak at a hot spring, so she agreed right away, and together they planned an overnight excursion.

The place they chose was an inn nestled in a pastoral landscape.

While they enjoyed the atmosphere of hot spring areas with traditional inns bunched together, this time they were inclined to visit a quiet little establishment that was all by itself.

They got off the bullet train at Mishima and rented a compact at the rental-car office in front of the station.

After putting her bags in the backseat area, Akane got in the passenger seat and immediately began operating the car navigation screen.

"Hey, Tak, tell me the phone number of the inn we're going to."

When he handed her the reservation confirmation slip that he'd printed out, Akane typed in the phone number of their destination with delight.

Finding the way she poked the screen with her forefinger adorable, Takanori purposely scowled at her.

"Hey, hey, it's fine. We can get there without relying on that thing."

He didn't like depending on car navigation when he drove. It annoyed him every time the system instructed him to turn right or turn left up ahead. But Akane—who didn't have a driver's license—had jumped the gun out of a desire to be helpful, and setting the destination, she slapped her knee with a proud look on her face.

"There, now we won't get lost."

Forcing a smile, Takanori started the car and took off.

The sun was strong for May, feeling more like summer weather. Clouds accumulated here and there, creating dark spots in the sky, and seemed to caress the peak of Mt. Amagi as they moved along.

Heading south along the national highway, they turned left onto the Nekkan road and continued for some time, and signs began appearing alongside the road for the inn where they would be staying that night.

Since the inn was listed in the car navigation system, they should have been able to get there even without the signs. Yet there seemed to be some discrepancy between the signs and the navigation's instructions.

Then Akane spotted a guidepost at the corner of a liquor store which read "** Hot Spring: Next Right."

"Ah, up there. Go right."

Because the right-turn arrow was also green, Takanori unthinkingly cut the wheel to the right.

"Weird," he murmured.

From that point on, the navigation guide and the places they were driving through began to differ sharply. The navigation was guiding them straight ahead, and when the monitor encouraged them to make a U-turn, there was an almost desperate quality to its voice.

He continued along, unsure of whether to turn around or not, but less than five minutes later they arrived at the inn.

The solitary establishment's garden offered a commanding view of the placid, rural landscape, and they were certain it was the one where they'd arranged to stay. The phone number she had input also matched.

Before cutting the engine, they took one last look at the monitor. The flag indicating their destination was planted in a mountain valley some three miles away from their location.

Takanori turned and removed the key, causing the image to vanish.

"The information you typed in must've been wrong. It's your fault, Akane," he said half-jokingly.

Akane didn't hold her tongue. "No way, it's the driver's fault. You must've been sending out some weird signal, Tak."

Still assuming that it was a car-navigation error, they didn't make much of the matter.

It was slightly after 3 p.m. when they checked into the inn. Having arrived much sooner than expected, even after taking a relaxing soak in the open-air bath, they would still have to kill time before the dinner hour. Thus, they decided to go for a little drive in the area. They got back into the car, and searching the navigation system for sightseeing spots in the vicinity, Akane came up with a suggestion.

"Hey, why don't we try going here?" she said, poking the destination flag on the monitor with the tip of her fingernail. They'd arrived at the inn just fine by following the signs, so she seemed curious as to where exactly the navigation had tried to guide them.

Now that you mention it, I'd like to know too.

"Looks like it could be interesting. Let's go find out," he agreed without hesitation, and when he was about to start up the car again, a thought struck him: *Better set the place we're at now as our return destination.* It was easy to lose one's way in the twists and turns of the mountains, and he was a bit worried about getting lost on the trip back to the inn.

This time, obeying the car navigation's instructions and led on by the voice guide, they drove along the mountain road. Once they passed a hairpin curve beyond a small cluster of homes and climbed a hill, the road straightened out.

On the right was a stony riverbed, while on the left the face of the mountain was covered in a tapestry of shrubs, and this scenery stretched on and on.

"Up ahead, take a left."

The arrow on the monitor indicated a course that would take them leftward for a time, away from the prefectural route, and over the mountain. At the corner in front of them stood a road guide, with the following words written in black paint on a white panel:

South Hakone Pacific Land

That seemed to be where they were being led by the car navigation.

After driving beside a field and continuing along a hill with sharp curves, they began to see ready-made vacation homes on both sides that were part of this "South Hakone Pacific Land." They opened the car windows, letting the brisk highland air blow in, and with it the first taste of early summer. There even seemed to be a tennis court; they heard the thwacking sound of a tennis ball being hit below them on the right. They saw an information center in front of the entrance, but the destination being shown to them by the navigation was further ahead.

Takanori drove on, proceeding onto a road curving to the left.

A look at the monitor made it clear that the destination was nearby. The voice guide indeed announced, "You are approaching your destination," in a cheerful tone.

At its urging Takanori reduced his speed, and they accessed a more detailed screen on the monitor and verified their location.

Their destination was diagonally to their right up ahead, and on the screen they gradually moved closer and closer to the flag. The view of the gentle mountain slope through the windshield showed no signs of any structures that could be the right spot.

A vague sense of desolation drifted into the scenery before them. Something just felt wrong. Not only had they found nothing as far as their eyes could see, but their surroundings were getting drearier. Where the hell were they being led?

"You are approaching your destination."

Stopping the car when the flag was to its immediate right on the screen, Takanori turned his gaze in that direction. Akane turned her head in an identical motion.

The shrubs had been cut back entirely, revealing the surface of the mountain, which was otherwise covered in grass.

A grassy field on a gentle downward slope...that was all there was to say about it. Takanori zoomed in on the monitor. The flag showing their destination stood directly to the right roughly sixty feet from the road. From the driver's seat, he couldn't see down the slope, so he unfastened his seatbelt and prepared to exit the car.

"Don't go."

Akane reached out and grabbed Takanori's hand. With his attention fixed solely on the scenery to the right, he hadn't paid any attention to Akane sitting beside him in the passenger seat. Though just a few moments earlier he'd seen her in such high spirits, now she was curled up and her whole body was shaking.

"I'll be right back," he said, "so just hang tight."

Rather than acquiesce to her plea, he chose to go outside. He was seized by a feeling—almost a sense of obligation—that he needed to know just what this place was. Chalking this up to a car-navigation error was too facile. Yet it wasn't clear to him whether their guide's intentions were benign or malevolent. If he knew it to be malicious, he wouldn't have come near this place, but he had no reason to draw that conclusion.

When he opened the door and stepped out, he was able to get a wider view thanks to his higher vantage point.

Some kind of facility, now cleared away, must have been present once. Here and there, he saw the lingering remnants of some structures. It looked more like the ruins of bungalows or shacks rather than a larger building requiring foundation work. The remains of concrete blocks were also arranged along the boundary separating the road and the field.

Among the scattered pieces of concrete was a wooden plate, in which some letters had been carved. Without picking it up, Takanori leaned over and brought his face closer.

Villa Log Cabin

It seemed to be the name of the facility that had once stood there.

Climbing over the small mound of rubble, Takanori took a step onto the grass-covered slope.

It felt like he'd moved from hard asphalt to softer, spongier earth… His feet sank surprisingly deep, and he could sense a water vein beneath him. Perhaps there was a pond nearby. Under the grass, the soil was saturated with moisture.

Despite trying to descend slowly, he picked up momentum and stumbled down some dozen or so steps before coming to a halt. He hadn't intended to stop. It was as if some sixth sense, together with the concerted effort of all his cells behind the other five, had forced his body to defy gravity and stop moving.

In front of him was a cylindrical object projecting a few feet out of the ground. It was shaped like the fat stump of a tree cut down just above the root, and around it the smell of soil was especially potent.

He could see some moss and weeds stuck to the surface as if they'd taken root in soft earth, but there were also stones stacked like bricks with a concrete lid on top, conveying a palpable sense of weight.

There before him, close enough to reach out and touch, was an old well.

Unconsciously, Takanori took a step backward, then another. A ghostly breath seeped out from a small gap beneath the lid and drifted over to his feet. Repulsed by this grim air—*thou shalt not come near*, it seemed to say—Takanori took back another few steps.

Though the sun began to set, an abundance of light still fell on the slope. Nothing about the weather conditions should have made him feel cold. Only the short, old well rising up from the ground in front of him could be depriving him of his body heat.

He rubbed his forearms with both hands, but as soon as they touched his rough skin, a chill rippled through his body.

He turned away from the old well and started scrambling up the hill.

Arriving back at the car, he opened the door, slid into the driver's seat, and spoke to Akane.

"Let's go."

She didn't answer. When he looked at the passenger seat, Akane was pale and trembling. Since she hadn't even seen the old well, Takanori had no clue why she was so frightened. In any case, they needed to leave right now. He shifted into drive and peered closer at the monitor to check the way back.

"Ah," he let out despite himself.

He was sure they'd entered their current location just before leaving the inn's parking lot, but once again the destination flag on the monitor appeared someplace else.

The flag, which should have been pointing at the parking lot of the hot spring inn where they'd checked in, now appeared on the other side of the river running along the mountain road. There was no bridge in the vicinity to take them there, and simply from looking at the monitor, he saw that they couldn't reach the spot.

Once again, the car navigation was guiding Takanori and Akane to some destination.

Takanori couldn't decide. The weirdness was only mounting. Should they go back or follow the navigation to see what was there?

With his curiosity and dread offsetting each other, he was torn.

Let me tell Akane about it and ask her to decide, he thought. If she said no, then by all means, he would head straight back, the navigation be damned. He could get there without a map, back along the same road they'd taken.

Yet her answer surprised him.

"Seems like we have no choice."

She sounded resigned. Or perhaps her desire to know what was there had won out.

The flag stood almost halfway between their present location and the hot spring inn. The navigation showed a route bypassing the mountain road they'd taken that would end up being a shortcut.

When their destination was immediately to their right, Takanori stopped the car on the shoulder.

As expected, it was by the river, and with no bridge the other side was unreachable.

"I'll go and take a look. Do you want to stay?" Takanori said.

Akane shook her head and answered, "I don't think we both need to go. I'll leave it to you, Tak."

Hammering the positional relationship on the monitor into his head, he exited the car, crossed the road, and stood on the bank.

The slope across the river was forested with cedar trees, all nearly the same height. The flag's location was about ten feet above the river.

A single, imposing cedar stood a full head taller than the others, and he realized that its position and the flag on the monitor overlapped.

The wind was causing the branches of all the cedar trees to bend in the same direction, except for that tallest one, which stood as if unperturbed by the wind, almost contemptuous of the other trees.

Then he shifted his eyes downward. As he looked down the

trunk, all the way to the root, an artificial blue color that didn't match the natural surface of the mountain caught his eye.

And there—fluttering at the root with one side lifted up by the wind—was a blue tarp, the kind you saw at construction sites. It was exactly where the flag indicated. In fact, the tarp was also the kind you might find at the scene of a murder or some other crime.

Maybe a corpse was buried at the root of the tree... Was it why only that cedar tree grew up taller than the others, sucking the nutrients from the dead body? The way the blue tarp was fluttering, the will of a buried soul seemed to be waving a hand and inviting, "Come, come."

With that image in mind, Takanori closed his eyes and opened them again after counting to three. The vivid blue color disappeared from the root of the cedar tree, leaving only dark brown humus peeping out between the blades of grass.

Taking a good look at this scenery and imprinting it on his retinas, he returned to the car to find Akane leaning out the window of the passenger seat.

"What happened?" she asked.

He didn't know how to answer. If there had been an abandoned car on the grassy slope, he might have replied, "There was a car." But the only lasting impressions of what he'd seen were a tall cedar among a cluster of shorter trees and a blue tarp fluttering at its root. He understood that the tarp didn't exist in reality and had only been an illusion. The real scenery had overlapped with a scene from somewhere in his past and become distorted.

"There was nothing there," Takanori answered out of desperation, unable to explain what he'd seen.

Akane sighed, and an expression of relief returned to her face.

It was already past 4 p.m. The early summer days lasted long, and there was still some time until sunset. Having confirmed where the navigation had wanted to lead them, all that was left to do now was to return to the inn.

It was a mere five minutes away. During that brief span, Akane

kept on talking. Takanori had never seen her so loquacious. She usually listened to other people as they spoke and then responded in
turn, but now, ignoring the context, she went on talking all by herself.

Mouthing halfhearted replies, Takanori continued to think. Why
hadn't the navigation worked properly? Was it just some accident, or
was it some premonition of the future?

If the mysterious phenomena had any meaning, it was important
to scrutinize them for a hidden truth, taking care not to overlook
anything.

Takanori's intuition was telling him that the phenomena
couldn't possibly have been an accident.

After returning to the inn, they went out together to the open-air
bath. Even the continuous flow of the hot spring water couldn't wash
away the two sights planted in his head by the locations where the
navigation had led them.

6

More than a month had passed since then. Takanori had failed to
ascribe any sort of significance to the old well poking out from the
grassy field or to the tall cedar tree on the other side of the river, and
meanwhile the freshness of that scenery was fading away.

He remembered exactly where they were located. They were
places that he could easily revisit if he so wished. And if he did, he
would discover that old well in the same spot. But he would never see
that blue tarp spread out at the root of the cedar tree. He was able to
distinguish reality from illusion.

Yet what worried him now, as he read the information in front of
him about the death-row prisoner Kashiwada, was not the unnatural-
ness of the two locations. Their deed the following day had taken on
greater importance. The result of that intercourse resided in Akane's

womb now, and it certainly was real.

Whether he counted based on her menstrual cycle or from the time between their dates, there was no doubt. She'd gotten pregnant when they'd embraced just before checking out of the inn.

The next day, they'd had a late breakfast at the dining hall and then returned to their room. They'd laid down on the futon, which was still spread out; as they'd caressed each other, one thing had led to another, and when it was over, he'd looked at the digital clock beside his pillow.

The time had been branded in his mind because he'd been worried about their 10 a.m. checkout.

...*10:04.*

And now he saw the very same date and time on his monitor.

"*On May 19th at 10:04 a.m., Seiji Kashiwada, convicted of abducting and murdering several young girls, was executed at the Tokyo Detention Center...*"

Having risen at some point from the sofa, Akane was now standing beside him, her eyes riveted on the same screen.

With so many things that he needed to think about, Takanori's mind was on the verge of shorting out. He couldn't even spare the energy to speculate about what Akane was trying to glean from the pieces of info lined up on the monitor. He had to focus all his mental power on whether it meant anything that the time he'd finished being intimate with her matched the hour of Kashiwada's execution.

Then it struck him that perhaps a hint might be hidden in the circumstances behind the Kashiwada case. He sent the content on his monitor to the printer.

Meanwhile, he led Akane over to the sofa to make her look away from the info on Kashiwada. It may have been mere information, but he wanted to keep the man at a distance from her.

Seeing that the print job was finished, Takanori went over to the table and began reading the article. The incidents had occurred over ten years earlier. Only a high school student at the time, he'd forgotten nearly all the details. As he read, he began to recall the facial expressions and tone of newscasters reporting on the story and other little nuances surrounding the case.

"Seiji Kashiwada was arrested as a suspect in a series of kidnappings and murders of young girls across Tokyo, Kanagawa, Shizuoka, and Chiba Prefectures, and after being tried and convicted he was sentenced to death and executed..."

Skimming over the description of Kashiwada's childhood and family makeup, Takanori reached the section detailing the first incident only to have to interrupt his reading.

"On July 28, 2003, the body of the first victim, aged eleven, was discovered near the ** River in Kannami Hirai, Shizuoka Prefecture."

Having stopped right there, he was unable to proceed. His eyes went back over the same passage, again and again.

A bell had rung in his head. Putting the article on Kashiwada to the side for a moment, he brought up a map on his monitor.

The route down which he and Akane had been led by the car navigation system, starting from the hot spring inn where they'd spent the night one month earlier—he tried tracing it on the map again. Hirai, in Kannami...he was certain there was a tall cedar at the spot the navigation had registered all on its own as the second destination.

Takanori's mind flashed back to old news footage. The slope near the river, the blue tarp covering the root of the cedar, detectives inspecting the area... Overlapping the vivid imagery flying around in his head was the voice of a female announcer.

"Today, at 4:30 p.m., the remains of a young girl were discovered on a mountain path in the township of Kannami in Shizuoka Prefecture. Investigators are calling it a homicide..."

Takanori knew that his intuition was correct. That news footage from over ten years ago had remained in the depths of his memory, revived when he'd beheld the same scenery, and shown him a false vision of a blue tarp.

If the second site to which they'd been mistakenly led by the navigation system was where the body of the first victim was discovered, then what was he to make of the old well at the first site? At this rate, he could hypothesize that the spot was connected to the Kashiwada case.

Takanori read on furiously, searching for an answer. No doubt, that old well on the outskirts of South Hakone Pacific Land was a place where one of the victims had been abandoned.

Yet the second victim's body was discovered in Miura City in Kanagawa Prefecture, the third in Hachioji City in Tokyo Prefecture, the fourth in Kamogawa City in Chiba Prefecture, and the fifth...

Takanori looked up from the document. Akane was lying on the sofa with both hands folded over her heart. The shallow rising and falling of her chest was proof positive that she was alive.

You idiot. There was no fifth victim. Akane just barely escaped from the clutches of that monster.

He resumed looking at the document and proceeded to read about when Kashiwada had been caught in the act.

"Having been tipped off by local residents, Atami police rushed to a tangerine farm in the Kamitaga area of Atami City in Shizuoka Prefecture, where they discovered Kashiwada hiding in a patch of shrubs holding a young girl, and arrested him on the spot..."

Takanori brought up a map again and checked where the arrest had taken place.

The distance from Kamitaga in Atami City to South Hakone Pacific Land was about four miles as the bird flies. That was indeed close, but he couldn't find anything in the document indicating a connection to the old well.

It looks like I have no choice but to revisit the site.

He could no longer afford to remain a bystander. Though he didn't know the reason, the Kashiwada case was intimately involved with his and Akane's lives.

Events which had seemed unrelated at first glance were starting to come together and form patches of black spots as though on a piece of flypaper.

It had all started with the live stream of a suicide by hanging saved onto a USB stick. Though it was saved data, the man in the video had begun to move, and the revelation that he was the serial murderer Kashiwada had thrown various connections to Takanori and Akane into relief. She had nearly been the next victim. The place where the first victim was discovered and the one they'd been led to by the car navigation were identical. And their deed, performed at the same time as the execution, had made Akane pregnant.

All these seemingly unconnected events were neatly lined up on that single piece of flypaper.

The problem was whether these strange phenomena—beginning with the USB stick brought by Kiyomi Sakata to Yoneda and passed along by Yoneda to him—could have a physical effect on him and Akane. If he just felt it was a bit spooky, the answer would be simple, and he could brush it off. Yet if there were some foreseeable physical harm, he needed to analyze the phenomena as far as he could perceive them, gauge the nature of the danger, and come up with some way to deal with it.

Unless he solved this mystery, his life with Akane would be far from peaceful.

His foe was likely not a person with any physical substance. But even if it were some unfathomable opponent, beyond all imagining, running away didn't cut it.

Takanori made up his mind. He may have led an easygoing life, but the time had come to test his mettle as a man.

7

All of the spaces in the small bicycle parking lot were occupied.

If Takanori moved about three of the bikes to the side, perhaps he could make enough room for his, but that was a bit of a hassle. He also felt reluctant to touch other people's bicycles, so he parked his on the sidewalk and entered the branch ward office. He was just getting a marriage registration form and family register, so he should only be a few minutes.

He'd never come to the branch ward office before, not even to get a copy of his resident card, and had been a stranger to the place until now.

After entering, he looked around. A female receptionist who was sitting on a round stool stood up right away and greeted him.

"How may I help you?"

"Hi, I'd like to get a marriage registration form."

The woman smiled pleasantly and pointed to the leftmost counter.

"You can get one at the counter over there."

When he went there as directed and applied, they gave him three things—a sheet of instructions, two marriage registration forms, and a relatively large-sized envelope.

He thought he might need his family register as well, so he asked the woman who had greeted him earlier.

"I need my family register for the marriage registration, don't I?"

"Well...it was such a long time ago that I don't remember," she said.

"Huh?"

At a loss for words, Takanori looked at the woman's face closely. She seemed to be in her sixties or so and gave the impression that she must have been quite a beautiful woman in her youth.

"Oh, I'm sorry. It was such a corny joke." The woman gave him a big smile and continued, "For family registers, please fill out a pink form and submit it at the counter."

Takanori burst out laughing at her response, which had caught him off guard. Yet he didn't feel annoyed. In fact, she'd put him in a cheerful mood, and he wanted to thank her for it.

"Thank you."

Walking away, he wrote his address and name on the pink form and submitted it at the designated counter, and almost immediately his name was called. The woman there held out his family register and an envelope but tilted her head for some reason. He wondered whether that was simply her habit or if something was wrong, but still in the dark, he paid the fee and received his family register.

All done, he thought. He put his knapsack on his back with all the necessary documents and was about to head for the bicycle parking lot.

"Best wishes," a voice came from somewhere, and when he looked around, it was the female receptionist waving at him with a smile.

"Thanks."

He raised his hand slightly in acknowledgment, and exiting through the automatic door, found himself in front of the cafeteria.

He'd intended to stop off at home and then drop by Studio Oz, but now he had second thoughts, preferring to have an early lunch before leaving. Slipping his arms out of the straps of his knapsack, he entered the cafeteria.

Thinking he'd kill time reading a book until the pasta lunch he'd ordered arrived, Takanori opened his knapsack and reached for a paperback titled *Beyond the Darkness*.

It was a nonfiction report on the details of the Kashiwada case. The author, Tsuyoshi Kihara, was a well-known nonfiction author held in high regard in the industry for his impartial research, persistence and patience in approaching his subjects, and refusal to be influenced by trends in forming his views.

It was a compilation of weekly magazine articles that originally appeared five or six years ago, and at the time Kashiwada's death sentence hadn't been declared yet. There were other works on the Kashiwada case as well, but none surpassed this book in terms of both quantity and quality.

Learning everything about the case could provide the breakthrough he needed to solve the puzzle thrust in front of Takanori... It was a time-honored method that he'd chosen to follow.

As he took out the book, his eyes fell on his family register, which he'd just obtained. Simply curious, never even having looked at his own before, he picked it up instead of the paperback.

There were two sheets bearing a flower print at the bottom left, the first one having to do almost entirely with his father and mother. His father's birthday and his grandparents' names were written on it, as was his mother's birthday and the names of her parents.

Flipping to the second page, Takanori saw his own name.

Person recorded in family register: Takanori
Date of birth: February 17, 1986
Father: Mitsuo Ando
Mother: Ryoko Ando
Relationship: Eldest son

He failed to comprehend the content recorded below at first glance. Thus, initially, he was able to remain calm.

Person's registry / Past status

Deletion date: July 22, 1991
Deleted item: Death
Reason for deletion: Court judgment permitting correction of family register due to mistakenly recorded death
Court judgment date: July 2, 1991
Filing date: July 22, 1991

PAST RECORD
Date of death: June 18, 1989
Time of death: 10 p.m.
Place of death: Toi-cho, Shizuoka Prefecture
Date of notification: October 11, 1989
Filed by: Mitsuo Ando
Date of removal: October 16, 1989

As Takanori read it again and again, the significance of what was entered in the record gradually dawned on him. He was compelled to admit that there was but one possible interpretation.

He had died in June of 1989 somewhere in Toi-cho, Shizuoka Prefecture, and four months later, a notice of death had been submitted by his father. On October 16th of that year, his name had been stricken from the register. That was his "Past Record."

However, two years later, in July, it became clear that he'd been mistakenly declared dead. Still, it was no easy thing to undo an entry in the register, and a court had decided whether a correction was permissible. On July 2, 1991, his father's claim was accepted and the correction was permitted, and then, on July 22nd of that year, his past record was deleted.

In other words, according to the register, Takanori would have been dead from June 1989 until June 1991, a full two years.

Looking up from the register, Takanori turned his face toward the ceiling. He inhaled and exhaled deeply and shut his eyes tight.

Only his sight was cut off; all his other senses were alive. His ears could still hear, and his nose could still smell. If he dug his fingernail into his neck, he would feel pain.

Well, seems like I'm still alive.

Opening his eyes again, Takanori confirmed that the world was still there.

"I think, therefore I am."

The French philosopher Descartes had said that. What should someone who'd found an entry in his family register about his own death say about life and death? The mere presence of a subject contemplating its own death didn't guarantee that it was alive.

It felt as if the world before him was becoming warped. A waitress had brought his pasta and salad set, but he hadn't noticed.

His formerly robust appetite had disappeared completely. Now his stomach was hinting that he was about to become violently upset.

If there's any way to accept that I was dead for two years between the ages of three and five, I'd love for someone to tell me.

The places to which the navigation system had led them had some significance—it couldn't have been a malfunction. This time, as before, it would be easy to chalk it up as a mistaken entry in his family register. The series of events, however, were refuting such a facile and convenient explanation.

He couldn't help thinking that he really had been dead for two years.

The last tarot card I picked at Yoneda's urging was "Death," which meant "Rebirth from death," didn't it? Was it really just a coincidence that I picked "Death"?

When signs match, it often means that phenomena that appear unrelated at first sight are connected underneath.

He'd wondered for a long time why his parents treated him like a fragile object. He understood now. If he really did die once and come back to them, of course they'd be thankful just to have him.

Though he'd made up his mind only the day before not to flee from his enemy, no matter who it was, his resolve now seemed to be crumbling. It felt like the strength was slipping away from his toes as though he'd stepped through the floor and his body was falling away.

What Takanori needed was to feel and know that he was alive.

Please. Somebody hold me up, anybody.

He twisted his body and looked for the female receptionist on the other side of the smoked glass. He wanted her to reassure him about the family register in his hands, to smile and say:

"Oh, I'm sorry. It was such a corny joke."

As if to cling to her, Takanori followed her from the corner of his eyes. Guiding another visitor to the counter, she glanced at him, as though she'd read his mind. It was only for a brief moment that her eyes met his through the glass, and soon she reverted her gaze as if no one was there.

She had a blank look on her face, completely different from her expression when she'd cracked that out-of-place joke just a while ago.

"Best wishes," she'd told him, but now he almost felt those same lips were murmuring, "My condolences."

CHAPTER THREE *Ring*

1

What kind of clothes should he wear to a meeting with a renowned nonfiction writer?

After some vacillation, Takanori settled on a safe bet: black cotton pants, a white polo shirt, and a dark-blue jacket. Considering that the person he was meeting was a freelancer, a suit and tie might be too much.

Takanori would be taking the subway to Shinjuku, transferring to the Yamanote line, and riding it to the second stop, Takada-no-baba. The office address was on the map he'd printed out. Whenever he needed to walk to a destination, Takanori preferred to rely on a map printed out on paper rather than his cell phone's small display. The office was less than five minutes on foot from the station.

Since getting the appointment, Takanori had gathered as much info on Tsuyoshi Kihara as possible from the internet and from books.

Kihara was born in 1953 in Kodaira City, Tokyo, which meant he was sixty-two now. After graduating from the Second Department of Literature at W University, he'd started working at a publishing company and gone on to edit more than a hundred nonfiction titles, five of which became bestsellers. After quitting the company over union issues and earning a living as a freelance weekly magazine writer, he built rich personal connections and acquired a knack for tracking criminal cases to emerge as a fully independent nonfiction author.

He'd gotten his break with his third hardcover, *The Birth of the Gods.*

S

It was about the founder of a religious cult that had brought about social problems. A major work, it appealed to the public to consider the contradictions of modern Japanese society and depicted the struggles of the devotees who'd sought to show the strength of their faith through acts that were a hair away from being crimes. The book had won him the Ooya Prize that year. Afterwards he'd become a household name and appeared often as a commentator on TV gossip shows. As for his personal life, at the age of forty-seven he'd gotten married to a woman ten years his junior who ran a bar and restaurant, and although they didn't have any children, they were a loving couple. One of his hobbies was standing behind the bar and entertaining customers in between bouts of writing.

Takanori had actually never seen him on TV but knew Kihara's face from a newspaper photo.

It had appeared alongside a column Kihara had written calling the capital-punishment system into question. Takanori had been moved by the piece.

Kihara was opposed to capital punishment. When he'd worked at the publishing company on true crime titles, coming face-to-face with so many brutal cases had built up his hatred for the perpetrators, and he'd maintained a position in favor of the death penalty. Yet, after becoming a freelance writer, the more he gathered information on criminals and probed into their lives, the more inclined he'd become to oppose the system.

In the column, he cited two reasons why.

To explain the first, Kihara used a hundred apples in a box as an example.

The number didn't matter, and it could have been strawberries, rather than apples. Say there were a hundred apples lined up in a wooden box. Left outside in the elements, at least one of the apples would start to spoil and become rotten. Call this first rotten apple "A." If one got rid of A when it started going bad, the decay could be prevented from spreading, but if one did nothing, the decay would be transferred to the next apple and then the next apple, and thus the damage would spread everywhere.

Now, assuming that the good apples had the right to isolate apple A, which had gone bad, there were two conceivable ways to stop the infection from spreading. You could transfer the bad apple to another box and cut off contact forever, or burn the apple and erase its existence completely.

Nevertheless, apple A hadn't wished to become rotten. It was simply a law of nature that one apple in every hundred goes bad, and in keeping with this law, it gathered up all of the other apples' potential to become spoiled and borne their sins all by itself. The good apples should sigh with relief that decay had come not to them but to apple A first, and they ought not demolish it out of hatred.

Could there even be a society where not one of the hundred apples would ever go bad? Trying to make it so would necessitate the use of a lot of very powerful antiseptics, and then things such as liberty, vitality, pleasure, and joy would all vanish. Making a perfect society where rotten apples never existed represented a dilemma in that all apples would be deprived of the chance to be happy.

One could either agree to a society where decay would arise according to the laws of nature, or agree to a draconian, fascist society, where the causes of decay would be suppressed and removed beforehand.

If one desired the former, then the good apples should bear no hatred toward apple A's misfortune. Rather, they should isolate it out of a sense of sympathy, mercy, and pity. The only ones permitted to abhor apple A were the ones directly harmed by it, and it would not be right for the entire box of apples to uniformly adopt the emotions of those individuals.

That was the first reason Kihara opposed the death penalty.

As a precondition for applying the apple example to human beings, he noted that people would have to have almost no free will, but space considerations didn't allow him to go into the issue in detail.

The second reason was more practical in nature: the capital punishment system wasn't serving to deter heinous crimes.

S

In destitute prewar Japan, someone might have had the simplistic motive to commit murder and steal the victim's money. In such an era, capital punishment might have been an effective deterrent to some degree. The prospect of paying the ultimate price would probably have put a stop to such barbarous crimes.

Yet now, decades into the postwar years, murders motivated by robbery or rape and other brutal cases had sharply declined, and the motives had become vastly more complicated.

Especially in the case of heinous crimes committed by young people, their childhoods and household environments had influenced them in complex ways, giving rise to a certain darkness in their hearts, and simply obtaining money could no longer be established as the motive.

After interviewing a certain youth who had committed murder and hearing his laments, Kihara had come to oppose the death penalty.

"You're still young," he'd said, "so there's no way they'll give you the death penalty."

"Huh?" the youth had replied, a lump in his throat. "You mean I won't be executed?" he'd asked with a look of disappointment on his face.

Knowing nothing of the Juvenile Act, he'd assumed that anyone who committed murder would be put to death.

Now, it was difficult enough for any criminal to analyze his or her motive in perpetrating the crime. But this was even truer of the very young and tender for whom accurately discerning one's own motive was a herculean task.

It was because Kihara was an observer that he could understand something of the young man's motive. Somewhere in his heart, the youth had hoped to receive the death penalty.

In his life thus far, he'd never enjoyed any moments in the spotlight and always been shoved into the corner. His mother's love had been reserved for his siblings, and he'd been baptized in violence by his father. He'd had no friends, nor had he ever known a girl's affection. When he hoped to shock the world and prove that he'd been alive, at least at the end there, and to die spectacularly, the only option available to him was to commit a horrendous crime and be sentenced to death.

A criminal act intended to announce him to the world and to establish his identity...that was how Kihara evaluated the young man's crime.

When someone perpetrated a heinous crime with the express desire of receiving the death penalty, the point of that penalty was naturally called into question. Not only was it not a deterrent, it arguably even promoted such behavior...

Takanori got off the Yamanote line at Takada-no-baba, took a passage under the tracks, and then turned left, recalling Kihara's column as he walked, and without even realizing it he arrived at a bridge spanning the Kanda River.

As soon as he crossed it, he spotted the condominium he was looking for on his right. Actually, he thought, the three-story condo facing the river was more just an ordinary apartment building.

Takanori didn't have a solid opinion on whether or not capital punishment should exist. He'd discussed it with his friends before but maintained a noncommittal position the whole time. It was true that after reading Kihara's column, he'd strongly sympathized with his ideas, but that didn't mean Takanori was now against capital punishment.

Having sensed an ominous shadow stalking Akane over the past few days, there had been moments when he let his imagination run away. Akane was carrying his child in her womb. If somebody showed up and tried to harm his wife and child, he wondered, would he be able to protect them?

If his wife and child were murdered by a criminal, he was sure he'd scream, "I'll kill you!" with a visceral rage. If it were allowed, he'd probably want to kill him with his own hands. Lacking that power, all he could do was to rely on the judgment of the law.

He could understand Kihara's assertion and felt the author was right about that. Yet, another part of Takanori felt it was perfectly natural for a member of society to put himself in the victim's shoes and be furious enough to favor the death penalty. It was understandable if the waves of hatred emanating from the victims and their loved ones resonated with society at large.

Kihara's idea didn't seem realistically achievable unless people were saints. To view every point on a two-dimensional plane, you needed to stand at a higher, three-dimensional vantage point. Likewise, you needed to be able to view the entire world with a fair mind to cast away your emotions.

But that would be akin to a god's view—could every member of society reasonably be expected to adopt such a perspective? As long as you lived in the real world, where good and evil coexisted, it was natural to be lost between reason and emotion, ideals and reality, and questions like capital punishment had no simple answer.

Takanori came to a halt in the middle of the bridge and looked at his wristwatch. Just as he'd thought, it was five minutes or so earlier than the designated time. Kihara had promised to spare an hour for him, from 11 a.m. to noon. Arriving too early would be like breaking a promise, too.

He put his hands on the balustrade, bent forward, and stared at the river to kill time. Black sludge had gathered here and there where the shallow current got slowed down by the concrete bulkheads. When he shifted his gaze upstream, above the railroad bridge of the Yamanote line, he could see small patchy patterns made by the summer clouds in a sky cropped out by the buildings.

Wanting to stretch out his body, Takanori raised his arms up toward that sky.

No matter how far he tried to reach, he couldn't grab any of the clouds floating by. Nor could he dip his hands into the water and grab the black sludge. The moment he began to wonder why he'd gotten those strange ideas, a chill ran through his spine.

When the chill slowly formed into a distinct fear, he couldn't identify the source at first.

His shivering was getting more severe and synchronizing with the vibration of a two-ton truck driving past behind him.

He couldn't see the true form of whatever was trying to harm them; the ominous mood that enveloped him and Akane was like dark mud and as nebulous as a cloud.

"I'll kill you!" only worked if your enemy was a flesh-and-blood person. He couldn't combat something that wasn't human, some unknown presence.

Can I really fight this? Can I remove a threat menacing my wife and child without having grasped it?

No matter how powerful the enemy, it was better to have one you could fight physically. If you could beat it with a weapon, then there was a way.

Just visualizing facing a ghost devoid of flesh—and imagining how ghastly that would be—made him shiver uncontrollably.

Takanori started walking. After crossing the bridge and entering the building, he saw rooms lined up on both sides of the hallway.

He walked to the middle and stood in front of a door.

The plate said Apartment 104. That was Kihara's office for sure.

Taking a deep breath to calm his fears, Takanori rang the bell.

2

When he entered the room, the first things that caught his eye were two garbage bags, so full they seemed ready to explode. Facing the entrance door as if they were huge *daruma* dolls squatting on the floor, they seemed to be watching out for strangers.

He could tell through the translucent plastic that most of the trash inside was paper.

Takanori introduced himself at the entrance door, and then took his shoes off and went inside. When prompted, he sat down in a chair in front of the table. Moving only his eyes, he looked around the room. It seemed rude to stare at everything, but since this was the office of a famous nonfiction writer, it was filled with fascinating things, and Takanori found it difficult to suppress his curiosity.

"Doesn't it stink in here?" Kihara asked as he made coffee.

He probably asked because he's aware of the garbage bags sitting there.

"No, not particularly."

To be honest, he did notice an odor, but it wasn't too offensive. Just as Studio Oz was filled with the peculiar smells of a video production company, so too did this office smell like the workplace of someone who wrote for a living.

"I'm not sure if you know this...but many serial killers aren't sensitive to foul odors."

Takanori felt an urge to rephrase what he'd said—he *did* detect a faint smell—but since it didn't seem like Kihara had meant any offense, kept his mouth shut.

"No, no, I'm not talking about you," Kihara said. "I've been doing this work for so long that I really can't smell anything at this point, so every now and then I ask people to make sure, that's all."

His tone was very gentle toward Takanori, who was young enough to be his son.

In some ways, Kihara bore a resemblance to Yoneda at Studio Oz. His height and apparent age were about the same, and he also shared Yoneda's comforting aura, which didn't put people on edge when they first met him.

"It doesn't bother me," Takanori said. "I can faintly make out a pleasant smell here that has a human touch."

Kihara gave a big smile, nodded, and looked at his wristwatch.

"I'm sorry to have to rush, but I've got a meeting with my editor in an hour. So, how about we get down to the business at hand?"

Though a little surprised at this abrupt transition, Takanori briefly touched on his impression from reading Kihara's nonfiction book about the Kashiwada case, *Beyond the Darkness,* and described how a video that seemed to be a live broadcast of the execution got uploaded to the internet.

"Oh, did that really happen?" asked Kihara. "Well, I guess it was about a month ago that Kashiwada was executed."

"That's right. The sentence was carried out on May 19th."

"A similar incident happened once before. An anti-death penalty group illegally obtained the video of an execution from the Ministry of Justice and put it online. This is probably the same sort of thing, right?"

"I can't really explain it well," Takanori replied, "but it wasn't like an execution video got leaked. I can't help thinking that some effects were added to it. To me, it looks like some footage shot in a totally different place got edited in."

"I see. So, what's the connection between that video and you? You wouldn't be thinking of turning it into a book, would you?"

Takanori was at a loss for words. He hadn't a shred of confidence that he could make anyone believe the series of events that had beset him and Akane concerning the Kashiwada case. Even so, he needed to give a clear reason, or else Kihara's interest would evaporate, and Takanori might not be able to ask the writer for help.

Sympathizing with Takanori's struggle to come up with an answer, Kihara continued.

"It's quite rare these days for me to meet one of my readers. Nothing good ever comes of it. Lots of folks—and I mean lots—have given me an idea and told me to write a book about it, when really they'd just brought me some boring old drivel. When I got that phone call from you, at first I thought, 'Here we go again,' but I could sense that something was different this time. In your words I could hear a sort of desperate cry, like you'd been dragged into the Kashiwada case and gotten stuck in a bind. At the same time, it gave me some hope. I thought that maybe, you would bring me some hint to solve these questions that I've been dealing with for years now... So that's why I decided to go ahead and meet you.

"The Kashiwada case is the most mysterious of all the subjects

I ever dealt with. That remains true even now. I myself am not convinced by what I wrote. You might call it unfinished business.

"A moment ago, you told me about the impression you'd gotten from *Beyond the Darkness*. Is it true? I want you to tell me your honest thoughts about it, without any hesitation."

Takanori made up his mind. He knew that if he made something up or misled him with words of praise, they'd never have a relationship of trust. "In all honesty, it left me with a hazy impression."

"Oh, why is that?"

"When I read the first part, I felt that the author was clearly convinced that Seiji Kashiwada was the one who'd kidnapped and murdered those young girls. But after making it three-quarters of the way through the book, I got the impression that your conviction had been shaken somehow."

Kihara nodded, with apparent satisfaction. "That project proceeded as a series of installments in a monthly magazine. As you know, Kashiwada was caught red-handed as he was taking that fifth girl around. When his house was searched, they found hair belonging to the third victim in his room, and a man who looked like Kashiwada had been spotted in the vicinity of the victim's home. Since a number of people gave testimony, there was no doubt it was him. That's about the clearest possible evidence you can have. Everyone was certain he was guilty. Naturally, I believed it too. But the more I searched in order to proceed with my writing, the deeper my questions became, and I just ended up getting lost. It's easy to start writing a book. The hard part is to follow through to the end with a definite conclusion. With *Beyond the Darkness*, I tried to finish the book after giving the reader a unified viewpoint that summed up the whole case, but when I reached the final chapter I was left with an even deeper mystery."

When Kihara went for a sip of the coffee he'd made, Takanori got in a word. "At the time of the incident, I was in high school. I only knew bits and pieces about the case, but now that I've read your book and searched around online, I think I've gotten the picture. What's available to the average person, like me, doesn't seem to be all that complicated. What we believed was that a homicidal fiend named Kashiwada abducted several young girls and took them from place to place before gratifying his perverted sexual cravings and killing them. It was obviously the most despicable, cold-blooded case of murder for pleasure in Japanese criminal history. Mr. Kihara, what do you find so mysterious about it?"

"Everything you just said."

"Everything..."

"First of all, we have no idea what his motive for the crime was."

"You're saying he didn't kill for pleasure?"

"There were no traces of Kashiwada's bodily fluids, either inside the victims' bodies or at the crime scenes."

"The prosecution provided evidence suggesting that his bodily fluids had been found..."

"That was something they made up to make the case easier to understand. Of course, the fact that no semen was found doesn't mean that the murders weren't committed for pleasure. Maybe it was just absorbed by the criminal's clothes and never spilled out. Plus, there're lots of cases reported around the world of sexual killers who aren't aroused by female genitalia or breasts, or who are impotent. In that regard, there's a clear distinction between such cases and more common instances of rape."

"So, what you're saying," Takanori tried to confirm, "is that Kashiwada's case is different from any other pattern we've seen?"

"That's right. Perverted sexual killers tend to mutilate the corpse. Oftentimes they'll dismember the body, or cut open its belly, and right in the middle of the act they'll have an orgasm and ejaculate. In this case, however, all of the victims were simply strangled to death, and there were no other signs of bodily harm."

"But it was reported that the bodies were partly destroyed..."

"Just the fingernails. The nails of the index and middle fingers on the fourth victim's right hand had been removed with pliers. This is only my speculation, but he might have done it to remove any trace after the girl unexpectedly fought back and scratched him. He couldn't afford to leave any of his skin under her nails at the crime scene. If his DNA were collected, it would be definitive proof, wouldn't it?"

"I see," Takanori said. "Kashiwada treated his victims' bodies a little more carefully than those other sexual killers."

"Exactly. Not just a little more—he was *too* careful. His method of killing was always strangulation. He seemed to have used a soft cloth, so that it was done cleanly, with no red marks or lacerations on their necks. It's just that all four victims had their underwear removed. I'm sure you knew that."

"I did."

Every piece Takanori had read stated that these were perverted sexual murders since the victims' underwear had been removed.

"But that's all," Kihara said. "None of their other clothing was disturbed. Only their panties were pulled off from under their skirts. There were no injuries to their genitals, of course. Well, what do you think of all that?"

"Maybe he was satisfied just looking at them."

"I think it was more like he observed them, like it was a routine. That's what I got from the evidence. The criminal removed their underwear so he could inspect their genitals."

"Does that mean it was a type of fetishism?"

"No, it was more dispassionate. It was a simple inspection, unrelated to any sexual impulse."

"Listening to you, I find myself somehow even more confused," Takanori said. "So...what *was* Kashiwada's purpose?"

"That's the biggest puzzle of all. What was his motive for abducting and murdering those girls?

"The prosecution tried to cover up the complexities of the case. They decided beforehand that they were absolutely going to go for the death penalty, and that's how they proceeded. That's why they needed to make the outline of the case as easy for people to comprehend as possible. His motive had to be to satisfy a selfish, perverted sexual urge. The fact that he remained silent was taken as proof that he didn't feel any remorse. One interpretation that was put forward suggested that Kashiwada had a personality disorder and believed his alternate personality had committed the crimes. The personality controlling him after his arrest had no recollection of the killings, and therefore he couldn't confess even if he wanted to.

"That's why so many psychological tests were done on him, but with those too, the conclusion that he was legally accountable came first. If he were judged not responsible for his actions on grounds of lunacy or diminished capacity, he'd end up in a mental asylum, and not an execution chamber.

"The prosecution staked their prestige on obtaining the death penalty for a criminal who'd kidnapped and murdered several girls for his own selfish pleasure, and the mass media and the public vigorously supported this. There was practically nobody who defended Kashiwada.

"Well, his defense counsel did raise an objection to the results of the psych tests, and they did file an appeal, but with all the denunciation they faced from the public, they got bogged down and lost their steam.

"The trial went ahead, propelled by the prosecution's arguments, and the death penalty was finally handed down. Then about a month ago, the sentence was carried out.

"But even now, it's hard for me to swallow," Kihara said. "What was his motive, really? All of his victims were found leaning against a tree trunk in the woods, with their legs extended neatly together, both hands placed on their knees and their heads facing slightly downward and their hair hanging in front. None of the books described how they looked when their bodies were found, of course. I saw the crime scene photos myself. Just one look gave me the impression that this had been some sort of ritual."

"A ritual...as in a religious ritual?"

"Right. There were elements in the crime scene photos that made me think it'd been the act of some fanatical cult rather than a murder for sexual pleasure."

"Was Kashiwada a follower of a cult?"

"He hadn't been involved with any specific group—only a cult that his own delusions had created, where the founder and the follower were one and the same. That is, I believe there was a cult that existed only inside his head, and his crimes were committed in accordance with its doctrine."

"I see. And because he remained silent until he was executed, the content of this doctrine was never revealed, and his motive remained unknown to the end."

"There were some unusual common traits which strongly suggested that these crimes were rooted in this doctrine of the 'Kashiwada cult.' No mention of this is made in any of the books. This information was known only to a very small number of people in the media, and it was a matter of privacy for the victims' families. Plus, there were human rights issues in the mix, so the press exercised self-restraint in this instance. Have you heard any kind of rumors about the victims' families?"

"No, none." If the media didn't make something public, there was no way Takanori could catch wind of it.

"First of all, the victims were all nearly the same age. All four of them were born in 1991 or 1992, making them roughly twelve at the time of the incidents. Why was their age range so narrow? Perverts who're sexually attracted only to young girls might actually be more prevalent overseas, but I've never come across any instance where the target age was so set. The first, third, and fourth victims' birthdays were only one month apart. With a random attacker choosing targets indiscriminately, that's just inconceivable."

That made Takanori recall Akane's birthdate. She was born in June 1992, which would have made her the youngest of all the victims, but the date was only about half a year off.

"There were other things that the victims had in common," Kihara went on. "What I'm about to tell you is something almost nobody knows. In fact, three of the four victims had been born out of wedlock. They didn't even know who their fathers were. Only the third victim had been born to a married couple, but a year after she was born, the parents got divorced. In other words, all four girls were raised by single mothers, and one of them was from a foster-care facility."

Takanori gulped. Naturally, he thought of Akane. Once again, she was a perfect fit.

"One more thing," Kihara said. "Since the papers and magazines didn't publish pictures of the victims' faces, this is also something nobody could know. I have some snapshots of the victims that were taken when they were still alive. Their builds and faces were very much alike."

Takanori had never seen a picture of Akane from when she was twelve, so he had to imagine what she'd been like based on her current appearance.

"You have pictures of the victims?" he asked.

"Would you like to see them?"

"Please."

Kihara opened a cabinet and pulled out several photographs of the young girls from a file containing all his materials on the Kashiwada case.

The four pictures lined up on the table were all taken from the bust up, and the girls strongly resembled each other. Their hairstyles were different, as were their weights, so each girl had a distinct aura about her, but their facial features looked exactly the same.

Takanori felt as if he were seeing Akane's image among the four girls.

As he stacked the four photographs together and returned them, his expression grew serious. "By the way, I still haven't answered the question you asked me earlier. About what my connection to the Kashiwada case is… There's a woman I'm in love with, and I plan to marry her. She's carrying my child. Her name is Akane Maruyama, and she was going to be his fifth victim. You know, she really does resemble these young girls."

Kihara let out a deep sigh.

"Ah, so that's why you contacted me. No wonder... So I wasn't mistaken, then. You really were in a bind, weren't you? But Kashiwada was executed. I'd say the problem has been cut off at the root."

It was true that with the sentence carried out, the physical entity known as Kashiwada had been terminated. But that fact fell within the province of "science" as commonly understood—he might not have lost the power to exert his influence while lurking in the paranormal realm.

After all, even I died once and came back.

Takanori was about to say so aloud as a joke, but he swallowed his words and reached into his knapsack.

"Please, take a look at this."

He pulled out his computer and turned it on. One of his reasons for coming here was to show Kihara the video of the hanging saved on the USB stick. Loath to waste time while the computer was starting up, Takanori posed another question.

"After listening to you, I can definitely see what's mysterious about the Kashiwada case. But what's your personal take on it, Mr. Kihara? Do you really believe Kashiwada had to be the killer?"

"The thing is, I'm not sure at this point. Would you mind looking at the photos of the victims that were taken where the bodies were abandoned?"

At the writer's invitation, Takanori lined up the four photographs on the table as if they were tarot cards.

"Anything you notice?" Kihara asked.

"No, not really..."

Since each girl resembled Akane, just looking at the pictures made him uncomfortable, and he wanted to avert his eyes.

"When I saw these photos," said Kihara, "I had a certain intuition. It's sort of like an instinct I've developed over the years. All of the girls were in the same pose. Why? Because they were his subjects."

"His subjects..."

"Like how people make the peace sign when they get their pictures taken. The culprit must have taken the victims' pictures with a camera or recorded them on video."

Takanori found himself drawn in by the photos. Now that Kihara mentioned it, all of the girls indeed were in a fixed pose, turned into perfect subjects.

"Yes, you're right about that."

"And yet...no matter how much they searched Kashiwada's house, they couldn't find a single video or photo of the victims."

That wasn't necessarily proof that Kashiwada hadn't been the killer. The very presumption that he must have photographed or filmed the victims was nothing more than speculation.

As they talked, the background image appeared on the computer screen.

First, Takanori showed Kihara the original video saved on the USB stick.

The man appeared, moving about the studio apartment with a video camera in hand.

He set the camera on top of the desk and connected it to the computer. Up to that point his face was not shown, meaning they couldn't tell if it was Kashiwada. The man turned his back to the camera and moved away from the computer, placed one foot on the chair in the middle of the room, stood up, put the rope around his neck, turned around, and kicked out the chair. His body fell vertically across the screen and through the floor and momentarily disappeared, only to fall again from the ceiling, coming to a stop with his face out of view. His hands and feet convulsed, his crotch grew wet, and his vital reactions gradually ceased.

Although Takanori had seen the video repeatedly, every time he watched it, he got goose bumps.

"It looks exactly like an execution scene," Kihara voiced his initial impression just as the body began to rotate with the rope around its neck.

"I thought so too," Takanori said.

"An execution chamber is a dual structure with a first floor and a sublevel, and the way it works is that when the prison guard pushes a button, it sends electricity to the floor plate. That opens it, and the condemned person's body falls down into the execution sub-chamber. But the room in this video isn't an execution chamber, obviously. Where was this?"

"Room 303 at the Shinagawa View Heights, in Aomono-Yoko-cho. The person living there is named Hiroyuki Niimura."

Looking surprised, Kihara turned toward Takanori.

"How do you know that?"

"I managed to piece it together."

"That's some detective work," Kihara praised.

"No, I just happened to figure it out. But the one I really want you to check out is this one."

Takanori closed the original video on the USB stick and proceeded to call up the version he'd saved on his hard drive. This was the copy where some unnatural phenomenon was at work, and the hanged man—who appeared to be Kashiwada—moved downwards as time passed. It was always the same room, No. 303, Shinagawa View Heights. It was only the body that kept on changing.

When Takanori last saw it, the blindfold had come off and revealed the man to be Kashiwada. He'd been swinging in the middle of the frame with his eyes rolled back.

But now, as Takanori and Kihara watched the video together, every last trace of a human presence had disappeared. The room appeared exactly the same, but without the raw presence given off by the body, the video felt completely different.

The subject in the original video on the USB stick was Kashiwada, and his every last movement had commanded the viewer's attention. But in the video Takanori saw now, the subject was nowhere to be found. There was only the rope hanging from the ceiling, swinging slightly from the recoil.

He's just gone.

Only the bottom part of the rope, blackened by sweat and a small amount of blood, hinted that a dead body had been there.

The rope's job had been to tightly constrict Kashiwada's neck and to hold his body up in the air. Yet, like an escape artist, Kashiwada had pulled his neck out of the loop and vanished.

Positioned in the center of the screen, the ring of the rope was rotating slowly as if to provoke and mock the viewer.

Kihara, who hadn't beheld the ongoing change, remained calm, but Takanori was simply dumbstruck, and his breathing grew more and more panicked.

The fucking guy got away, he cursed, uncharacteristically. *Where the hell did he go?*

The hanged man's whereabouts worried Takanori. There was no way the guy could have come back to life. But if he had, where might he be headed?

3

It was only about ten seconds or so, judging by the second hand of the clock. Yet as Takanori stared and waited, time seemed to stretch forever.

Even if a person's heart stopped beating, if proper treatment could be administered within eight minutes or so, it was possible for the patient to be resuscitated. A few cases had been reported around the world where dead people had come back to life. But in Takanori's case, the span had been two years. It was beyond anything that medical science could explain.

With his left hand on his chin, Mitsuo Ando was looking down at the family register, lost in thought, as Takanori watched him and wondered how he was going to explain this as a doctor and a father. Placed atop his desk in the director's office, the register arrested Mitsuo's movement like the muzzle of a gun that was pointed at him.

Takanori had thought it best not to call his father in advance and tell him the reason for his visit. Knowing his father, if he'd known why Takanori was coming, he would have made up some elaborate, convincing explanation beforehand and created a smokescreen to conceal the truth.

There was no way to extract it from him without taking him by surprise.

Mitsuo kept looking down because he didn't want Takanori to see how agitated he was.

Surely Mitsuo was deeply regretful that he hadn't dealt with this problem sooner. He hadn't even considered that his son would decide to marry so soon, without consulting his parents at all. If he'd known, there might have been some other way to handle this matter. Or perhaps he hadn't known that the matter of Takanori's death had remained in the family register as a past record. It was hard to believe that Mitsuo, always so prudent and prepared for everything, had forgotten about that. He'd simply been too busy to check the content in the family register.

When exactly twenty seconds had passed, Mitsuo raised his face.

"By the way, why did you need to get the family register?" he asked.

He tried to pretend to be calm, but his eyes were wandering. In the first place, it was not an answer to the question Takanori had asked: *How are you going to explain the fact that I was dead for two years?*

"Because I'm getting married, dad."

"Oh, married, eh? When I got married, I was the same age as you are now. So, whom do you want to marry?"

"Akane Maruyama."

As her name permeated his mind, many memories came flooding back. Seeing his father's expression become a bit more cheerful, Takanori assumed that he had a good impression of Akane.

"Oh, that girl. She was the one who truly proved how valuable Fureai was for society."

Since Akane Maruyama had entered the foster home Fureai at

the same time that it was founded, Mitsuo had known about her since she was little.

"I agree," Takanori said.

"She was a nice girl. I admit it. But why have you chosen her as your marriage partner?"

"Because we're alike."

"Alike? I don't understand what you mean. Isn't it more accurate to say you and she are complete opposites?"

She had been all alone in the world, while Takanori had been showered with affection by his wealthy parents growing up. Mitsuo was merely talking about how different their childhood environments had been.

"I know what you're saying, dad. Because I thought so, too. I asked myself why I feel we're the same even though we're from completely different backgrounds." Then Takanori cast his eyes down at the family register, as if the answer to that question might lie there.

Mitsuo defied Takanori's inducement and fixed his gaze straight ahead, brushing off the family register as if he were getting rid of something detestable.

"I don't see why you had to barge into my office like this. I mean, why don't you visit us at home more often? Your mom wants to see you."

"I'll go there soon, with Akane."

Takanori had a reason for coming to his father's office instead of the house—he didn't want to involve his mother in this. He couldn't ask his father to explain the entry about his death in the family register in her presence. That would be all right if his parents had gotten on the same page beforehand, but if Mitsuo had told a nonsense story to her, Takanori would be stirring up a hornet's nest. Only Takanori needed the truth to be revealed, and the merciful thing was to let his mother go on believing the fake story.

"It was an unfortunate accident," Mitsuo said.

With that preliminary remark out of the way, he began to describe what had happened.

"Every person has different types of memories. Memories of scenery or sounds, of smells or tastes... They're obtained by the five senses that human beings possess. The story I'm about to tell you started with my sense of touch. My hands still remember the feeling. For two years, I'd been pained by the memory of being touched by soft skin, and the feeling had soaked into my hands...

"I don't even remember how many times I was tortured by nightmares... Every time I had a bad dream where I was sinking under the sea and being buffeted by the waves, I'd wake up in a cold sweat and put a hand to my chest to calm my heart. There was always this feeling of small hands trying to grab my shin at the end of my nightmare. Their soft fingers would slip away from my skin and disappear down into the bottom of the sea. How it frustrated me that I couldn't grab those hands, even though I felt like I could reach them if only I stretched my arms farther...

"Those small hands were yours.

"It was about twenty-five years ago, in the early summer. You were still two or three, I think. The three of us went to the beach for a swim, in Toi, West Izu. It was before the beach opened, so there weren't so many people there, and it was almost like our own private beach.

"You and I were on our chests on long inflatables, and we were paddling out to the open sea. Every time the waves came, you sounded like you were having so much fun. I heard your mother's voice from behind, telling us to 'Come back,' but I ignored it and paddled further and further. I just wanted to see you having fun some more.

"Just as your mother's voice became hysterical, this big white wave appeared in front of us. It turned our plastic floats upside down, and we got thrown out into the sea.

"I didn't realize until my head went under that it was so deep that even an adult's legs couldn't reach bottom, and I nearly panicked. I stuck my head above the surface and looked around for you as I kicked below the water to stay afloat, but you were nowhere to be found. I saw your mother running toward me from the shore, splashing through the water. She was half-crazed, coming out into the sea with her clothes still on.

"That's when I felt your hands clinging on to my leg. It was only a brief moment that you touched my leg. I took a deep breath and dove into the dark sea to search for you, but I couldn't find you. I knew you were somewhere near me, but I couldn't reach you.

"When I looked closer toward the shore, I saw your mother flailing, her arms raised. The way her screams were mixed with this dull gurgling, I knew she was drowning.

"As you know, your mother's a poor swimmer. She's helpless in the water if she can't stand up, but she was possessed by the desire to save you. She was panicking and starting to go under.

"I was 'between the devil and the deep blue sea,' as they say. I grabbed the inflatable floating nearby, lifted your mother's body on top of it, and went back over to the spot where you'd disappeared. The slightest loss of time made such a difference. I swam around the area, holding my breath and going down so many times, but I was never able to get ahold of you again.

"All I had left of you was some of your hair caught in my wedding ring on my left hand. But you were gone.

"The Coast Guard searched for days, but even after they were done, we paid out of our own pocket and kept looking for you. We were never able to find you, though.

"Afterwards, your mother and I started hurling abuse at each other, vile stuff. She'd sob and tell me to 'give me back my baby,' and I'd shout back that her reckless behavior cost us the chance to save you. The two of us were one step away from divorcing.

"Those two years, we kept on struggling in the depths of that blackness. It makes me shudder every time I recall those years..."

Getting choked up, Mitsuo turned his face to the side, and his expression softened somewhat.

"But then a miracle happened. It was exactly two years after you drowned. In a small fishing village north of Toi called Odoi, there was this elderly couple—a retired fisherman and his wife—who quietly passed away one after the other, without anyone at their side. When a distant relative came to visit and searched the house, a young boy was found in the back shed.

"The old fishing couple never had any children, so naturally they couldn't have had any grandkids. The boy showed symptoms of memory loss, and no one had any idea who he was, where he came from, or how he ended up there.

"He was properly dressed, and well-fed, so it was clear that he'd been raised with care by the old couple.

"It didn't take all that long to realize that the boy was you.

"It was a miracle. Your mother was beside herself with joy, and I thanked God for our unexpected good luck. I used it as an opportunity to quit my job at K University's Faculty of Medicine and took over at the hospital run by your mother's family, developing it into something much larger and venturing into charitable work.

"A precious treasure, once lost, had been returned to us. It was only natural that I'd want to give something back to society..."

Takanori remained silent and calm as he listened to his father speak so earnestly.

At the time, his father had belonged to the forensic medicine department in the Faculty of Medicine at K University. He'd likely had many opportunities to take part in autopsies and must have formed deep connections with the police. Surely he had managed to pull a few strings and to offer some money to get others to cooperate with him—all to concoct a coherent story so that he could put the register back the way it was before.

Yet the story that his son had been raised by an old fisherman and his wife went beyond belief. As it went, a childless couple had gone out in their boat to fish and picked up this young boy, who'd slipped through the search dragnet and floated his way to them, and after reviving the boy, they'd raised him discreetly and no one had ever noticed.

Just like Momotaro.

When Takanori recalled the tale of Momotaro—the "peach

boy" whom an old couple found floating down a river inside a giant fruit—he nearly burst out laughing, forgetting that it was his own story, too.

As he tried to stifle his laughter, his father went on talking. Making heavy use of medical terms, Mitsuo described how the after-effects of having nearly drowned had erased Takanori's memory of the two years spent living in Odoi. Apparently, similar examples had been reported overseas.

There was a period after Takanori entered elementary school when his body was remarkably small. Mentally, too, he fell behind the other students and had trouble keeping up in class. As he grew he got better, and once in middle school, he closed the gap with his fellow students academically. By the time he started high school, he was of above-average height and could boast the highest grades of anyone in his year.

This wasn't a matter of memory loss. To him, it made more sense in every way to suppose that the two-year period when he was two and three had been excised from his life.

Listening to his father spin his yarn, Takanori didn't feel especially angry.

As Mitsuo talked frantically, his eyes seeming to plead for forgiveness, Takanori found his inclination to scoff at him subside.

It was immodest of his father to make up some ridiculous fairy tale about a matter of life and death, but mocking someone who was trying to work things out somehow, who was struggling to live with himself, seemed even worse.

For two years, his father and mother had believed their beloved son was dead. That belief was an unmistakable fact. As he imagined their desperation and sorrow, Takanori's heart was filled with gratitude.

Forgive me, his father seemed to be saying. *Right now, this foolish excuse is all I can give you.*

Witnessing this appeal made Takanori realize how loved he'd been by his father.

The immediate prospect of marrying Akane and becoming a father only intensified his appreciation.

Wiping his eyes with his hand, he stepped away from the table and sat down on the sofa.

"I understand, dad. Now I know how it all happened. I have a vague recollection of it, too. I can dimly remember that sometime before I entered preschool, we went swimming in the ocean with nobody around."

Even when Takanori said this, Mitsuo kept his guard up. Perhaps he couldn't help wondering what it was that his son remembered.

"Oh? Right, the three of us did go out a lot together."

"No, what I remember is a time that you and I went out, just us two."

"Hmm, that's odd. Your mother was usually with us."

Until hearing his father's story, Takanori hadn't known that the beach in Toi was where he'd drowned. Previously, a vision of a tranquil seaside area would sometimes pop up in his head. Some of his memories were accompanied by a fear of getting pulled down to the dark depths of the sea, and so it seemed that the part about him drowning was true.

However, he had an even more vivid memory. The timeframe was incoherent, and the scenes came to him in fragments, and whenever he tried to remember, he had to labor to put together all the little pieces of the jigsaw puzzle.

"No, mom wasn't there. There was another man there, instead."

His mother was absent from the beach scenery, with a strange man in her place.

"A man," Mitsuo echoed...

Bored of playing with the sand under the blazing sun, young Takanori was about to return to his father, who was sitting on the embankment and watching him.

A man was walking toward Mitsuo on top of the embankment, which stretched straight along the shoreline.

Although this man appeared to be a stranger, he began talking to Takanori's father. Despite his young age, Takanori could tell that they were talking about some serious matter. Although the stranger was grinning, his father reacted with an angry look.

Takanori felt so thirsty that he walked over to his father and mumbled, "I'm thirsty, dad," while studying the stranger's face.

His father held out a bottle of oolong tea that he'd been drinking. Takanori took it and was about to drink, but there wasn't much left. Seeing this, the man muttered something unintelligible before asking, "Want another?" in a tone that was overly familiar, coming from a stranger.

Takanori declined the offer, instead finishing off the last drops of the tea his father had given him.

While he didn't know why he remembered this, the scene had left a major impression on him...

"Dad, who was that man?"

A tiny spasm ran across Mitsuo's face. He always looked that way just before getting sullen.

"There's no such man... Well, anyway, he's gone now, so don't worry about it. Just forget about him."

Mitsuo wore the same angry expression he'd shown back then, when Takanori was a boy.

4

Thank goodness it's early summer, Akane thought as she took in the view outside the window. Though it was after 7 p.m., it was still light out. If it were closer to winter, the scenery alongside the train line would long since have been covered in darkness.

Takanori had told her to come home quickly, and she had tried to do just that, but she'd had to attend a meeting of the drama club in the role of assistant moderator and ended up leaving quite late. They'd been unable to decide the program for the school festival to be held in the fall, and every time someone suggested a potential play to perform, the group discussed the option in detail. Then the club president Miho Iizawa proposed that she write an original work, and the meeting devolved into bickering.

Iizawa had the highest grades in her class and was a precocious girl all around, so it wasn't as though she lacked the literary talent. Yet the dramas she'd written previously were rather awful and even traumatic for the other club members, and the fact that she was oblivious to it exacerbated the problem.

The ensemble that she'd written last year about the behind-the-scenes doings of the club members—except for the care taken to assign the performers equal roles—had met with severe criticism. Every emotional peak had been expressed in shouts and roars, and the whole play was full of the sort of overacting that only the Takarazuka Revue could pull off, so neither the actors themselves nor the audience were able to get emotionally involved. It was arguably a work meant to satisfy the club president herself, and although the members had all had their fill of her, she hadn't taken the hint, offering to write another drama for them to perform. Even Akane had sighed as the assistant moderator.

Finally wrapping up the meeting and leaving school only ten minutes ago, she jumped on the inbound Keihin Express train.

Since the question of what to do for the school festival had been put on hold, inevitably, they would soon be rehashing the same agenda item.

While she fretted over how to go about placating young Iizawa, the train slid in to Aomono-Yokocho station. With no train on the opposite track, Akane could see the outbound platform as she leaned against the doors.

Just before they came to a full stop, her gaze was drawn to a lone man around the center of the platform. He was using his cell phone and started walking. Almost bumping into another passenger, he raised his hand with the device up high and spun on his tiptoes like a dancer. At that moment, his face slowly turned to reveal itself, dominating her field of vision.

That might be the guy I saw that time.

A light bulb went off in her head. It wasn't only his face but also his sharp style that stood out, with his white jacket coordinated with a summer necktie. He resembled the strange man she'd seen near Takanori's condo. That time, the man had been standing on the sidewalk on the other side of the street so she couldn't make out his facial features, but the gestures of his hands as he used his cell phone and the way he looked around as he talked were a dead match.

This time, all that stood between them was one side of the tracks, meaning they were considerably closer than before.

The man, his back turned to Akane and using his cell phone, didn't seem to notice that she was right behind him and separated only by the glass of the train doors.

At such times, Akane's cognitive faculties sped up. In her mind, she rapidly lined up all the pieces of info that she'd received from Takanori as if she were a professional card dealer.

...The live-streamed suicide by hanging was filmed in a studio apartment, not a prison execution chamber.

...The apartment was right near Aomono-Yokocho station on the Keihin Express line.

...It was Room 303 at the Shinagawa View Heights.

...The person living there was named Hiroyuki Niimura.

...Was there any chance that the strange guy she saw near Takanori's place was this Hiroyuki Niimura?

The doors on the opposite side were still open.

People on the platform were waiting for the passengers onboard to get off.

In a flash, Akane decided to get off, slipping between the other passengers onto the platform. She didn't want to waste this opportunity. It was her chance to reverse the disadvantage of being stalked by an unknown person. If this man in front of her went into Room 303 at the Shinagawa View Heights, her hypothesis that she was being followed by Hiroyuki Niimura would be correct. That would put her one step ahead of him in terms of the info they each possessed.

I can do this, she encouraged herself.

Just as the train began pulling away, Akane walked toward the stairs leading down to the ticket gate. Then she took her cell phone out of her bag and turned it off. If her activity were being monitored via a GPS tracking app, turning off the phone would surely disable the feature.

Yet she knew that she was also severing her connection to Takanori.

Around the time that Akane turned off her phone, Takanori was in his kitchen. An FM station on the radio on the counter directly behind him was playing a lighthearted bossa nova tune.

He sipped from his glass of red wine and poured a little into the beef curry that he had simmering away. He vaguely recalled seeing a recipe somewhere that said red wine paired well with beef curry. The bloody color mixed together with the curry roux and gave off a faint aroma. The beef had become nice and tender.

Once their child was born, Takanori would be working from home more often, and if Akane were to keep her job as a full-time teacher, he would have even more opportunities to cook their meals. His repertoire was still rather limited at the moment, and curry and fried rice were the only dishes that he could cook decently. That said, he was reluctant to attend a cooking class or consult a cookbook.

He certainly wanted to fulfill his responsibilities as a husband and father, but he believed the way to do that was to make the most of his masculinity rather than to copy the manner of a typical house-wife. His features were the furthest thing from those of a rugged man, yet there were times when Takanori wished to be just that type.

How long has the curry been simmering? he wondered. He poked his head out from the kitchen to check the living-room clock and saw that it was long past 7 p.m.

Before leaving that morning, Akane had told him she would be home around seven or so.

Where could she be? Perhaps she'd gotten off at Roppongi and was walking over to his place, or perhaps she was still on the subway. She couldn't possibly still be on the Keihin Express, Takanori figured. As he imagined Akane in transit, he remembered the GPS tracking app installed on her cell phone.

On top of concerns about her mental state, there was also the possibility that she was being targeted by some stranger, and thus Takanori had decided to install the software with Akane's consent, much like a parent giving his young child a cell phone equipped with a GPS feature.

As a tool that let you know where your loved ones were, it really was useful.

Takanori lowered the heat under the pot of curry and wiped his hands. Moving to the living room, he picked up his cell phone. When he launched the application and searched for Akane's whereabouts, he noticed that her phone had been turned off.

Why would she turn it off?

Since she almost never turned off her phone, something felt amiss to him.

When he proceeded with his search, the place where her cell phone had been turned off appeared onscreen.

The point on the map indicated Aomono-Yokocho station on the Keihin Express line. Moreover, the phone had been turned off after she'd stepped onto the platform, and not inside the train.

As far as Takanori knew, there was no connection between Akane and Aomono-Yokocho. To begin with, she had no relatives nor any friends around there.

Why Aomono-Yokocho?

Naturally, he associated the area with the live video of the hanging. The apartment where the video had likely been filmed was just a stone's throw from the station.

Could she really be heading there?

This was one of the biggest puzzles he was contending with. He had no idea how the series of events surrounding the Kashiwada case, Shinagawa View Heights, and Hiroyuki Niimura—the resident of that unit—were connected. The only things he knew were the address and the name, and he had no leads as to what kind of man Niimura was. However, Takanori could be almost certain that there was something creepy about him.

An ominous premonition came over Takanori, and at once he lost his appetite.

The distance was not even far enough for it to be considered tailing. Akane went through the ticket gate and entered an alley in the residential area, and within only two minutes she spotted the apartment she was looking for. It was an old seven-story building with rows of studio apartments that were all the same size: the Shinagawa View Heights, which Takanori had also visited once.

On the short trip from Aomono-Yokocho station, Akane kept surveilling the man from behind. If it had been brighter outside, she could have made out all of his features, but in the dim light after sunset the man's contours melted into the darkness.

He appeared to be in his thirties and had a slender, tall build, and even from behind she could tell that he was neat and well-groomed. The more she observed him, the more he seemed to be the same person as the stranger from the other day.

The man, who was walking about thirty feet in front of her, came to a halt. Seeing this, Akane headed toward a nearby greengrocer, pretended to pick vegetables from the outdoor stands, and tracked him with just her eyes.

Aiming the tip of his shoe at the base of a utility pole, he kicked it at a dramatic speed and went back to walking as if nothing had happened.

Akane resumed her pursuit. After he entered the lobby of the Shinagawa View Heights just as she'd expected, she looked at the base of the pole where the man had kicked it and found the remains of a moth stuck to its concrete surface. The splatter of the squashed bug's bodily fluids was much larger than the size of its wings.

Akane shuddered. The act seemed like the opposite of how a man who projected such a clean appearance would behave. She simply couldn't fathom the point of obliterating the moth.

She peered into the lobby, but there was no sign of him. The elevator was running, and she could hear the groaning of its motor. The display panel showed the elevator stopping on the third floor. As soon as she heard faint footsteps walking down a corridor, the motor produced a different sound and the elevator descended.

There was no guarantee that the man wouldn't be there when the door opened. She looked around to see whether there might be some place she could hide and noticed a space set back from the residents' mailboxes, just beside the janitor's room, whose curtain was drawn now that it was after work hours.

The mailboxes were lined up along both sides in the space, and on the far wall were three pairs of coin-operated washing machines and dryers. One of the washers was in use, and the whole unit was shaking just before the end of its spin cycle as if it were suffering death spasms.

Just as she was about to step toward the building entrance, Akane glimpsed the number "303" on a mailbox. Room 303—Hiroyuki Niimura's apartment.

Akane peeked inside and found a single postcard that had been tossed in at the bottom. The slot opened right away when she pulled it down with the tip of her finger. *Go on*, the postcard seemed to say, ripe for the taking.

After looking around behind her and verifying that no one was there, she picked up the postcard and placed it in her bag. The elevator had begun to move again. With the mailboxes on the walls to her left and right, and the washers and dryers set against the wall further down, she found herself at a dead end with no avenue of escape.

Perhaps someone was coming down, timing when the washer would stop.

Akane held her breath as she stood in the recessed space with the mailboxes, just her nose sticking out into the hallway. Without making a sound, a woman passed right in front of her face. Caught off guard, Akane stood still, her arms folded across her chest, and a tiny shriek escaped her lips.

With an elegant gait, the woman was heading toward the bicycle parking space when she heard Akane's cry and stopped.

The lady wore a sleeveless dress and a large pair of sunglasses and had slipped on pumps on her otherwise bare feet. Her profile was right there; her hair came down to the middle of her back, and her upper arms, the nape of her neck, and her chin line were practically pure white. Akane's nose detected a peculiar scent unlike any perfume, and she instinctively held her breath. It was not that the smell offended her, but it was ever so faintly redolent of soil, a smell to which Akane was particularly sensitive.

You've come back to me.

So spoke a gentle voice, seemingly from nowhere, jolting Akane.

"Mom...why are you here..."

Just as she uttered this, the phantom of her mother vanished. The woman had looked exactly like Akane's mother in her youth.

Her illusion always appeared about once a year, but with this instance, it seemed she was beginning to manifest more often.

Her head a jumble, Akane went outside and around to the front of the building and looked up at the third-floor windows. Only the third unit from the right had its lights on.

She was sure that was Hiroyuki Niimura's apartment.

Having made certain of that much, she set out toward the station, turning her phone on as she made her way there.

All right, I'd better just get to Aomono-Yokocho.

All that linked Akane to Aomono-Yokocho was Room 303 at the Shinagawa View Heights. Takanori had identified where she was, at least.

Not being able to narrow down what lay in store for him there irked him. After changing out of his sweatpants into jeans, he rushed to his entryway.

He shoved his feet into his sneakers, but in his haste the momentum caused him to stumble and bash his head into the door, and just then he heard his cell phone ring.

Akane's name showed up on the display. As relief washed over him, the strength left his body, and he nearly sank down onto his entryway mat.

There was no end to his anxieties. Yet he supposed that in essence, that was what it meant to love someone. You had to accept all that love entailed, worries included.

Sitting down properly on his mat, Takanori pressed the call button on his phone and heard Akane's voice on the other side.

5

After scouring the bookstores, including secondhand shops, Takanori had finally acquired it. He placed the paperback on his table and proceeded to inspect it carefully from every angle.

Looking at the colophon, he saw that the first edition had come out in June 1991, with the paperback released two years later.

Five thousand copies had been printed of the first edition. It was exceedingly difficult to obtain one; scarcely any could be found in libraries, let alone in used booksellers, and even a search of online auctions yielded no hits. The first edition had vanished entirely from the marketplace, perhaps having been gathered up and collected someplace. The only copies that he could even hope to obtain were reprints and paperback versions.

There was a chance that the origin of the series of inexplicable events was explained in the book, that some hint to elucidating the mystery lay hidden within... The circumstances of the book's discovery intimated as much.

None of the occurrences so far had been a coincidence. Phenomena which at first glance appeared to be unrelated were linked in remarkable ways, ways that were invisible to the eye. The spot to which they'd been guided by the car navigation was where the first victim's body had been dumped in the Kashiwada case, and the young girl who had nearly become the next victim was Akane, the woman he would be marrying.

Given the flow of things, this development couldn't be a coincidence, either.

Since the rare and valuable book appeared in both the live suicide video and the photographs taken during the house search, it had to be connected to all this somehow. What was more, the photos of the interior of Kashiwada's room revealed a whole bundle of first editions sitting at the entryway.

It was Kihara who had noted this strange coincidence.

Takanori had learned of it yesterday morning at Kihara's office.

Yesterday morning...

It was a muggy day, reaching about ninety degrees during the daytime. Just walking the few hundred yards from Takada-no-baba station to Kihara's office, Takanori broke into a sweat. Yet the temperature wasn't the only reason he was perspiring so much. On the previous occasion, he'd been able to kill time on the way there with a casual stroll, but this time his impatience made him walk faster.

He'd received a call earlier that morning from Kihara, who'd discovered that the live video of the suicide and the photos taken during the police search of Kashiwada's place ten years prior contained an item in common. Upon hearing this, unable to contain himself, Takanori had dashed over to Kihara's office.

"An item in common..."

That was how Kihara had described what he had found.

Responding to the bell, Kihara opened the door, and upon seeing the beads of sweat on Takanori's face, lowered the temperature of his air conditioner by several degrees.

"Oh, so you ran here in this heat. Well, please come in."

Assuming that Takanori was eager to know what was going on,

Kihara didn't waste any time serving coffee and instead loaded the video on his computer screen.

Kihara had given the two videos that Takanori had brought and copied for him repeated viewings, and after running a comparative analysis, he'd found something.

On the computer screen was the video in which Kashiwada had slipped out of the rope around his neck like an escape artist and run away. The disorderly studio apartment was full of inanimate everyday objects. What now occupied the center of the room was not a human being, but simply the ring of the rope hanging from the ceiling.

Kihara moved the cursor to focus on the ceiling where the rope should have been fastened. To support the body of a man, a rope needed to be affixed to a point on the ceiling. Yet in a typical studio apartment, there was surely no place on the ceiling to tie a rope.

With that question as his starting point, Kihara had searched for where the rope might have been fastened, but in the middle of the ceiling was a small, black, cavernous hole stretching even further above, with no place for a rope to connect. It was as if the rope had been hanging from this darkness like the thread of a spider's web descending from another dimension.

"When I watched this video, right away it made me think of a magnifying glass."

He's right, Takanori thought. Hanging in the middle of the screen and ending in a ring, the rope resembled an inverted magnifying glass.

"Yes, that's what it looks like," he said.

"Taking that as a hint, I tried to enlarge the 'convex lens' section. I was curious about what I might see. At first, I was doing this half-seriously, but then..."

Working off the idea that magnifying glasses made tiny objects appear larger, Kihara had treated the ring of the rope as a lens and enlarged the image inside little by little.

When he'd done that, the focus had lined up with part of the bookshelf on the opposite wall.

S

"That's when I got the idea to compare it with the version on the USB. In the middle of the screen, Kashiwada was hanging and blocking the view, so the items on the bookshelf behind him were hidden."

After putting the USB version on the screen and confirming this, Kihara reverted to the video saved on his hard drive.

With Kashiwada's body gone, the view to the back was clear and revealed a single volume lying on its side where the lens was focused.

The title of the book was *Ring*.

Go on, take a look, Kashiwada seemed to beckon, leading Takanori's eyes to the copy of *Ring* in the enlarged, ring-shaped hanging rope that so resembled a magnifying glass.

Could this really be a coincidence, too?

With everything around it a blur, the lone volume asserted itself emphatically.

"But that's not all," Kihara said, going through the materials related to the Kashiwada case and pulling several photographs from the file. "These photos were taken right after Kashiwada's arrest. They were shot about ten years ago, when the cops searched his home, and they show every inch of the place."

The mere mention of photos of the living space of a serial kidnapper and murderer of girls put notions in Takanori's head and made him search for something abnormal. Banishing those thoughts, he peered closer and observed the room in the snippets captured by the camera until his nose nearly touched.

The unit was a studio apartment, larger than those at the Shinagawa View Heights, with a single bed positioned at one wall and a bookshelf stretching all the way to the ceiling at another wall. The bookshelf was stacked full of volumes with no free space.

The photos allowed him to read their titles.

They belonged to all sort of genres—natural science, mathematics, medicine, philosophy, religion, history, and literature—and a cursory scan was all Takanori needed to discern the resident's high level of education.

He recalled that Kashiwada had worked as a college-prep teacher.

He'd been at one of the leading schools in West Funabashi and supposedly taught three subjects, namely mathematics, physics, and
English. It was therefore only natural for the books' genres to be so
wide-ranging.

There were also some magazines stacked on the table beside the
bed. Many of them were critical and scientific journals, the furthest
thing possible from obscenity.

A dozen dictionaries surrounded a laptop on a fairly large desk
by the balcony door.

On one side of a mini-kitchen was a small two-door refrigerator,
with a wardrobe right next to it. Its doors were closed, preventing
them from learning what types of clothes were stored inside. The
cabinets contained few dishes, and here and there were signs of the
occupant's frugal lifestyle.

Beyond the bookshelves lined up all the way to the entryway was
a cheap colored box, and heaps of books were visible in between this
colored box and a shoebox. Takanori leaned in even closer, trying to
count the number of volumes.

Seventeen. The books were bundled together with vinyl rope tied
in a cross shape.

All seventeen of them bore the same title: *Ring*.

"It's perfectly clear, all of them are the first edition of the book,"
Kihara explained to Takanori, who was speechless with shock. "I
know because *Ring* had a different jacket starting with the reprint.
Only the first edition had the image of a woman's hand holding out a
videotape. You can tell just by looking."

"*Ring*... Do you know what the book's about, Mr. Kihara?"

"I haven't read it. But it's fairly well known, and hard to find."

"Is it a novel?"

"No, it's supposed to be nonfiction." The genre was Kihara's specialty, so of course he would know about the book.

"But how is it connected to the Kashiwada case?"

"I can't really say, at this point. I'm going to be looking into that
next. It was published right around when you were born, or possibly

before, so you probably don't remember. If you don't mind my asking, how old are you?"

"I'm twenty-eight."

"It was a quarter of a century ago, so I'm not surprised you don't know. There was this urban legend about a videotape that was utterly cursed, and anyone who watched it would die in a bizarre way one week later. The story was circulated as if it were true."

Takanori would have been only two and had no clear recollection of those times, but back when he was in elementary school, he'd caught the lingering scent of the rumor. A demonic videotape that killed the viewer after one week... Yes, he felt certain that it had been regarded as a new incarnation of chain letters.

"Yeah, I kind of remember something. I seem to recall my friends and I talking about it just after I entered elementary school..."

Indeed, it felt as though he'd caught the tail end of the urban legend as it was going away.

"The inspiration for it was this book," Kihara said. "Supposedly, a weekly magazine reporter named Kazuyuki Asakawa met with an untimely death after compiling exhaustive notes about a certain case, and his brother, who worked at a publishing company, released them in book form. Sure, it's an unlikely story. Probably drummed it up to get attention. My assumption is that it's a fictional work repackaged as nonfiction."

"I see. I'll read it right away."

"Well, it's a hard book to get your hands on. There were only 5,000 copies printed of the first edition. Including the second through the fifth reprints, only 22,000 copies sold before it went out of print. Then it was published as a paperback two years later, and a total of six runs sold 62,000 copies before going out of print in 1999. That means all together there were 84,000 copies of the original and paperback versions for sale, so it did okay overall. What's strange is that the first edition is the only one to have nearly disappeared from the market. That said...take another look at this."

Kihara showed him one of the photos again, pointing to the stack of books placed beside the colored box at the entryway.

"Kashiwada had a total of seventeen copies in his apartment, right?" Takanori said.

"Look very closely. What impression do you get from this stack of books?"

All seventeen of them were neatly bundled together with vinyl rope tied into a cross shape. It almost looked like what people did when they were throwing out a bunch of newspapers or magazines.

"Could he have been planning to burn them as garbage?"

"That's what I thought, too. By all appearances, it looks like he was going to get rid of them. But why? I can't understand why he'd want to throw away books that were so rare. If he'd sold them at an online auction he could've gotten over ten times the original price, no question. Instead he bound them with vinyl rope and left them at the entryway like they were about to be tossed out. Don't you think that's a crude way to treat something so valuable?"

When he put it that way, Takanori had to agree. Why would someone needlessly discard books that could fetch a high price at a used bookstore? With seventeen copies, Kashiwada couldn't have been unaware of the books' value.

Takanori asked, "Had he ever been involved with a publishing company?"

If Kashiwada had worked at the publisher of *Ring*, it wouldn't be that odd for him to own so many copies of the same book.

"No, he never belonged to any publishing house. For my part, I'm planning to pursue this avenue. Kazuyuki Asakawa—the author of the notes—may be dead, but his brother Junichiro might still be alive. Besides that, I'm thinking of tracking down some of the people who were involved in publishing *Ring* to ask them about it."

"If you do learn something—even something trivial—please let me know as soon as you find out. I'll get here right away."

At that moment, Takanori's best bet was Kihara's talent for ferreting out information, which he'd cultivated over many years.

While the paperback in Takanori's hands wasn't especially valuable, in terms of learning what the book was about, it'd do just fine.

It was a story about a cursed videotape that killed those who watched it one week later... Before reading it, Takanori already doubted the book's credibility. Still, he told himself to remain calm and composed no matter what details he found.

The urge to laugh off this story as a likely fabrication clashed with a sense of caution that he'd best not dismiss any non-scientific phenomena. The conflicting emotions mingling inside him made his vessels throb.

He made up his mind and flipped open the cover, and immediately he was shocked stiff by an enormous eye.

Inside the cover was a color illustration with a motif of eyeballs. Within a black frame that resembled a memorial photo were countless eyeballs on a yellow and orange background.

A complete picture of a human eye popped out from the background in the middle of the upper part of the page. In between the upper and lower eyelids, the iris was looking straight out at him. For some reason, one part of the lower lid was cut, giving it the shape of a severed ring.

Fighting an oppressive feeling that someone was watching him, Takanori began to read the main text.

6

"It all started with a single videotape."

So read one of the catchphrases on the band of the paperback.

"This is a true account."

The second catchphrase insisted that its content was based on a true story.

Simply put, that meant what was written in the book was a report of actual events resulting from a single videotape.

Takanori turned the pages of *Ring*. At no other time in his life had he read a book with such intense concentration.

The narrator was a man named Kazuyuki Asakawa, a weekly magazine reporter. Encountering some mysterious incidents and investigating their causes, and forced into an inescapable situation, he'd compiled his experiences into a text. At the end of summer a quarter-century ago...

Asakawa learned that by coincidence, four teenage boys and girls had met with unnatural deaths in Tokyo and Kanagawa, on the same day, at the same time, and for reasons unknown.

Given that they'd died at the same time though in different places, he surmised that the four of them had some point in common.

At first, Asakawa imagined that perhaps the four teens had been at the same location and contracted food poisoning, or some new type of virus—something of that nature.

As he pursued his investigation, he uncovered that the four had been friends, and one week prior to their deaths they'd spent the night in Building B-4 at a rental cottage called Villa Log Cabin in South Hakone Pacific Land.

Having read that far in one sitting, Takanori stopped flipping the pages and looked up.

He remembered the name South Hakone Pacific Land distinctly. That was the first place to which the car navigation had mistakenly guided him and Akane.

Asakawa had gone alone to South Hakone Pacific Land in a rental car at nighttime in the rain, which was utterly unlike the sunny weather that afternoon when Takanori and Akane had taken their drive. Nonetheless, the writer's description of the scenery vividly conjured the mountain roads leading to the villa. Both sides of the narrow path winding its way through the terraced fields were covered with tall grasses, grown thick like willows, such that here and there the road had been like a tunnel.

After inquiring at the information center, Asakawa proceeded to the left in his car.

Takanori remembered that road. It was exactly the same one they'd been led down by the car navigation.

Later, Asakawa parked in the lot in front of the building manager's office at Villa Log Cabin.

Takanori knew that there were no longer any structures onsite. The several cottages had been demolished, with the gentle slope leading into the ravine now a grassy plain. And about a hundred feet from the road, there was a lonely old well.

Poking out from the bushes, the well appeared like a deformed gravestone, or like a human being whose torso was buried in the earth, with only the neck sticking out. When he'd taken a step back, and then another, Takanori had felt goose bumps on both his arms.

Where were the well and the cottage in relation to each other back when Asakawa visited? he wondered, but putting that question aside for the moment, he read on.

Asakawa concluded that what linked the four teenagers was a videotape they discovered at Villa Log Cabin and that the images on the tape caused their unnatural deaths. The video consisted of a series of eerie, fragmented scenes and didn't make much sense, but the final part warned, *Those who have viewed these images are fated to die at this exact hour one week from now.* A bit that described how you could escape death had been taped over and erased.

Apparently, the four teens had watched the video in that room and mischievously decided to erase the scene explaining how to avoid dying one week later. Then they'd left the tape behind for the next guest to watch.

Though they'd seen the images on the tape, they hadn't acted on the key to avoiding their fate. Not only had they not believed the warning, they'd taken a mocking attitude.

Having watched the video purely by chance, Asakawa was stricken with panic. He knew that the warning on the video was genuine. Were he to do nothing, he would surely meet the same fate as those four teenagers. At that point, he couldn't simply laugh off the supernatural as being unscientific.

Asakawa returned to Tokyo, and judging that he couldn't handle the situation on his own, he turned to an old friend from high school. This friend's name was Ryuji Takayama. Famous since high school for his smarts, he was an oddball. After graduating from his college's medical department, he switched his focus to end up as a lecturer in philosophy. He was also highly knowledgeable about paranormal phenomena, and was fearless. To get to the bottom of the mystery, Asakawa absolutely needed his help.

After listening to Asakawa's story, Ryuji scoffed through his nose. "Okay, just show me the tape," he said, displaying not the slightest fear of death, determined to confront this occult phenomenon.

As soon as he received a copy of the tape made by Asakawa, Ryuji went about logically analyzing the video, which at first glance seemed preposterous.

Meanwhile, misfortune befell Asakawa's wife and young daughter: they accidentally watched the video. Now Asakawa was forced to battle an unknown terror to save not only his own life but those of his wife and daughter.

Takanori understood how Asakawa felt so well that it hurt.

Heedless of Asakawa's agony, Ryuji went on analyzing the video with great excitement.

The first problem was the origin of the videotape. Why had something like it been created? Elucidating the reason was the key to canceling out the fate of dying one week later, he surmised.

He tabulated all the disjointed scenes, finding twelve in all, and further managed to divide them into two major groups. One consisted of abstract scenes depicting what could be considered imaginary landscapes. The other comprised actual scenes that seemed to be reflected on retinas. And he noticed a feature found only in the realistic scenes: brief moments where the screen went totally black appeared at roughly equal intervals.

Ryuji speculated that these instants looked rather like the blinking of an eye and concluded that scenes actually witnessed by somebody, along with imaginary scenery harbored in that person's mind, had been projected onto the videotape.

If the images really were mentally projected, that person possessed extraordinary occult powers and would surely have drawn considerable attention. Reinvestigating the data on persons with paranormal abilities in Japan, Ryuji eventually tracked down a woman who could well have projected the images.

Her name was Sadako Yamamura.

Ryuji and Asakawa began looking into the life of this Sadako, who was closely connected to the demonic videotape. She'd been born in 1947 on the island of Izu Oshima as the daughter of Shizuko Yamamura—a psychic of unparalleled spiritual power—and a psychologist named Heihachiro Ikuma. After graduating high school she'd gone to Tokyo and joined "Theater Group Soaring" as an actress.

With her graceful features, she'd cut a brilliant figure in the group, but before realizing her ambitions, she had disappeared without a trace.

But where?

As they tried everything possible to find out, Ryuji and Asakawa learned that a tuberculosis sanitarium had once stood where South Hakone Pacific Land was located. Sadako's father had been a patient at the facility.

Ryuji uncovered that tragedy had struck Sadako on a visit to her father. Raped by a man named Nagao—a doctor at the facility who'd also been the last carrier of the smallpox virus—she'd been thrown down a well.

Takanori looked up from the book again and pictured how the area had transformed over time.

Beginning as a tuberculosis sanitarium, it had turned into Villa Log Cabin of the South Hakone Pacific Land resort, and now there was only a gently sloping grassy field... Yet, throughout, the well alone had remained, hiding in the shrubs in the backyard of the sanitarium and lying low beneath Villa Log Cabin.

Ring

Tossed into that well, Sadako Yamamura met an untimely end when she was only twenty or so. It must have taken a while for death to visit her, and during that time she nurtured a deep-seated grudge, filling the small, sealed, saturated space with it.

Takanori remembered vividly how a sinister air, carried by a tepid breeze, had crawled out from the gap between the concrete lid and the stones and swayed the grass before swirling up and stroking his legs.

The demonic video had been born in Building B-4 of Villa Log Cabin, situated directly above the old well.

The living room had been above the floorboards, and the TV and video recorder had been in the corner. Sadako's grudge had soaked into a videotape that had been inserted with the record mode on.

Considering the circumstances, Ryuji and Asakawa assumed that the way to escape death one week later was to dredge up Sadako's bones—in order to give them a proper burial for the repose of her soul.

Ten p.m. that night—that was when Asakawa's time would run out.

The two of them went beneath the cottage, lifted the concrete lid, and climbed down to the bottom of the well to scoop out the muddy water with buckets.

Takanori wasn't claustrophobic but felt suffocated just reading the scene. Could someone really climb down a rope into a hole barely big enough for a person to fit and bring up muddy water? He shuddered to think of it. Even if you had to in order to save your family, it wouldn't be easy. In fact, his imagination was resisting the possibility that he, too, could face such a terrible choice.

Yet Ryuji did precisely that out of a superhuman fearlessness and curiosity, and Asakawa braved his harsh predicament determined to save his wife and daughter.

Their effort paid off, with Asakawa discovering Sadako's skull amid the mud, scooping it up, and bringing it out into the open air above.

Even after his time had run out, he remained alive. Believing they had solved the mystery, he and Ryuji brought Sadako's remains to her family home in Oshima and laid her to rest.

They thought the case was closed. But it wasn't as simple as that.

The next night, when his time was up, Ryuji met an unnatural death in his apartment. His body was found by a student of his, a young woman named Mai Takano.

Paralyzed with shock, Asakawa's mind practically shut down. He had no idea why Ryuji had died. Hadn't the curse been expiated when they solved the mystery of the videotape? If they failed to solve it, why was he still alive?

There was but one logical conclusion.

The way to escape the tape's diabolical power didn't lie in bringing up Sadako's bones and performing that service for her soul. During his week, Asakawa had unwittingly done what the demonic tape had instructed him to do.

What was the act that he had taken but Ryuji had failed to that ended up satisfying the videotape's desire?

Asakawa desperately tried to recall all the things he'd done the previous week.

He found his clue in the concept of a virus. Since the start of this case, he'd sensed that a virus was somehow involved. Plus, this Nagao person who'd murdered Sadako had been Japan's last smallpox carrier. The virus' drive could have blended with Sadako's supernatural powers in her physical form.

Viruses propagated with the help of their infected hosts. If that drive applied to the videotape, then one possible answer was apparent. Perhaps the cursed videotape's wish had been for someone to copy it and show it to a third party who had yet to watch it.

Without realizing it, Asakawa had fulfilled its desire. He'd taken the videotape from Villa Log Cabin, made a copy, and shown it to Ryuji.

The moment he realized that the way to break the curse of the video was to copy it, he came up with a concrete means of rescuing his wife and daughter. The only thing he could do was to beseech his wife's parents to sacrifice themselves. Her parents would surely give their own lives and assume the danger for themselves to save their daughter and grandchild. And if they were to copy the videotape and show it to someone else, they could avoid their own deaths as well.

And thus, to save his wife and daughter, Asakawa elected to unleash the cursed videotape upon the world.

The story known as *Ring* ended with Asakawa heading to Ashikaga where his wife's parents lived.

When Takanori finished reading, his back was drenched in cold sweat. It had soaked through his shirt and reached his seat rest, making the leather fabric of his chair stick to his back unpleasantly.

His breathing was shallow and painful. He could hear his own heartbeat.

Asakawa's final choice weighed heavily on his mind.

Was it better to release a cursed videotape into the world or to sacrifice your family and minimize the damage likely to spread through society?

Faced with such a momentous decision, Takanori's imagination was on the verge of folding.

He was reminded of something his father always said.

"Those who are born into privilege have a duty to give back to society."

If he were abused by someone close to him, and his heart were filled with hatred toward the world, he might very well unleash evil upon it without hesitation. Even worse, he might become evil incarnate and take revenge on a world that had created him.

He balked at the very idea of choosing between such alternatives. He felt inordinately afraid because that predicament perhaps wasn't a figment of his imagination.

Asakawa had obtained the cursed videotape at South Hakone Pacific Land, copied it, and given it to Ryuji.

Takanori had copied the video on the USB stick he'd received from Yoneda and given it to Kihara.

Asakawa's wife and daughter had viewed the video inadvertently while it was in the tape deck.

Akane had ended up seeing the video saved on his computer, and Takanori's child was now growing in her womb.

What was he supposed to make of those similarities?

As if he were being strangulated little by little, the circumstances in *Ring* were gradually coming to haunt him.

7

It was 11 a.m. all three times that he visited Kihara's office.

Perhaps because of the time of day, the everyday scenery he saw on his walk over there was largely unchanged. Moreover, when the apartment building with Kihara's office came into view, Takanori tended to do the same thing.

He halted somewhere along the bridge in front of the building and cast his eyes down at the river's surface.

Standing still, Takanori attempted a little analysis on how his conscious mind worked. The time before last, he'd come earlier than his appointment and had needed to kill time. Why was he doing it now?

When he put both hands on the bridge balustrade and leaned over, he thought he saw dark river water gushing towards him. Though it hadn't rained the day before, the volume of water seemed to be greater somehow.

In fact, Takanori was sure that the quantity of water hadn't changed. The image of dirty water accumulating at the bottom of a well, as depicted in *Ring*, was overlapping with the actual scenery and intensifying it. A dark, mysterious reality was now bulging before him.

Every time he met and listened to Kihara, he received valuable info. No doubt, yesterday, the writer had put to use his special knack for gathering facts and looked into the circumstances surrounding *Ring*.

Contemplating what sort of developments he might become privy to just moments later, Takanori suddenly felt that he'd rather not find out, and his eagerness to visit the office diminished.

Tsuyoshi Kihara was to him what Ryuji Takayama had been to Asakawa. Ryuji had been bold and fearless, and compared to him, Kihara was quite a bit older but also calmer, more judicious, and gentler in appearance. While their personalities differed greatly, if not for Kihara's aid, Takanori wouldn't have been unable to make even the slightest progress, and thus he was in the same position as Asakawa.

His reality was very similar to the circumstances recorded in *Ring*. The only difference was that the video of the hanging saved on the USB stick—while abundantly creepy—in no way constituted a lethal warning.

With his hands still on the balustrade, Takanori felt no inclination at all to start moving again, fixated on that point.

If the information I'm about to get from Kihara does involve some warning of impending death, will I be able to stay sane?

If he could leave things in a nebulous state, it'd be so much easier. If possible, he wanted to retrace his steps and go right back home. He wanted to toss the whole creeping, supernatural weirdness into a well and cover it up with concrete.

Takanori gave the base of the balustrade a kick, sending pain through his toes. The physical response brought him to his senses.

Unless he accurately grasped the true nature of the peril that lay in store, he'd be unable to target his enemy. If he tried to escape into vagueness without gaining any clarity, he might end up courting tragedy, with the lives of his loved ones slipping through his fingers and vanishing.

Decisions born of cowardice tended to worsen your situation. Even if a dire warning was in store for him, he could only tackle it head-on and think carefully about how to evade it. Ryuji Takayama had tried to do just that.

Looking at his wristwatch and confirming that it was five minutes past 11 a.m., his appointment time, Takanori started walking.

He crossed the bridge and entered the lobby of the building, and when he was face to face with the door of Kihara's office, he pressed the intercom.

The previous time, and the time before that, Kihara had responded quickly from inside, but this time the tiny speaker didn't let out a single peep.

A disturbing premonition came over Takanori. If Ryuji Takayama from *Ring* corresponded to Kihara, the writer would meet an unexpected end.

Takanori rang the intercom again, holding his breath.

There was still no response. Pressing his ear to the door, he tried to perceive what was happening in the office, but there was no sign whatsoever that anybody was present. With a gulp, he placed a hand on the doorknob. As the door hadn't been locked from the other side, the knob turned easily, producing a small gap.

"Oh, Takanori. Sorry about that."

The voice came not from the office interior but from behind him. The shock nearly drained the strength from Takanori, who clutched the doorknob. He twisted his body around to keep from falling over, and only inches away there was Kihara, holding two bottles of oolong tea.

"My refrigerator was empty," Kihara said. Apparently, he'd just bought the bottles of tea from the vending machine in front of the building.

Not wanting Kihara to see him shaking, Takanori adopted a cheery tone.

"Good morning!"

Yet the shivering of his legs reverberated in his voice, and the last syllable came out hoarse.

He wanted to kick himself for allowing something so trivial to make him lose his composure.

"Well then, please, come on in."

At Kihara's urging, Takanori entered the office and practically tore off his shoes.

After speaking at length about their impressions of Ring, the two of them reached out for a bottle of oolong tea simultaneously and slaked their thirst. The bottles of the now lukewarm tea left behind little ring-like pools thanks to the droplets streaming down their surfaces.

"It's kind of a waste of time to wonder whether the events in Ring really happened," Kihara said. "After looking into it a bit, I realized the people who appear in the story are all real, and real names were used for nearly all of them."

Takanori let out an involuntary sigh. Things were not proceeding in a good direction. If characters that actually existed had taken the specific actions portrayed in the book, no elements of fiction entered into the narrative.

"So Kazuyuki Asakawa and Ryuji Takayama were real people," Takanori paraphrased rather pointlessly.

"They were. But since these events happened twenty-five years ago, a lot of the people in the story have passed away. Even Asakawa's brother Junichiro who published the book died of cancer six years ago, I'm afraid. I'd hoped to talk to him, as the only person I could ask about the details…"

Takanori could tell where this was headed from Kihara's tone. Not wanting to ask, but unable to afford staying in the dark, Takanori made up his mind and posed a question.

"Afterwards, what happened to Asakawa and his wife and daughter?"

At the end of Ring, Asakawa was driving toward Ashikaga where his parents-in-law lived, to save his wife and daughter. It was unclear whether things turned out as he'd hoped and if his family had been saved.

"They died," came the pitiless answer.

"Died..." rasped Takanori, leaning forward.

"Asakawa's wife and daughter suffered acute myocardial infarctions at the same time, due to an aortic aneurysm, and they didn't make it. Asakawa himself died due to a traffic accident. He was seriously injured and slipped into a coma and breathed his last without ever waking up again."

Takanori held his head in his hands. Reading *Ring*, he'd identified with Asakawa the most. No, it was more than identification—he felt as if Asakawa were his alter ego. Spurred by his sense of duty as a husband and father, he'd accomplished an extraordinary feat, descending into that old well and retrieving Sadako's bones. Despite all that, his struggles had come to naught?

"What a cruel end..."

Sensing what Takanori was thinking, Kihara remained silent for a moment. It wasn't somebody else's problem for the writer, either. Going by the calculus that Takanori and Asakawa were counterparts, Kihara, not Takanori, would feel the first physical effects.

"The people involved with *Ring* who've passed away can be divided into two major groups," Kihara said. "The first consists of everyone who clearly died thanks to watching the videotape. Everyone in this group had a sarcoma in their coronary arteries and suffered an acute myocardial infarction. The four teenagers with whom it all started, Ryuji Takayama, Asakawa's wife and daughter...all of them had the same symptoms. Conversely, Kazuyuki Asakawa, his brother Junichiro, and Mai Takano all died of illnesses or in accidents, and their deaths seem unrelated to the influence of the videotape."

"Mai Takano..."

It was a name Takanori had seen somewhere before, but he couldn't recall from where.

"She was a student in the philosophy department at K University and a pupil of Takayama's. She was also the first person to find Ryuji's body."

Getting up as he said this, Kihara retrieved a bundle of files from his cabinet.

Takanori picked up each one and checked the materials inside. The data on the persons connected to *Ring* were sorted into two main categories, the living and the dead, and further subcategories. There were two sets of each file, one of them evidently copied for Takanori.

The five files were labeled: "Family / Friends and Acquaintances," "Publishing-Related," "Medical-Related," "Film-Related," and "Other." Takanori wondered why one of them had the "Film-Related" label.

"What does 'Film-Related' refer to?"

"Twenty-five years ago, plans were drawn up to make a movie based on *Ring*, and they even decided on a cast, but for some reason the project ended up getting shelved. What you see here in that file is data on the staff and cast. Since your job is related to film, Takanori, it's a perfect fit for you. Why don't you get in touch with some of these people and ask them about the events from that time? All of their contact info is included. Starting tomorrow, let's split up the work and get some intel."

Taking advantage of his production connections, Takanori could surely get in touch with the director and producer who'd been attached to the project.

"Understood. I'll get right on it. Now, about this one..."

There was one more category with which he was familiar. It was the file labeled "Medical-Related."

"Obviously," Kihara said, "autopsies would have been performed for those who died unnatural deaths as a result of watching the videotape. It may say 'Medical-Related,' but it has nothing to do with curing diseases. It deals with the forensic specialists and medical examiners who performed the autopsies on the victims, and the pathologists who biopsied the tissue. I'm planning to follow up on this myself tomorrow."

Reacting to the mention of medical examiners, Takanori removed the materials from the file and flipped through the loose documents. In the upper part of one printout, he found a familiar name. Placing a finger on it, he looked up.

"This name..."

"Mitsuo Ando. A lecturer in forensics at K University's Department of Medicine. He was the surgeon who performed the autopsy on Ryuji Takayama. I was thinking I'd get in touch with him tomorrow..."

It couldn't possibly be a coincidence. That much was certain. The images projected from the mind of Sadako twenty-five years earlier and the suicide video on the USB stick were connected by a single line.

"That won't be necessary," Takanori said. "I can do it."

Perhaps Kihara was just surprised by the offer, but he looked confused. He was clearly doubtful that an untested rookie could get an appointment with such a prominent figure as the director of a major hospital.

"But he's..."

"No need to worry. He's my father."

"What?!"

Kihara opened his eyes almost comically wide. To be sure, twenty-five years ago, Takanori's father Mitsuo had belonged to the forensic medicine department at K University. Since there weren't that many university medical examiners in the metropolitan area, forensic specialists often doubled as medical examiners, and it wouldn't have been at all unusual for Mitsuo to perform Ryuji Takayama's autopsy.

This case may have originated with a video saved on a USB stick, but its roots were deep and extensive. Parts of the roots, which had spread deep underground, were poking through the surface at last.

The mystery of the family register recording Takanori as dead for two whole years was perhaps about to be solved, too.

The clock on the wall indicated that it was ten minutes to noon. Not tomorrow—Takanori needed to move on this right away. He decided to get lunch in front of the station and to rush over to the director's office at the hospital.

Last time, he'd compromised and pretended to believe his father's little fairy tale, but this time, he'd do no such thing.

Father or not, I'm not going to go easy on him.

Takanori intended to keep up the pressure until he had proof that his father was speaking the plain and honest truth...

Determined, he bid Kihara farewell.

CHAPTER FOUR   *Nightmare*

1

"Please have a seat on the sofa while you wait."

Disregarding the secretary's words, Takanori walked over by the window and put his cheeks against the glass. Having a location that let one look down upon one of the greatest parks in Tokyo as if it were a private garden was magnificent—there was no other word for it, and he could definitely understand why his father had taken a liking to this office.

"The director will be here in five minutes," the secretary said before bowing and taking her leave.

It seemed the wind had intensified in the afternoon, which was quite unusual during the rainy season.

A few leaves flittered across the massive windowpane. Seeing the wind forming ripples in the park pond brought to mind images of Lake Haruna, which Takanori had visited just after entering elementary school. He recalled children on skates going around the surface, which was covered in ice, as the cold winter winds blew.

The surface of the pond that he was viewing now through the thick glass reminded him of that unseasonably cold lake.

Takanori's father had made good use of his leisure time taking his son out to all kinds of places. After going around and seeing the scenic beauty of Japan's national parks, he'd expanded their ventures to overseas locales and shown Takanori around world heritage sites to broaden his knowledge. Takanori treasured the many experiences afforded him by his father and mother, but when he looked back on his past, for some reason, one scene after another involving water came to mind.

Hearing the door open without a knock, Takanori reflexively looked behind him.

Mitsuo slowly entered the room, a hint of dissatisfaction in his eyes.

Why do you always come to the office instead of the house? he seemed to be saying. *And without getting in touch first.*

Seeing his father's displeasure, Takanori likewise communicated with his eyes only: *You do get it, right? I can't have mom hear this kind of conversation.*

Following this wordless exchange, Mitsuo went around behind the sofa and invited Takanori to take a seat. Takanori did so but chose a spot where he'd be seeing his father's face not directly from the front but obliquely to his right.

"Dad, I want you to be honest with me. Or else your nightmare from twenty-five years ago might come back to haunt you."

By this, he meant that his father would lose someone dear to him, and of course Takanori was referring to himself.

Having warned his father to be frank and forthcoming, Takanori started relating the series of events thus far. He was trapped in a serious predicament, and once his father saw that, Takanori hoped, covering up the truth with a patently fake story would no longer be an option.

Even after his son was done, Mitsuo kept his eyes fixed on one spot on the wall without blinking. This was a habit of his. Whenever he pondered the future, his eyes moved rapidly, and whenever he tried to recall the past, they remained locked in one place.

"I've read *Ring*," Mitsuo said. "Not in book form. It was a printout of a document saved on a floppy disc."

"Okay, then since you know the story, this should go quickly. I want you to tell me everything you learned when you autopsied Ryuji Takayama."

"Usually, a myocardial infarction is caused by a blood clot where the artery stiffens and the lining gets narrow. But in his case, there was a blockage right before the left circumflex coronary artery. The cause of the blockage was a sarcoma..."

Takanori put his hands out with his palms facing Mitsuo to stop him. He already knew about the sarcoma in the left coronary artery from the material that Kihara had gathered.

"Dad, enough with the medical interpretation. What I want to know is what those nonsensical events mean. Starting with the four teenagers, then Asakawa's wife and child, and Ryuji Takayama... They all died from watching the images projected psychokinetically by a young woman named Sadako Yamamura. Is it some kind of silly joke? That's impossible, you know that. As a doctor, how do you explain such a total farce? I want to know what you really think, dad."

"It does defy logic."

"So, what, has the world gone mad?"

"You know," Mitsuo said, "I sometimes suffer from hallucinations. At those times, it feels like the world we've come to know has gone insane and vanished. I can't help thinking the world we're living in is completely different from the one we used to inhabit."

"But isn't that exactly what scientists are for? Pinning down the mechanics of how things work no matter what the world is like?"

"We tried to come up with the most logical explanation for the absurd phenomenon. We tried everything. A certain possibility occurred to us: an unknown virus."

"A virus..." Since the term appeared many times in *Ring* as a sort of keyword, he felt like it made sense when Mitsuo mentioned it.

"We gathered as much data as we could and divided the victims into two main groups: those who watched the videotape and died without following the directions, and those who followed the directions and escaped the effects. Kazuyuki Asakawa and Mai Takano followed them but died in unfortunate accidents and were autopsied. Asakawa was the victim of a car crash, while Takano wasted away after she fell into a vent on the roof of a building. Thus the two belong to the category of people who escaped the tape's effects by following its directions.

"We autopsied both groups, took their tissue, and turned it over to our pathologists. The unknown virus was found in the bodies of both groups."

"That's the gist of it. A conscious viewing of the video imagery produces the unknown virus in your body, and the virus creates a sarcoma in the coronary artery, which interferes with blood circulation, which causes an acute myocardial infarction. It's not so rare for consciousness to produce a physical effect."

"But the people who followed the directions didn't have sarcomas. Had the effect of the virus been suppressed?"

"No, there was a manifest difference in the virus between people who hadn't followed the directions after watching the tape and those who had."

"Are you saying that the virus mutated?" asked Takanori.

"Yes. In the case of the former, it formed a ring shape, so we named it the ring virus to make it easier to distinguish. But with the latter group, part of the ring was severed, and it looked like sperm. It formed the letter S, and when I saw it under a microscope, it wriggled like a snake."

"You mean, the virus can be categorized into two types, the ring-shaped version and the S-shaped one, and the former could produce a sarcoma, but the latter had lost that effect. Is that right?"

"Right," Mitsuo affirmed.

"What does the latter type do? How is the S virus harmful to the human body?"

"It does nothing..."

"That can't be! Asakawa and Mai Takano both died."

"Their causes of death had nothing to do with the virus, they just died from unfortunate accidents."

Takanori couldn't believe it. It was hard to accept that a simple mutation of the virus—so pernicious that it could form a sarcoma in the coronary artery—rendered it completely harmless to the human body. He found it rather more reasonable to think that the virus, once transformed, had grown even more virulent.

"Dad, what if I'm already infected with the virus? What would you do?"

"Impossible. It can't be..."

"What makes you so sure?"

"Because it's all over. Twenty-five years ago, the virus became extinct, and the human race overcame the crisis of potentially losing its diversity."

From his diagonal vantage point, Takanori peered into Mitsuo's eyes. Unable to bear his son's gaze, Mitsuo shifted his eyes in the opposite direction.

He's lying.

Takanori knew this in his heart. For the most part, his father was trying to give an accurate account of what happened. But after a certain point, it seemed his intention was to hide something.

"Dad, please. Please tell me the truth."

"I'm not lying about anything at all."

"If you're hiding something, it's the same as lying to me," Takanori said.

"You're still young, son. You'll likely live more than twice as many years as you have already, and I sincerely hope you do. But in order to live happily over those long years, it's better not to learn certain things. Your promising life might turn out to be a hard and painful one thanks to what you learn. Well, I'm only saying this by way of example..."

"You underestimate me, dad. You're assuming the truth will crush me and that I'll lose heart. Since I was little, I've learned at your knees. You used to say I shouldn't avert my eyes from impending danger...that I shouldn't be blind to the truth, even if I don't want to face it... That's what you always told me. Have you forgotten?"

"Well...I only borrowed those words from somebody else," Mitsuo said, wiping the sweat on his forehead with the back of his hand.

"No, those words came from the heart."

Mitsuo's face contorted and turned red. He nearly pounded the table with his fist but halted it midair. Barely stifling the desire to raise his voice, he swallowed his words, put his elbows on the table, and covered his eyes with both hands.

"I just have one wish," he said. "I want you to lead a happy life. It was a blessing, please don't waste it..."

"I know, that's why I'm asking..."

"Please just let this go. It's for your own sake."

As Mitsuo weakly hung his head, Takanori found his own ardor dampening. Bursting into this office in pursuit of the truth, he'd been determined not to go easy on his father, but now his stance was softening. If Mitsuo had yelled without listening at all, Takanori could have been more emotional and adamant. But the weaker his father became, the more discouraged Takanori felt. They were father and son, and not strangers, and their states of mind couldn't but correspond to some degree.

Mitsuo pressed the intercom and called his secretary.

"The guest is leaving," he said.

"I have no intention of leaving yet."

"It's not for you to say. I'm busy here. And anyway, it's all over now. There's no cause for concern. The virus can't be resurrected."

"What makes you say it's over? Tell me the reason."

At this, Mitsuo sprang up from the sofa, and the momentum seemed to give him the strength to say, "Because Kashiwada's dead. There's no overturning that fact."

Mitsuo seemed convinced of Kashiwada's death, but Takanori had his doubts. The video on the USB stick began transforming the moment it was transferred to his hard drive, and Kashiwada's figure was gone without a trace. Almost as if he'd been sucked into a network that floated like a cloud...

And the empty ring of the rope had brought the first edition of *Ring* into focus.

It felt so much like there was some powerful intent at work.

But whose?

Kashiwada's, of course. That was why Takanori couldn't believe so easily that the man was truly dead.

2

After meeting up with Yoneda in the hotel lobby, Takanori took the elevator with him down to the first basement level.

With the press conference about to begin, the basement lobby was a mess of media representatives clutching their camera equipment.

Takanori cast a sidelong glance at them as he entered the meeting hall. Then they both found empty seats and took them.

Television cameras were packed tightly in the space between the wall and the last row of the two hundred folding chairs lined up there, while the seats in front were filled by TV, weekly magazine, and tabloid reporters.

The hotel that was serving as a press conference venue stood right next to the building where Studio Oz was located. Not in any position to help with the promotion, Yoneda and Takanori had come purely as spectators. Having found themselves a couple of empty chairs, they kept a low profile.

In a few minutes, the press conference to announce the completion of the new film *Studio 104* would begin, with the main cast coming out on stage followed by the director and the producer.

With his small eyes wide open, Yoneda leaned over and whispered into Takanori's ear, "You know, there was talk about how the suicide video on the USB stick was uploaded on an online video site and leaked, but that seems not to have been the case."

"It was a lie?"

"It was unrelated. Live streams of suicides were causing a stir on the net, so Kiyomi Sakata simply took advantage of that. Turns out it was sent directly to her email as an attachment."

Takanori had felt that it didn't quite make sense back when he'd first heard about it from Yoneda. When some lurid clip got uploaded to an online video site, there were always people who made copies, and as soon as it was taken down, it popped up elsewhere, and round and round it went. It just seemed strange for the only surviving copy of the video to be on a USB stick that Takanori happened to receive.

"But why would Kiyomi Sakata have lied like that?" he asked.

"Beats me," replied Yoneda. "It looks like some complicated circumstances are involved here. Speak of the Devil—look, here comes Her Highness."

The entire conference venue lit up with a multitude of flashes, and the starring actors came out on stage, followed by the director and the producer. Bringing up the rear was Kiyomi Sakata. From under a skirt that ended above her knees stretched her long, slender legs; when she placed one of them on the end of the platform and raised up her well-proportioned body, the number of flashes noticeably increased. Described as being of uncertain age, she had to be around fifty judging from her career. On top of that, she'd given birth to two children by different fathers, once when she was a teenager and then again in her late thirties. Perhaps her beauty and sex appeal, which belied her age, was captivating to the attendees, and it seemed to Takanori that the number of flashes for her exceeded those for the leading lady, Yoko Aso.

The movie *Studio 104* had been planned and produced by Kiyomi Sakata, and that was prompting a lot of extra attention.

The lead actress, Yoko Aso, occupied center stage. Yuji Nakahara and Yoshihiro Tachiki, who played supporting roles, sat on either side of her, the director Anzai on the far left, and Kiyomi Sakata on the far right. With the actors and the staff, there were five people seated on stage in total.

In his mind, Takanori was overlapping the view with an imaginary press conference that could have taken place in the past.

Twenty-five years earlier, Kiyomi Sakata was supposed to have appeared front and center at a press conference as the female lead for the movie *Ring*. But just when the first draft of the script was completed and the casting was nearly complete, the movie was cancelled.

The file Kihara had handed Takanori the day before briefly described the circumstances—part speculation—behind the cancelation. Takanori had read that part repeatedly, so he remembered it in detail.

Each file Kihara made was brilliantly ordered. Some of the info had been obtained through interviews over the phone or in person, but more than half of it owed to online searches.

It would have taken Takanori more than a week, but Kihara had spent just one day collecting all that info.

According to his file, the lead actress for *Ring* had changed more than once. At first, a totally fresh face was almost chosen through auditioning, but she ended up declining for personal reasons. Subsequently, the starlet Kiyomi Sakata (screen name: Nao Aizawa) landed the main role.

In the file, it was implied that Kiyomi Sakata was ultimately responsible for the movie's cancelation. The truth was shrouded in mystery, and so with the proviso that the cause remained a matter of speculation, Kihara had related the following account.

Supposedly, Sakata had been suspected of using stimulants and other types of drugs, and there'd been an anonymous letter demanding that the movie be called off. Furthermore, she'd lied about her age and passed herself off as an innocent young girl, when in fact she'd had an affair with a family man and given birth while still a teenager. With so many factors piling up, the producer had lost his nerve.

An illicit affair might have made for suitable marketing material. A criminal offense on the part of the lead actress, however, would sink the movie. If the studio went ahead with production and a scandal erupted past the point of no return, it meant taking a huge financial hit.

It was best not to court danger...and thus the producer had chosen to shelve the film before it could suffer fatal damage.

With her career as an actress besmirched, from that point on Kiyomi Sakata lived in obscurity, driven into an early retirement.

What brought her back into the limelight was her marriage to the famous television newscaster Shuichi Sakata. Kiyomi had made a name for herself as a fortuneteller, and Shuichi had come to her for advice after falling into a slump. They'd fallen in love and married when Kiyomi was in her late thirties. It was Shuichi's third marriage but her first.

She had a baby boy the following year and then gotten involved in television and film production through her own venture, remaining active on the TV gossip show circuit to the present. She was naturally gifted at attaining fame in the celebrity world.

Her background was full of the sorts of episodes common in show business, and Takanori was engrossed as an observer. However, Kiyomi Sakata was now working under her real name, and when Takanori had seen her maiden name in the file, he'd let out a little yelp of surprise.

It was Niimura.

In pursuing the strange phenomena surrounding the USB video, the shadow of Hiroyuki Niimura had appeared and disappeared time and again, yet Takanori hadn't the slightest idea who he was or how he was connected to the case. If the child born to Kiyomi and her adulterous partner were Hiroyuki Niimura, then a tangled web of relationships lurked behind the events.

The file did not state the name of Kiyomi's child. Devoted to her career, she practically abandoned her baby and left its care in the hands of her mother. The file did list the address of the grandmother who was entrusted with raising the boy.

Funabashi City, Chiba Prefecture.

Takanori remembered that place name as well. Seiji Kashiwada had been employed as a teacher at a college-prep school, and both his residence and workplace had been in Funabashi.

There was a good chance that the connection between the condemned prisoner Kashiwada and Niimura lay in Funabashi.

Nonetheless, there was no chance that they were the same person or even siblings.

Kashiwada was in his late forties when he died; Niimura had to be in his early thirties. And prior to marrying Shuichi Sakata, Kiyomi hadn't given birth to any other children.

Another major commonality worth noting was *Ring*, multiple copies of which had existed in Kashiwada's home in West Funabashi. A single volume was visible in Niimura's studio apartment in Aomono-Yokocho. Each owned the rare first edition.

As Takanori thought of the many connections rising to the surface from Kiyomi Sakata's past, his mind drifted away from the stage for a moment, but when he heard the entire hall stirring, it snapped him back to reality.

The host had asked Kiyomi to predict whether *Studio 104* would be a hit, and she'd gently admonished, "If we could tell our own futures, we fortunetellers would all be rich." That seemed to have set the hall abuzz.

Kiyomi Sakata seemed to know all too well that a fortuneteller couldn't predict his or her own future, no matter how skilled. The current situation attested to that much; fearing that she couldn't, she'd brought the USB stick to a video expert, though she'd concealed the circumstances in asking for it to be analyzed. Takanori didn't doubt that she held some secret that she couldn't afford to let slip.

Then a notion flashed through his mind. Although she'd practically thrown Niimura away, in all likelihood Kiyomi knew his address. She might have visited his apartment in Aomono-Yokocho and been familiar with its interior. Astonished to receive a live suicide video as an email attachment, she noticed that her son's apartment had been the venue, even if the hanged man was somebody else. In the absence of anything like a threatening note, not knowing the sender's intent would have only intensified the creepiness.

Being unfamiliar with modern imaging technology, Kiyomi had sought to learn if CG could be used to create such a composite image. If she could tell whether the video was genuine or fake, she'd be able to discern whether the whole thing was a nasty prank. Perhaps she also desired any information she could get on it, and drumming up some perfunctory reason, she'd brought her request to Yoneda at Studio Oz as a last resort.

Twenty-five years ago, Kiyomi had lost her chance to star in a movie, *Ring*, thanks to unsubstantiated rumors. This time, on the cusp of producing her first major picture in quite some time, she was taking the greatest care to avoid repeating the same mistake.

Previously, a film had been scrapped when a scandal threatened to turn into a criminal case. If the same formula applied to this occasion as well...

Takanori wondered whether a specific crime might be hiding behind all these various events.

But first, he needed to test his hypothesis that Kiyomi's son was this Hiroyuki Niimura.

Once all the actors and staff finished expressing their enthusiasm and expectations for *Studio 104*, the host proceeded to the next segment, questions from the media.

"Now, are there any questions?"

Right away, some people in the front row raised their hands, and the questions shifted the discussion to the romance scandal of the female lead, Yoko Aso. It seemed that the same questions were coming from multiple persons, and all of them were focused on her.

With press conferences, most of the questions tended to be pointed at the actors, so the director and producer could take a back seat and let their minds wander. Barraged by the reporters, Aso was fumbling her answers and inviting sniggers from the audience. Seeing this from the corner of her eyes, and equipped with the wisdom of age, Kiyomi tried to take on the role of mediator.

"I think that's quite enough bullying for this young girl. Why don't you try someone a little more seasoned?"

This is my first and last chance to find out if Hiroyuki Niimura is Kiyomi Sakata's son—I can't miss it.

Timing it just right, Takanori strained his voice.

"Miss Sakata, how is Hiroyuki doing?"

The smile on her face froze, and her narrow, carefully maintained eyebrows rose gradually. She held her breath and kept her body completely still. Glaring around the hall as if shining a searchlight, she scanned for the source of the voice, and when she got to Takanori she fixed her eyes on him.

Her consternation was so fierce that just looking at her made him sorry. Restoring a cheerful mood back to the hall was now utterly out of the question. Kiyomi Sakata tapped her chest lightly and blinked repeatedly, and her breathing grew heavier and heavier. Unable to come up with something clever to say to create a smokescreen, she released Takanori from her gaze and glanced up at the ceiling.

"I don't remember the names of men from my past," she said, barely getting the words out in a hoarse voice.

"Who's this Hiroyuki?" Yoneda whispered, poking Takanori with his elbow.

Takanori was convinced.

No mistake. That was almost a confession.

Hiroyuki Niimura indeed was the son she'd given birth to as a teenager.

Niimura's existence was a bomb laden with the power to destroy everything in Kiyomi's life.

3

Until a little while ago, Akane was lying down on bed and talking about what had happened at school that day. Miss Ohashi had been chosen to lead the summer mountain-climbing class, and now she was nagging Akane relentlessly. Even as Akane complained to Takanori, the span between the words coming from her mouth lengthened little by little, and once she was fast asleep, her nose started emitting a tiny snore.

It seemed as though she'd timed it, quietly falling asleep with Takanori's right arm as her pillow just as the hands of the clock struck midnight. He felt a slight change when she transitioned from being awake and entered into the dream world.

Whether or not you could fathom the recesses of your partner's heart determined the depth of your love.

Seeing that Akane had fallen into a deep sleep, Takanori slid his right arm out from between the back of her head and the pillow. Lifting his upper body a bit and keeping that pose, he continued to gaze upon her sleeping face.

Despite his fatigue, sleep seemed unlikely to visit him anytime soon. On the contrary, he grew only more and more alert, and from his toes to his hips and back, intermittent chills were running through his body.

When his left hand touched her hair, Akane smiled faintly and brought her face towards him. She wasn't awake, merely getting closer to him unconsciously.

From the gap of the man's shirt she had on, her well-rounded breasts were peeking out, while her belly underneath was covered by a towel blanket. Growing inside was a life almost three months old. A little while longer and it would probably be visible on an ultrasound scan.

His heart was in chaos. The vision of his future, which had been so clear until yesterday, was now shrouded in a haze and being shut off behind a black veil.

Takanori had no idea what he should do next. As he sighed, tears began welling up in his eyes, but he stifled them.

The information he'd received from Kihara that evening was hitting him slowly but steadily. Viewed according to a certain hypothesis, several puzzles that the writer had compiled and set aside looked to be connected by a single line. No matter how Takanori rearranged them, they appeared to lead only one way.

Their fourth meeting had been held at a location other than Kihara's office. On the way back from visiting one Professor Miyashita of the Department of Pathology at K University's Faculty of Medicine and hearing what he had to say, Kihara had dropped by a family restaurant and called upon Takanori, realizing that his home was nearby. Takanori had rushed over there and gotten the latest info.

A former colleague of Mitsuo Ando's, Professor Miyashita was the pathologist who'd performed the biopsies on the videotape's victims twenty-five years ago.

The professor had been reticent at first, but then he'd opened up. Starting out by saying that the matter was all over and done with, he'd provided a full account of those bizarre, quarter-century-old events.

His story was a continuation of what Takanori had heard from his father the previous day at the hospital director's office.

Apart from the parts that overlapped, when Takanori sorted out Professor Miyashita's story, what caught his attention besides the keyword "virus" was the phrase "mutation."

The ring-shaped virus produced a sarcoma in the coronary artery. However, the S-shaped virus, a broken ring, had been stripped of that effect. That was just as Mitsuo had related. Yet the suggestion that the S-shaped virus posed no danger whatsoever was a lie.

According to Miyashita's explanation, a mutation had given rise to a new effect.

Miyashita had explained the odd phenomenon using the autopsy results for Mai Takano as an example.

A student of Ryuji Takayama's, Mai Takano had watched the images projected by Sadako Yamamura's mind, and yet certain physical features had rendered her immune from the effects of the ring virus. In the end, though, she'd fallen into a drain ditch on the roof of a building and died an untimely death. As the medical examiners who performed her autopsy, Professor Miyashita and Mitsuo Ando detected something unusual afoot. There were signs that while she was stuck in that ditch, Mai Takano had given birth. Moreover, Mitsuo Ando was certain that Mai was a virgin. Thus, the question became: how had she become pregnant, and to what had she given birth?

The hint lay in the shapes of the ring virus and the S-shaped virus. Finding the form of the S-shaped virus reminiscent of a sperm cell, Mitsuo Ando had looked into Mai's activity during her lifetime and surmised that she might have been ovulating when she watched the images on the videotape. Assuming that the ring virus targeted the coronary artery for attack, the S-shaped virus—as its very shape suggested—might well have targeted a woman's uterus. That was why Mai had been immune from the effects of the video. Instead, an egg newly released into her womb had been invaded by the S-shaped virus, and presenting symptoms of pregnancy in the span of just one week, she had given birth at the bottom of a ditch without anybody knowing.

This had not been a normal baby. The child whom she'd birthed was Sadako Yamamura.

It was Sadako who had originally projected the images onto the videotape. Her genetic information, imbued with extraordinary occult power, might have survived inside the virus in the form of video data, or so Professor Miyashita had suggested.

To make matters worse, in a brief time, the medium itself had also undergone a change, in concert with the virus, which had mutated and found a new target of attack. Like a snake wriggling its body and shedding its skin, perhaps the virus had experienced a bewildering transmutation and altered the medium so as to prolong its own life.

Initially, the medium had been the images on the videotape. Those who saw the images became hosts to the ring virus in their bodies. Yet after the tape was eradicated, the medium responsible for propagating the virus had transformed into written matter, namely *Ring*.

A quarter-century ago, Professor Miyashita and Mitsuo Ando had contemplated how this situation would unfold and presaged the end of the world.

This document called *Ring* was written by Kazuyuki Asakawa, and his brother Junichiro had proceeded to publish it. What was more, plans had been made to turn it into a film, and a studio had taken steps toward doing so. With this change in medium from a book to a movie, the contagion would have spread much faster than by videotape, at an almost incomparable speed.

What was the fate of the infected? An ovulating woman who came into contact with the medium—in other words, who read *Ring* or watched the film version—would get pregnant without sexual reproduction and give birth to Sadako.

Professor Miyashita and Mitsuo Ando feared that the individual known as Sadako Yamamura would explosively multiply and thereby deprive the natural world of its diversity, leading the world toward extinction.

However, things had somehow proceeded down a different path, contrary to their prediction, and the threat of the virus had suddenly subsided.

Though it was unclear how it had happened, the plans to make the film had fallen apart and the first edition of *Ring* had vanished from the market, and the nightmare of Sadako spreading throughout the world had been averted.

Even after that, as far as they knew, there had been no abnormal incidents indicating the effects of the S-shaped virus, and they'd been forced to conclude that the case was closed.

That was why Professor Miyashita had prefaced everything with the remark that it was all over. If it were an ongoing issue, he would have kept his mouth shut so as not to cause society-wide panic.

After the series of cases surrounding the cursed videotape had retreated into the distant past, everything felt like a dream when the professor thought back on it. As the nightmare receded, its credibility faded away, until finally he felt more at ease talking about it as if it had all happened to somebody else.

Spreading out the microscope photographs of the ring virus and S-shaped virus on the table of the family restaurant and looking around, however, Kihara had lowered his voice and said he didn't believe the evil of the virus had been contained.

Takanori felt the same way and was beginning to think that it hadn't ended at all—it was more fitting to say that it had been smoldering.

There is a novella by a certain famous author about an old man who spends one night watching a nude young woman sleeping beside him. While the old man appreciates the woman's youthful form, beyond her he sees the shadow of his own death drawing near.

Looking at Akane's face while she slept, Takanori tried to recall the story. He wasn't sure which one had died at the end, the old man or the young woman, but one thing he couldn't forget was its dense, wafting image of death.

Takanori asked himself, *Can I really love her from the bottom of my heart?*

Having just seen the microscope pics of the virus, he remembered the shape so clearly and felt uneasy, as if the virus had arisen and was spreading in his body. Triggered by the images in the photos, perhaps the virus had proliferated and was now crawling in the folds of his brain... Its wicked hope to strike on a woman's ovulation date showed how truly sinister it was.

After meeting with Kihara, Takanori had gone on thinking about it the whole time on the way home. It was apparent to him that Kihara had thought along similar lines and reached the same conclusion, but he'd refrained from spelling it out.

No matter how they connected the dots, there was only one line that they could see, and it seemed that no other interpretation was tenable.

Kashiwada had killed four young girls, but his motive remained totally unknown. Not even the prosecution had believed that he'd murdered for pleasure to satisfy abnormal sexual urges.

In the home of the condemned Kashiwada, there'd been seventeen first-edition copies of *Ring* bundled up and left at the entryway.

The birthdays of the girls he'd slain were concentrated in a short span of roughly half a year, from the summer of 1991 to the spring of 1992. On top of that, all of the girls had looked so alike.

The first edition of *Ring* had been published in June 1991.

Three of the four girls killed by Kashiwada had been born to single mothers.

All of the girls had breathed their last leaning against a tree trunk, with their underwear removed, but their bodies had been neatly arranged, imparting an impression of some kind of ritual.

When these background facts were linked together, they spun a coherent story.

The horrible effects of the S-shaped virus as mediated by the first edition of *Ring* hadn't subsided but hidden and festered. Almost twenty-five years ago, women who'd read *Ring* while they were ovulating had actually given birth due to the effects of the virus. Some of the children might have been aborted, but at least four of them had been born into this world.

What the young female victims had in common was that every one of them was Sadako.

And now Kashiwada's motive was clear as well.

He was hunting Sadako.

Kashiwada had wanted to eradicate all the Sadakos who'd been born into the world, and he'd searched for the girls one after another and killed them all.

Yet the story wasn't over. A crucial fact was lying in wait for Takanori.

The fifth victim, who had nearly been killed by Kashiwada, was sleeping beside him now. The only Sadako left in this world...was Akane.

Can I really love this woman with all my heart?

He repeated this same question over and over.

Was he really going to be part of the same family tree as such a deformity of a woman, who had died time and again only to come back from the dead? Was he really to be her husband and the father of their child?

What am I supposed to do? Somebody please tell me the answer, Takanori silently screamed.

Then, even though she seemed to be asleep, both of Akane's arms moved. Behind Takanori's back her hands linked, and he found himself getting pulled to her with great force. He was now on top of Akane, in her embrace. Holding him affectionately from beneath, she put her lips close to his ears.

He felt a subtle breath on his earlobe, and then came her words.

"Tak, you don't have to suffer alone. I can help you. Believe me. I have that power..."

You're right about that, he thought. Akane did have the power, the same extraordinary power that Takanori feared.

4

Akane was an early riser. At 7 a.m., she was out the door and headed to the school.

Having tossed and turned the night before, Takanori awoke feeling like he hadn't slept at all, and when he looked beside him Akane was gone. His clock showed it was past seven.

Perhaps Akane had used that sliver of a moment when he'd drifted off as her cue to leave. He almost suspected that it meant she was trying to be considerate, to avoid an awkward moment.

It was possible that Akane would never come home, and this thought nearly became a desire, but he banished it before it could take root in his heart. Takanori considered indulging in the now vast bed to catch a few more winks, but with little chance of falling asleep, he promptly abandoned the idea and instead hopped in the shower.

He grabbed a glass of milk and a banana for breakfast and proceeded to drink two cups of coffee.

February 25th next year. That was the expected due date for their child.

As he tried to picture the infant's face, those of the girls who'd fallen victim to Kashiwada came and went, one after another.

The alternative—not having the child—wasn't unthinkable. If he was going to ask Akane to get an abortion and leave her, he needed to go about it immediately. Yet how would he explain his reason for leaving?

It was impossible for Takanori to dump his lover because she was Sadako. Akane was completely blameless. The same went for Akane's mother, too.

Takanori wanted to know how Akane had come to be born. Her mother had given birth to Akane without knowing who the father was, and she'd died when Akane was around three. As for whether her birth had truly been caused by her mother's reading *Ring* on her ovulation date, or whether there'd been some other mechanism at work, he couldn't say.

Takanori remembered that the photos of those who'd been involved with *Ring* were still in the large brown envelope, sandwiched in the file. After seeing them once in Kihara's office, he had yet to take a look at the pictures in his apartment.

Dwelling on the victims' faces' resemblance to Akane's, Takanori took all of the girls' pictures out from the envelope and lined them up on the table.

All four girls did look so much alike. Each one was pretty enough to catch a person's glance. Due to the differences in their hairstyles and how full their faces were or weren't, the resemblance wasn't enough to judge that they were the same people—it merely gave the impression that they were lookalikes. Even though they were born from the same DNA, the environments in which they'd grown up made them all look a bit different.

Akane was a little unlike the girls who'd been killed by Kashiwada. She was one step behind in terms of sheer beauty but was the absolute victor in terms of womanly softness and endowed with a supple charm. Looking at all the female victims, Takanori felt that their faces were perfectly well-proportioned and more neuter in appearance, whereas Akane's looked perfectly feminine. Maybe it was simply because of the differences between a young girl and an adult woman, or perhaps he was biased because he loved her...

Comparing them from every angle, Takanori was amazed after all this time as a video specialist at just how much info could be gleaned from pictures.

There were still a lot of photos that Takanori hadn't seen yet in the brown envelope. All of them had been printed out by Kihara. Eager to read the written materials in the file, Takanori had failed to realize the value hidden in those photos.

Putting the pictures of the four girls aside for a moment, he placed the other photos on the table one by one as he took them out from the envelope.

The picture of Kiyomi Sakata when she was young was worth beholding. It gave off the kind of bewitching aura that could seduce a man—"impish" was the word for it. It was a woman's charm, clearly distinct from those neuter girls.

Asakawa, the weekly magazine reporter, could be called a good-looking guy. A fine young man, nice and lean, he seemed the type to be popular with women.

From Ryuji Takayama's picture, Takanori could sense a masculine presence in contrast to Asakawa's. His hair was very short, and his broad neck sat solidly on his shoulders. Given his physique, it made sense that he'd been a prominent shot-putter in high school. His jawline was sharp, hinting at an iron will. He had the face of a physical laborer rather than a scholar.

Takanori looked at Ryuji Takayama's picture for a little while. Somehow he gazed at that face much longer than he did at the photos of Sakata or Asakawa. For some reason, he found himself unable to look away.

The more Takanori stared at the face, the more he came to feel that he might have met the man somewhere. He'd had the same feeling about the death-row inmate Kashiwada.

Takanori took out some photos of Kashiwada from the envelope.

Born in Maebashi, Kashiwada had spent all his years locally from elementary school to high school, and after graduating from college in Tokyo he'd joined a travel agency, but it hadn't lasted long. He'd changed jobs one after another, knocking around overseas, but afterwards he'd settled down and worked as a college-prep school instructor in West Funabashi.

His father had passed away when he was in high school, and his mother had died during his college years. After losing both parents in such a short span, his connections with his relatives had been severed. He'd never married, and he'd had few friends. His profile painted a picture of a lonely life.

He'd grown a beard, and his face had looked lax while he was working as an instructor at the school. In the pictures, his lusterless hair was long and shaggy. He wore black-rimmed glasses, and there were signs that he'd neglected his health. The photos of him shown to the public after his arrest were all alike, and in the average person's mind Kashiwada's face was the one in the pictures from his instructor era, which Takanori was now viewing.

Yet the ones from after he'd been locked away as a condemned man gave a completely different impression. The photos that Kihara had obtained using his connections hadn't been available to the public, so the difference Takanori was seeing now was practically unknown to the world.

After he was locked up, his beard and his hair had been shaved so that his head was as bald as a monk's, and the plain, restricted diet had made him leaner, making him look like a whole other man.

The two men were so different that Takanori was inclined to suspect Kashiwada had purposely disguised himself.

Now lean and sharp, his face looked exactly like Ryuji Takayama's.

Placing side by side the picture of Ryuji taken from his bust up and a photo of Kashiwada, Takanori compared the two.

They were very much alike, the resemblance surpassing even that of the female victims.

Being an expert at image processing, Takanori could see through to their skeletal structures under the skin of their heads. To make sure of it, he scanned Ryuji's picture and Kashiwada's and put them on his computer, and then overlapped the two after enlarging them to the same size. The space between the eyes, the position of the eyes and nose, the length of the lips, the shape of the ears, the forehead—every constituent part of their faces—matched perfectly.

What the hell?

Doubting his own senses, Takanori looked up from the screen and thought through it all.

A quarter-century ago, Ryuji Takayama had died after watching the demonic videotape and contracting the ring virus, and his body had been autopsied by Takanori's father. The fact that he was dead was incontrovertible.

Kashiwada had been arrested more than ten years earlier as a suspect in the serial abduction and murder of young girls, and his capital punishment had been carried out just one month ago. That meant that Kashiwada had been alive until then, and this too was a solid fact.

How could the two of them be the same person? Takanori was only getting more and more confused.

Ryuji Takayama had died on October 19, 1990.

In the family register, Takanori had drowned and died in June 1989 and was found alive two years later in June 1991, after the old couple in Otoi had passed away.

Ring had been published around that same time.

June 1991... There was a certain scene that Takanori couldn't forget. His father had often taken him to the sea to conquer his fear and memory of drowning. Takanori didn't know the name of the beach, but given what his father had told him the other day, now he knew the exact place—the Toi coastline.

It struck Takanori as odd that he should still be so concerned with that scene. To be sure, it did contain a certain crucial element that involved his own fate. People could be indifferent to something unrelated to them, but they remembered life-or-death events down to the last little detail.

With his retinas acting as camera eyes, and his eardrums as recording devices, this one scene was saved to his consciousness. Yet as time passed it had become blurry, covered in a haze, and driven into his unconscious mind.

Comparing Ryuji and Kashiwada's photos side by side, however, had been like a gust of wind that dispelled the haze.

The scene was gradually coming into clearer focus. Triggered by the two photos, it was returning to him now in the form of images and accompanying sounds.

He could hear the waves crashing. His father was sitting on the embankment, his eyes fixed on the shoreline and watching over Takanori as he swam. Feeling thirsty, Takanori began walking to where his father was sitting to get something to drink.

At the same time, he could see another man coming from the opposite direction. In the bright sunlight, the man's face was like a dark silhouette.

"Dad, I'm thirsty."

When he said so, his father handed him a bottle of oolong tea. As there was only a bit left, Takanori drained the contents in one sip, at which point the stranger addressed him in an overly familiar tone.

To a young boy of three and a half years, the words that had come out of the man's mouth sounded so unusual, and their meaning had been utterly unclear. Yet now, as the scene became more vivid, his remark seemed more intelligible.

With a greasy sweat on his face, the man searched the plastic bag and produced another bottle of oolong tea, and then turned to face Takanori.

"Hey, brother. Want another?" the man asked.

Even not knowing what it meant, Takanori sensed something terrifying in that word, and staring upward at the man's face, he slowly shook his head no.

In his mind, Takanori saw that very same face now. The person who was standing on that embankment and looking down at him was Ryuji Takayama.

S

After dying more than half a year earlier and being autopsied by his father, had Ryuji come back to life?

"Brother" signified some sort of association. Ryuji Takayama had been clinically dead for some period—that much was beyond doubt. If he'd called Takanori "brother" as a statement of fact, and not as a joke, then Takanori's death in the family register for two years wasn't merely a mistake in the record. He'd been clinically dead, too, and for two whole years... Just as Ryuji had come back, so had he.

Oh, God.

Then it naturally made sense how Ryuji and Kashiwada could be the same person.

Leaving aside the mechanism by which he'd come back from being dead, supposing that were the situation, a revived person would need a new family register. In Takanori's case, it was fortunate that his body hadn't turned up after he drowned at sea, as this allowed his father to fabricate some plausible lie and bring him back to life in the register. In Ryuji's case, though, his body was autopsied and taken apart. Assuming he'd come back, there was no way he could have returned as Ryuji Takayama. To live as an ordinary member of society, he'd have been forced to obtain a family register illegally. Thus, he'd located a missing person of around the same age, one who'd lived a solitary life, and assumed his identity. That person had been Seiji Kashiwada.

Once Takanori grasped the fact that Ryuji and Kashiwada were the same man and looked over the entire case, a mystery that had been put on hold was resolved, while at the same time a new question arose.

By the entryway in Kashiwada's home, there had been seventeen copies of the first edition of *Ring*, all tied up with vinyl rope and left there.

Someone had gone around collecting the first edition of *Ring*, just as someone had sent a threatening letter to the movie studio so that the film would be shelved.

198

Nightmare

Professor Miyashita and Takanori's father had said that the danger of the ring virus had somehow been annulled, but Takanori could scarcely believe this was the result of some natural healing power at work.

Somebody had gathered up all the copies of the first edition, and somebody had made every effort to get the film project cancelled. That person had circulated a nasty rumor about Kiyomi Sakata and sent the threat.

The virus hadn't simply died out on its own; it was far more logical to think that somebody had pulled some strings behind the scenes and guided it along to its demise. The person behind all of this had to be Ryuji, a.k.a. Kashiwada.

The new question that popped up was: why had Ryuji, i.e., Kashiwada, done these things?

Had he sacrificed himself to limit the horror of the ring virus as much as possible and put an end to it? Perhaps, but following that line of reasoning only led to a contradiction further down the road.

Say Ryuji/Kashiwada had sacrificed himself so the harm wouldn't spread to all of mankind, so the world would retain its diversity. If you took the act of saving the world's diversity to be a good, then its opposing concept, fixity, was evil. Trying to eliminate heterodox genes ran counter to the notion of preserving diversity; it would be a tremendous evil that went against Ryuji/Kashiwada's governing principle.

Sadako getting copied on the scale of a few people would likely pose no danger to humanity. Or would the young girls have hatched some plot to steer the world in a dark direction? Takanori could find no evidence of that whatsoever.

Right, even if the person who wanted to avert the horror of the ring virus intended to take responsibility for failing to fully cleanse the world of it, he couldn't have plotted to kill the Sadakos, whose only crime was to be born. That was where the conflict between good and evil arose.

The one responsible for abducting and murdering those young

girls hadn't been Kashiwada. Though the four young female victims had been posed as though they were subjects, not a single photo had been found at Kashiwada's home.

Since Kashiwada had been intimately involved with this whole matter, he'd left traces of his involvement here and there. It had worked against him when he was falsely accused of the crimes.

The vague doubt Kihara felt was well-grounded after all. While writing *Beyond the Darkness*, he had slowly but surely come to doubt Kashiwada's guilt.

But if Kashiwada hadn't been guilty, that meant the real killer was somewhere else. For argument's sake, Takanori decided to call this person N. As there was absolutely no way a woman could have committed a crime like this, N was almost certainly a man.

One requisite for N to be the killer was a deep connection to *Ring*.

Another was that the person had to be connected to Kashiwada somehow. In the process of collecting the first edition of *Ring*, Kashiwada had been compelled to gather all the data he could on the Sadakos, who had been born into the world through no fault of their own. If there were no connection between Kashiwada and N, there was no way N could have been privy to this data on the Sadakos.

After getting his hands on the addresses of the four Sadakos and other information on them, N had systematically committed the crimes.

Who met all of these conditions?

N had to be connected to *Ring*; he'd had some contact with Kashiwada and was around his age; he was a male who possessed the arm strength to methodically strangle four girls...

Surveying the field, Takanori could think of only one man who satisfied them all.

He needed to find evidence to identify the true killer right away.

If Kashiwada had been the killer, then the threat had vanished when he was executed. But N—relieved that Kashiwada had been put to death in his place, and presently on the loose—might attempt what he'd failed to accomplish once before.

N had just barely missed his chance to grab Akane, his fifth victim. It was probably Kashiwada who'd saved her. With the data on the Sadakos in his possession, he'd discerned what the targets of the serial murders had in common and thereby identified the killer. He'd also anticipated what would happen to Akane, who'd been saved for last, and tried to rescue her. He must have picked her up in his arms and hurried away through the mountainside.

However, that very act had gotten him confused with the real killer.

Now that Kashiwada was dead, that devil's hand could be reaching out for Akane once again. It was entirely possible that their current address was already known to him.

Takanori's dark premonition was on the verge of coming to pass. If the series of events that began with analyzing the USB video merely fit in the category of the weird, they wouldn't be at risk of getting harmed. Yet the vague and nebulous menace had taken on a definite physical nature.

At the very least, N had killed those four young girls with malice aforethought. If he'd had the patience to wait for Kashiwada to be executed, he was truly a formidable opponent.

This was entirely unlike facing an enemy in a game. This one had the heart of a monster, yet possessed a fully developed body—he was a flesh-and-blood man.

As Takanori had never been in a single fight his entire life, he had no idea how to defend himself in such an emergency.

Right now, what he longed for was the ability to fight back.

5

Something about the way Minakami puffed out his cigarette smoke gave him a cool profile. As he squinted to focus on the faraway scenery, he seemed to be really enjoying his smoke.

Yoneda had never cared a whit about others as a heavy smoker, but once he quit, he mandated that everyone on staff smoke outside on the balcony. Feeling the breeze blowing in the patchy blue sky and breathing in the outside air was not so bad. Though not a smoker himself, Takanori had accompanied Minakami out to the balcony and was seeking his advice after briefly explaining the situation.

Minakami was five years his senior at Studio Oz, but only four years older. The man knew enough about computers to be a hacker, and the security of the office's computers was entrusted entirely to him.

Even as he listened to Takanori's account, Minakami's expression showed no change at all.

"Okay, got it. I take it you don't know this guy's email address."

"Not at the moment," replied Takanori.

"Do you have any leads I can go on?"

"I have a postcard."

"A postcard, huh? Do you have it on you?"

Minakami held out the palm of his hand and asked to see the item right then and there if Takanori had it with him.

Takanori went back inside, retrieved the postcard from his bag, and brought it out to the balcony.

It was the one that Akane had nabbed from the mailbox for Room 303 at Shinagawa View Heights. She hadn't called it stealing—she insisted that she'd only taken it on the sly—but it amounted to the same thing no matter how you looked at it.

Taking the postcard, Minakami flipped it over front and back several times, read the text, and let out a single grunt.

The addressee on the front read "Mr. Hiroyuki Niimura," but a mere glance at the text on the back told him this was an invitation to a class reunion.

The Funabashi Public ** Junior High Class of ** Reunion will be held at the following location, date and time. We hope you can join us!

The date and time, location, fee, and other necessary information on the reunion were all given below, with the name of the secretary listed at the end.

*Yoshio Matsuoka, Director, Class of ** Reunion*

Written beneath that was Matsuoka's email address.

"What do you think? Will this guy be useful?"

Akane had risked her life to obtain this trophy, and Takanori prayed that it might be.

"Yep," said Minakami. "If Niimura's on a mailing list, it should be simple. All right, let me give it a try."

Minakami put out his cigarette in the portable ashtray he was holding and, somehow happy, led Takanori back inside.

After taking a seat in front of his computer, he straightened his posture and faced Takanori with a rather serious expression.

"I want to make sure that what we're about to do is justifiable," he said. "This Niimura person is a pretty bad guy, right?"

Takanori nodded silently.

Niimura being the real abductor and killer of the four young girls was nothing more than speculation. However, all of the circumstantial evidence fit.

If Kiyomi Sakata had realized that Niimura was the real killer, then her rash actions made sense. She too was connected to *Ring*, and it was eminently possible that she'd noticed his strange behavior and figured out what was going on, simply out of maternal instinct.

Just when she was feeling relieved that Kashiwada had been executed, settling the whole issue, someone had sent her a video linking Kashiwada to Niimura. One could only imagine how astonished she must have been. And this had occurred just before the release of the film she had produced. Recalling how *Ring* had been shelved, she must have feared that *Studio 104* would suffer the same fate.

The circumstantial evidence pointed in one direction. All that remained was to find real proof.

"I can't explain it in detail, but Niimura could be considered an enemy of mankind," Takanori stressed.

"A criminal?"

"That's right."

"So, what we're about to do will expose his crime."

"If we can find the images we're looking for on the guy's computer, then yes."

"In other words, what we're about to do is a meaningful act, born of good intentions. Is that right?"

"Of course."

"Okay then. I'm not the type of guy who can do something bad. Here we go! It's on."

With that, Minakami faced his computer with great intensity and began tapping his keyboard.

"How are you gonna do it?" Takanori asked him.

"It's easy. The email address of the reunion director, Yoshio Matsuoka, is written right here. First, I'll send Matsuoka an email, and then get him to install some special software. Well, basically it's a kind of virus. It'll be like I've taken control of Matsuoka's computer, so I'll be able to use it remotely. I'll sift through every last bit of data saved on his machine and extract the information we need. If Niimura's on the reunion mailing list, most of our work will be done. I could contact Niimura while posing as Matsuoka, and hijack *his* computer, or I can take control by sending him an email with a 'special' attachment. If Niimura's not on the list, it'll be kind of a headache, but they were classmates together at the same junior high, so if I can get into their social network, I can definitely get to his computer. Leave it to me. It might take a little while, but as long as we're connected online, there's nothing we can't do. After I've set everything up to remotely access Niimura's computer, I'll hand over the reins, and the rest will be up to you."

"Understood."

Not wanting to break Minakami's concentration, Takanori stepped away.

Studio Oz had only four people on staff including the president, Yoneda. Each member had a distinct character and set of skills, and when they all worked together, there was a palpable sense of heightened efficiency in the office.

President Yoneda had a generous and laidback personality, but he enjoyed great trust from his subordinates. He always kept his promises and followed through when he said he'd do something.

Minakami was a capable video production director, but he was not cut out to be a film director. He was a hacker with a strong sense of justice, and a heavy smoker.

Kanako Nishijima, the youngest person on staff, had no interest in cosmetics and was bereft of feminine allure. Yet she could travel abroad just as easily as go down to the convenience store, and like a cat she could land at someone else's door and hide out there for weeks on end to gather information. That was her specialty. While she bragged that she also sometimes used her feminine wiles, not a soul believed her.

As for myself...

Trying to analyze his own character, Takanori gave up halfway. Grasping what kind of person he was seemed to be the hardest. The only thing he could say was that he didn't resemble Yoneda, Minakami, or Nishijima at all.

It was precisely because the four of them had such distinct personalities that when they worked together, they achieved more than anyone expected. If four people with the same qualities got together, they wouldn't be nearly as efficient.

As he pondered this, Takanori remained at a distance and watched Minakami tapping away at his keyboard.

"There's nothing I can't do when I'm at a computer."

Minakami always bragged about his skills that way, and with his help they were sure to succeed. Probably by the next day, he would take over Niimura's computer and enable Takanori to have remote access. If so, whatever image data were saved onto Niimura's computer would be Takanori's to view at will. He would be free to copy them to his own computer, delete them, process them, or do anything else he wanted.

The kidnapper and murderer photographed all of his young female victims—that was Kihara's take. As if they knew they were going to be pictured, the girls had been posed in the same way. Not of their own will, it went without saying, but the killer's. But no photos or films of the girls had been found at Kashiwada's residence. If Takanori could find the images on Niimura's computer, it would be incontrovertible evidence. Nobody besides the killer could have taken those shots.

For Takanori, it was a double-edged sword.

If he obtained conclusive evidence that Niimura was the real killer, then the inferences they had made thus far would turn out to be true. If a gray card that had been left aside turned white, all of the surrounding gray would also change white themselves. The shallows that only appeared when the tide receded would become a long corridor, never to be covered again.

Beyond the corridor lay facts that Takanori didn't want to acknowledge. The fact that he'd actually died once, the fact that Akane was Sadako...

Even if those things were true, he needed to confront and accept them. To reveal Niimura's crime, Takanori had to resign himself to that reality.

When Minakami had finished one stage of the work, he went out onto the balcony to light up again. He was prone to smoking more cigarettes the more smoothly his work went.

His back visible through the balcony door, Minakami was brimming with confidence.

6

The ground was muddy, and the grass was covered with drops of water. Both his hands and knees were on the ground, and when he tried to stand up his right leg slipped and sent him tumbling. He tried again, but the result was the same. He was so frustrated that he couldn't get any traction with his feet but just kept slipping.

"Welcome. I'm glad you made it."

Still on all fours, Takanori lowered his body, and that was when a man's echoing voice came to him out of nowhere. His way of speaking sounded theatrical, and the vibrato he appended to his words offered a hokey welcome.

My eyes need a little more time to adjust, Takanori thought, but with the darkness locking him up he still couldn't spot any figure. But the man most definitely knew where Takanori was. *If I stay still, I'm giving him a chance. I've got to move.* Yet Takanori didn't know where to go.

At that moment, he heard a woman's voice. While the man's voice fell upon him from everywhere, making it impossible to track the source, he could somewhat make out the direction of the woman's.

It had come from inside a deep hole behind him on his right side.

"Tak, you don't need to worry about me."

The voice was Akane's.

I don't need to worry about you? What am I supposed to do?

Takanori wished she'd just tell him what she wanted him to do.

"'Tak'? That's so sweet, normie. Wait, no, you're more like a big lure."

The man's voice was becoming more and more vicious. Takanori knew that he shouldn't allow himself to be provoked, but he just couldn't stand it. Listening to the voice deepened his anger, and propelled by it, he moved his legs furiously. When his feet touched something solid, at long last he stopped slipping and stood up. Looking around carefully, he realized that the solid object he'd touched was a brick, half of which was buried in the ground. It was a small footing carved into the earth.

"So, you can finally stand up. Okay, go on, Mr. Lure. Make my wish come true."

The man's tone was different now. Though it had sounded like it was falling from nowhere in particular, now it seemed to be coming from a more focused point. A black clump taking shape ahead of Takanori was the source.

"Two prey. A big one, and a small one. They're right behind you."

Takanori stepped forward, keeping his body low. His anger continued to swell, giving him the strength to press on.

"No, not this way, don't come here. Can't you see? There's a fishpond right behind you. The deep, round pond. It's small, but it goes very deep. The two prey are swimming around in the mud at the bottom, so fish them out with your lure for me."

Though his feet still got stuck in the wet mud, he wasn't slipping anymore. His anger rose and transformed into a murderous urge, and as his will grew more determined, the muddy ground grew harder. *Now I see—the uncertainty of my footing was my own will.*

"Oh, I oughta tell you this first: even if you fish for them well, those prey are mine. So don't complain, no matter how I cook them. Well, I'll be nice and give you a little of what's left after I've eaten."

The voice was coming closer. He was right there. Now that Takanori's eyes had adjusted to the darkness, he could see the area around the man's legs.

"Tak, please, just ignore him. Don't give him the satisfaction... Please, just leave it to me," Akane appealed desperately. Her voice had its own vibrato effect, and she clearly seemed to be in a small, damp space. Her voice sounded almost like a bell.

"See? Why don't you listen to her? Not this way, that way. Climb down to the bottom of the well and bring my prey to me. That's your job. You guys are the same, right? Both of you died once already."

Yeah. So what? Takanori felt ashamed now that he'd tried to push Akane away for being a reincarnation of Sadako. *Like you said. We're birds of a feather.* That was precisely why they shared a deep bond: both of them were unnatural beings. They hadn't simply imagined hearing their gears click upon meeting for the first time.

Akane is the woman of my destiny—we were fated to meet each other. Nobody can take her away from me. If you wanna tear us apart by force, all I can do is fight back with all my will.

Just ahead, the man's kneecaps appeared in the dim, weak light.

Takanori didn't know where the light was coming from. An old streetlamp might have stood at the end of a guardrail on the road. Though it was very weak on its own, if several mirrors were combined to reflect it, it might create a certain level of brightness.

When he joined the mirrors together, the spotlight that it made illuminated a pair of legs that were as thin as a scarecrow's. Takanori aimed at them and jumped forward to tackle the man. Linking his hands behind the man's back and ramming his head into the man's crotch, Takanori knocked him backward.

"What're you doing? Dumbass. That's not what you're supposed to do!" The man's voice sounded panicked now. "I just wanted to keep playing! You guys are totally lame..."

Taking care not to let go, Takanori butted his head into the man's chin over and over and sat astride him. Not even knowing what he wanted, or his purpose, his body simply moved by itself, obeying instinct. The man kept talking nonsense, so Takanori put his hands around his neck, wanting only to shut his mouth. Then it felt like he was touching something soft and rubbery, and its elasticity pushed against his hands.

"Hey, stop it."

The man started flailing his arms and legs even as he was pinned down, hitting and scratching Takanori's face, head, and wherever else he could reach.

His fingers and fists—his whole body, really—were as soft as rubber. It reminded Takanori of an invertebrate rather than a human being. The man was tangling him like a huge octopus.

When Takanori put his palms on the man's throat and pushed with his body weight, the sound of breathing echoed around his ears.

Just a little more and he'll stop breathing.

But no matter how long he pushed, Takanori kept hearing a whoosh like that of a balloon deflating, never reaching the point of finishing off the man.

His cervical spine was supposed to be in the center of his neck, but Takanori's hands couldn't find it.

They were growing numb and tired. With no strength left, he gave up strangling the man. Getting his own breathing under control, he groped on the ground with his hands, and his fingers touched something hard. It was the brick.

Pressing down on the man's shoulders with both knees, Takanori raised the brick in the air, and the spotlight enhanced by the mirrors revealed the man's face.

Takanori felt as if he were being told, *If you're going to kill your enemy, you must witness his face first.*

It fit perfectly in a ring of light. His skin was white, his eyes were wide open, and his nose line was nice and neat. His thin lips gave the impression of cruelty, but he could be categorized as handsome. His neck stretched out unnaturally long, with white lines visible here and there.

Back when he couldn't see his adversary's face, it had felt like an invertebrate, made of rubber, but as soon as Takanori saw the man's features, the reality dawned on him that he was trying to kill a human being.

He stayed his hand, the brick suspended in mid-air.

"No, don't! What are you thinking? Don't do such a stupid thing. Please!" the man begged for his life.

But Takanori couldn't afford to miss this chance. If he did, he would live in fear every day. The moment he let his guard down, his lover would slip through his fingers and be lost forever.

"You're too cocky for a guy who's already died once," the man said.

Those words gave Takanori the impetus to follow through.

Wanting to end it with a single strike, he aimed at the man's head and tried to crush it with the brick, but the man moved to avoid the blow. Missing its target, the brick smashed the man's chin instead. His bright pink gums, shaped like a fan, bent, and the blood spilling out stained his teeth red. His tongue was moving like a slug in the pool of blood. He coughed, choked by the blood flowing into his throat.

Yet it still seemed like he wanted to say something.

"Nnnah bahd fuh a dehh guy."

The man couldn't enunciate properly and sounded like a lisping little child.

That wasn't enough to finish him.

Once more Takanori lifted the brick.

I won't miss this time, he thought, aiming at the man's head and striking again. The blow caved in his skull, and Takanori could tell pieces of bone had jabbed into his foe's brain.

Yet the man still wasn't dead, and was trying to say something.

"Mommm...pleeese plaaay wishhh meee..."

Takanori couldn't stand hearing any more. He lifted the brick again to shut the vicious mouth for good...but then suddenly, the scene shifted.

He couldn't tell where he was at first.

Takanori sat up suddenly from his sofa and turned his head right and left. He was soaked with sweat from his back to his hips.

On his right was the window with the lace curtain drawn, and on his left was the table with his computer on it.

Oftentimes when he was dreaming, he would notice another part of him whispering, *This isn't real*. This other self would speak to him as he soared through the sky or struggled desperately, chased by a monster.

It was clearly playing the role of a buffer, to cushion his landing back in reality once he was finished with the dream's strangeness.

But in the one he'd just had, the objective viewpoint hadn't appeared until the end. He'd been unable to distinguish between dream and reality, understanding only after waking that it had all been a dream, and his heart shrank.

He'd been lying down on his sofa and thinking, and he must have fallen asleep at some point. Looking at the clock, he saw it was half past six in the evening. He'd dozed off for only ten minutes. And he must have been dreaming for an even shorter duration.

Nevertheless, the scene of that black mountain slope was stuck in his brain. What stayed with him most was the feeling of the man's neck stretching like rubber, no matter how tightly he strangled it, and the feeling through the brick when he'd crushed the man's chin and skull. The sensations lingered in every part of his body, and he couldn't wipe them away.

Takanori recalled one of Kihara's phrases from the book he'd written about serial killers.

"People can die so easily that you might be surprised how little it takes. But once you intend to kill a person, somehow, they can't be killed so easily. You can strike him with a stone or stab him with a knife, but he'll resist, and chase after you like a zombie. That's why killers tend to persist in attacking their victims, out of fear."

Takanori agreed. He too had kept on hitting with the brick until he was sure the man was really dead. If he hadn't woken up, his attacks would surely have continued.

He knew perfectly well why he'd had that sort of dream. It was, quite simply, wish fulfillment.

The hacking begun by Minakami the day before had succeeded, and as of that afternoon, everything had been in place for Takanori to gain remote access to Niimura's computer and take complete control.

Wasting no time, Takanori broke into Niimura's machine and looked for the images in question. There were an endless number of folders in the Pictures section of Niimura's Documents. Opening up the pics one by one and checking everything would take forever. He typed "Sadako" as a keyword hoping to locate the ones he needed right away, but there were no hits. He tried all the keywords he could think of—"Ring," "serial abduction and murder of girls"—to no avail. Then he thought of typing SADAKO in upper-case letters, but changed his mind and just typed "S." That was when he found something.

All of a sudden, five folders appeared onscreen, entitled S-1, S-2, S-3, S-4, and S-5.

As he'd expected, the pictures of the girls right after their murder had been saved in folders S-1 to S-4. There were no films, only still images.

The girls were sitting on the quiet mountainside and leaning against tree trunks, with both hands primly on their knees and their heads lowered slightly. If a flash had been used, the mysterious atmosphere would surely have been destroyed, but the photos had the perfect amount of shading. With neither too much nor too little natural light from the sunset, the picturesque compositions arguably reached the level of art.

The peculiar relationship between murderer and victim had imparted tension to the compositions, giving them a decadent aesthetic. No other situation could rival these pictures as far as how well they captured beauty in the moment before it vanished, in its very evanescence.

Analyzing the pictures, Takanori almost felt awe for Niimura's talent. The feeling disappeared right away, however, when he opened folder S-5.

Pictures with Akane as the subject were saved in S-5. Niimura had stalked her as she'd grown up, taking photos of her when she was in junior high, high school, and college, and leaving the gate of the school where she worked, or standing on the platform at a station, or walking through a shopping concourse. Given that the number of pictures of her far exceeded that of all the pictures in S-1 through S-4, Takanori could tell how strong the killer's obsession was. No, it wasn't just strong—it was obviously still ongoing and had never lapsed.

The last photo was from the day before yesterday. It showed the first floor of the condo where Takanori lived and had been shot just as Akane was about to go through the auto-locking entrance.

The culprit behind the serial abduction and murder of the young girls wasn't Kashiwada, but Niimura. Worse, he was roaming around the neighborhood and had a complete grasp of Akane's commute.

Wondering how to protect her, Takanori had tried to fulfill his wish in a dream.

Worried about where she was now, he looked at the clock. It was 6:35 p.m. Around that time, she was usually on the Keihin Express. He turned on the GPS tracking app to pinpoint her current location.

There was no guarantee that she wasn't about to be attacked by Niimura right then.

As he expected, she was on a train in motion. Skipping North Shinagawa, it was about to enter Shinagawa station.

Were she on the special express, the train would proceed without stopping. But evidently Akane had taken one that required a transfer, and she seemed to step onto the platform there. At Shinagawa station, her movement completely stopped.

The time kept ticking away on the display of Takanori's cell phone. It felt like it was taking too long, even if she was waiting for a connecting train to arrive.

He spent ten minutes on pins and needles. Unable to endure it any longer, he called Akane's phone, when suddenly the target disappeared from his screen.

Akane had turned off her phone.

The time was 6:44 p.m.

Takanori slumped over his desk and cradled his head. Once her phone was off, there was nothing he could do.

How long can it go on like this?

He banged his fists on the table. Doing that didn't make him feel any better, though, and the disturbing sensation from when he'd smashed Niimura's chin in the dream came back.

As long as Niimura was out there on the loose, Takanori and Akane would never know peace in their life together.

It seemed he was in store for another sleepless night worrying about Akane's every move. In fact, he'd been unable to get a decent amount of sleep for the past few days. No matter how long he spent

214

lying on his bed, unless his nerves calmed down, rest eluded him.

If their child were born into such circumstances, Takanori's worries would be twofold. When he realized that, he suddenly raised his head.

Niimura's probably waiting for Akane to have the baby.

He was leaving her be for now, letting her go free as he waited for his one target to become two. Having only one mark meant his enjoyment would quickly be over. Yet if he had two, the fun could go on.

Just thinking about it made Takanori feel like he was going crazy. Even if he copied the images and brought them to the police, there was no way that they'd take it seriously and make a move. Seiji Kashiwada had been sentenced to death as a serial abductor and murderer of young girls, and he'd already been executed. Japanese law didn't envision a scenario where the real culprit came to light after an execution had been carried out. And the only evidence he could offer were these photos, insufficient grounds for reopening an investigation; Takanori was a pro at processing images who made a living creating fake ones using CG technology. He knew full well what would happen if he went to the police. They'd just send him away.

No matter how hard he tried to devise a way to escape the threat, there was only one answer. The sole option was to eliminate it by force. In other words, he had no choice but to kill Niimura.

Takanori opened his hands.

Can I really kill somebody with these hands?

If the enemy attacked with murderous intent, Takanori's despair might give him the courage to lash out in self-defense. But it would be too late if he waited for his enemy to act first. Unless he moved preemptively, the likelihood of losing his loved ones would only grow.

In a dream, you could kill any sort of monster. In the real world, that didn't happen so easily. Takanori could scarcely picture himself killing somebody on purpose. Just imagining it made the tips of his fingers shake.

Next to those shaking hands, the GPS tracking app on his cell phone started working again. It seemed Akane had turned her device back on.

It was 6:49 p.m. Her cell phone had been turned off for only five minutes.

The app showed a change in Akane's location. She appeared to have exited the ticket gate and picked up a taxi proceeding north along the Keihin No. 1 Road.

Perhaps some kind of trouble at Shinagawa station had forced her to give up waiting for the train and to take a taxi instead...that possibility made the most sense.

In any case, he figured, she'd be home in twenty minutes or so.

7

Well, I've finally lost the ability to tell dream from reality.

Takanori rubbed his eyes and shook his head.

He was now sitting at the table, but it wasn't to turn on his computer. Its very sight disgusted him at the moment. But despite having no intention of sitting, with his head in a haze, he'd staggered around and come over to the table to rest his body.

The computer had been off, with no light coming from the screen, and the display background was completely black.

Takanori dug his fingernails into his thigh and slapped his cheeks, but the scene before him didn't change.

It meant that this was real.

There was a man standing in the display.

Poised there in the middle of the monitor's black background, he looked like an actor greeting his audience from the stage in front of a closed curtain.

He wasn't standing straight. Judging from the angle of his crossed legs and the position of his hips, he was perched on a stool. However, the black stool blended into the dark background and was invisible, so he looked like he was standing with his body distorted in some unnatural way.

"Hey, brother. Don't be so depressed."

That's Seiji Kashiwada. Or should I say, Ryuji Takayama.

Stuck onto the black display, he looked like a cartoon character.

"Mr. Takayama," Takanori replied respectfully to Ryuji, who'd been his father's friend.

"Do you remember me? We've met before."

"Yes." Intimidated by the man's powerful aura, Takanori felt like a schoolboy.

"There's someplace I gotta go, so I don't have much time. But there were some last words I definitely wanted to tell you before I go, and that's why I'm here. I couldn't just watch you suffer without doing something for you. You can think of this place I'm in now as a two-dimensional digital space."

Shortly after Takanori had copied the hanging video of Kashiwada from the USB stick, just the human figure had disappeared from the screen and run off to nowhere, almost as if he'd gained another life limited to digital spaces. Had he now come back?

"I think you know this already, but our pasts share a certain fact. We were both born from Sadako's womb. Your dad has been trying like mad to hide that. You know why? Because he believes that he released an evil into this world in exchange for your life. It's not that he's trying to hide his own guilt. He's simply worried that you might needlessly feel ashamed of yourself if you found out the whole truth. There are things in this world that are better left unknown, if you can do without knowing them. Don't blame your dad. Everything he did, he did to bring his beloved son back to this world. If Mitsuo had done nothing, you wouldn't be here.

"You know about Mai Takano. Twenty-five years ago, she lived in Room 303 at the Shinagawa View Heights. She happened to watch that demonic videotape on her ovulation date and gave birth to a girl who carried Sadako's DNA. Her name on the family record is Masako Maruyama. She was Akane's mother, and I knew her very well.

"Masako had a peculiar womb. If you took an ovulated egg out of her body, injected a dead person's genetic information into the egg, and put it back in her womb, she'd give birth in a week, and the baby would grow to the age when the person had died and regain his or her old memories.

"You must think that's impossible. But there's a mechanism at work that you people will never be able to understand. I couldn't explain it even if I wanted to, and I'm not even supposed to. Because this all has to do with a world that exists in a higher dimension than the one you live in. The denizens of a two-dimensional plane couldn't glimpse the world of those living in three-dimensional space, or even imagine that world. Yet the opposite is feasible: if you live in a higher dimension, you can interfere with and manipulate the lives of those residing in a lower dimension.

"You're good at that, aren't you? Processing images, I mean. It's the same thing.

"If a person living in three dimensions picks up an ant that's crawling on a two-dimensional plane, the ant will seem to have disappeared instantly from that world. Conversely, if the ant gets placed back down from the sky above, it'll seem like the ant has appeared from nowhere. Even so-called occult abilities can be explained easily if you posit a higher-dimensional world. The word 'psychic' means someone with the special power to access that higher dimension. Prediction, mental projection—you name it, they can do it. You can lead somebody wherever you want by manipulating their car navigation system or mischievously send them a video. Like I did to Kiyomi Sakata.

"The same goes for information. All the data from a lower-dimensional world are saved in the high dimension. That includes individual biological info. And that means you can easily call up any information that's been saved. All you need is an interface.

"You'll get what I mean if you see that the interface happened to be Masako's womb.

"Her womb was like an umbilical cord connecting the higher

dimension and the lower ones.

"Now, this is very important: information exists in units. For example, genes are units of collated info, and when the DNA's double helix is converted into RNA, there needs to be a start code to begin the read-in process as well as an end code. With a beginning and an end, information can then be treated as a single unit.

"Human beings are the same. You're born, you live, and you die, and then finally you can tell what kind of life you led. No matter how happily you live, if you lose somebody you love right before you die, your life will turn out to be miserable at the last minute. You have to complete your life at some point—it doesn't matter where—or else it won't become a coherent unit of information, and it'll be impossible to transcend dimensions. Maybe it'll be easier to understand if I put it this way: *Human beings can't go to heaven while they're still alive. Only after you're confirmed to be dead can you get there.* It's the same thing.

"I'm now alive in this two-dimensional plane. I came here after I was officially certified to be dead in your world. That happened when the moment of my execution was recorded digitally.

"It wasn't like I wanted to take Niimura's place. I did need to undergo a public death, though, and an execution perfectly met all the requirements.

"That's why I can be here now, in the same bodily condition I was in when I was filmed.

"You know why I have to transcend dimensions? Twenty-five years ago, your world was in danger of an outbreak of the ring virus. If we hadn't done anything, the individual Sadako would have spread rapidly, ended diversity, and put the human race on the road to extinction.

"I came back to pick up the seeds that were scattered, and did everything I could. With your dad's help, I acquired Seiji Kashiwada's identity, and I passed myself off as him. Your dad doesn't know anything that happened after that point. I think he probably believes that I'm the real serial killer. Please explain to him later that I couldn't be such a bad guy, all right?

"Well, anyway, I became Kashiwada and tried to stop the book *Ring* from getting published, but didn't completely succeed. Two thousand out of the five thousand copies of the first edition were sold in the Kanto area. I traced the route along which the books were distributed and collected them one by one, going around visiting bookshops and libraries. Unfortunately, by that time, four Sadakos had already been born.

"I succeeded in sealing off the effect of the ring virus by adding a little trick for the revised edition and the paperback, which came out after the first edition. If you have a chance to get both editions, compare them. The inside cover is black for the first edition, but in the revised edition and the paperback, there's an illustration of eyeballs. That illustration acts like a vaccine or an antidote. Even a glance is enough—once you start reading, the mechanism will kick in to erase the effect of the virus.

"As for the movie, that worked out splendidly. I managed to get it shelved, as you know.

"I've done pretty well in destroying the ring virus, even though some of it escaped. Sadako had been born, but just four of them wouldn't threaten our ecosystem. We could just let them live. But of course, I kept an eye on them. I had to closely monitor where they were and how they were growing up. I even managed to collect a hair sample from one of the four girls when an opportunity presented itself. I anticipated that I might need to check their DNA, you know? But then, the fact that I kept her hair with her name labeled on it ended up being solid evidence implicating me as the serial abductor and killer of those girls.

"Now, I have to talk about Hiroyuki Niimura. In order to come by some dirt that would force the *Ring* movie to get shelved, I needed to befriend his grandmother. In time, his grandma asked me to become her grandson's home tutor.

"She was mourning at every turn how pitiable her grandson was, practically abandoned by his mother because she was so focused on her career as an actress. I felt guilty for entrapping Kiyomi Sakata and making her suffer that setback, so I accepted the offer around the time that he entered junior high and started inviting him to my home and teaching him. He was a smart kid, but he made no effort to understand the purpose of studying, right until the end. For him, it was all about doing better than his rivals—beating others and scoring higher, nothing else. After a while he arrived at a simple logic: he started wishing for others to fail rather than working for his own success. He thought that if his rivals screwed up and got low scores, he'd still win, and it didn't make any difference, as far as winning was concerned.

"I taught him until he graduated junior high, and then that was the limit. He was the one who left me. At the time, I didn't realize that he'd copied all the valuable data belonging to me. I'd underestimated him, thinking he was only a kid. But he'd tamed a monster and raised it inside him.

"Having that information about the four living Sadakos stolen from me by Niimura was my worst blunder ever.

"I think he loved his mother Kiyomi a lot. Since she'd once gotten the lead role in a movie, he took an interest in everything about *Ring*, to a bizarre degree. He's insane. He's an abnormal maniac. And it got to the point where he ended up living in the apartment where Mai Takano used to live, so that tells you how crazy he is.

"For Niimura, Sadako was the only one he could play with. He must've frolicked with her in his fantasies all the time.

"Then he learned that Sadako really existed in this world. And not only one of her, but four...

"When I found out that the first copy of Sadako had been abducted and killed, I didn't know what had transpired behind the scenes. I just figured she'd happened to be involved in a case. And then when the second Sadako was killed, it sparked a certain wariness in me. *No way*, I thought. And with the third murder, I was sure of it. The criminal was targeting only Sadako, killing one of them after another. That meant the culprit had my data on Sadako. Who could have the data besides me, I asked myself. Of course, only one person could have known so much about *Ring* and surreptitiously seen the data in my file and stolen them—Niimura. After that, it was just a matter of time. I had to protect the fourth one before she got abducted and killed. But I couldn't make it, and the fourth Sadako also fell into his clutches.

"And he still didn't stop. He was about to dig his talons into the fifth one.

"That was Akane, your beloved.

"I made up my mind that I had to save her no matter what, and I barely outfoxed him and rescued her. I laid her down in the backseat of my car while she was still unconscious and started driving along the highway towards Kamitaga from South Hakone Pacific Land. But then a truck came toward me from up ahead, so I pulled onto the shoulder. That's when Akane woke up and opened the door to escape, and she fled into a tangerine farm.

"She mistakenly believed I was the killer. I couldn't let her go. I jumped out of the car and went to the farm to search for her. I really didn't want her to think I was the killer. And there was something I wanted to tell her badly. With just a little more time I could've told her the truth, but it didn't work out that way. The police, who'd been informed, rushed to the farm, and when I was about to hold her up, they found us and arrested me. Not only was I seemingly caught in the act, even worse, they found the evidence in my room, so all hope was gone.

"You might be wondering why I'm telling you all this. Isn't that right?

"The core of what I want to tell you isn't this confession of my deeds."

When Ryuji finished saying all that, Takanori heard the door open. He automatically looked at the clock and saw it was 7:22 p.m. The door had been locked from inside, but before long Akane appeared from the hallway.

Takanori stood from the chair and sighed with relief.

"I'm home," she said.

"Hi, Akane, welcome home."

She sounded more cheerful than usual.

"Akane's come home at just the right time. She's the one I want to talk to. Can you bring her here and have her sit down in front of me?"

Takanori worried about whether he should comply with Ryuji's request. He was sure that seeing Ryuji's face—engraved in her mind as that of the killer—would come as a terrible shock. But in truth, not only was he not the killer, he was the man to whom she owed her life. Deciding that she ought to know the truth, Takanori waved at her to come over.

"Hmm? What is it?" she asked. Walking around the table and standing in front of the screen, she saw the image and gasped.

Then she uttered a short scream, put a hand to her mouth, and screwed her eyes shut.

Takanori gently held the terrified Akane and whispered in her ear, "It's all a misunderstanding. He didn't try to kill you. It was the opposite. He tried to save you. That was Niimura who tried to kill you. This is the man who rescued you from Niimura's grip. Go on, open your eyes now, and look at him closely."

Seeing Akane weakly shake her head, Takanori continued, "Don't worry. You don't need to be afraid anymore. Trust me and open your eyes."

Perhaps because his words had reached her heart, she gradually opened her eyes.

When Akane met his gaze, Ryuji didn't miss his chance and spoke to her first.

"Hello, Akane. My, how you've grown. I've never been so happy as I am now, seeing you again."

Hearing her name called out with such affection made Akane recall something, and a tiny sparkle appeared in her eyes.

"Akane, I want to erase the fear engraved in your mind. You thought I was going to kill you, but the truth is what Takanori told you just now. Do you remember, dear? When I pulled the car over on that dark mountain road, you took that as your chance and opened the door and ran away to that tangerine farm. I followed you desperately because I really didn't want you to mistake me for the killer. But more than that, I wanted to hold you, and there was something I wanted you to know. That was why I had to find you. You know why? Because I once loved your mother, Masako. Akane, you are my daughter. I wanted to tell you this."

Takanori nearly shot up from the shock. Akane had told him her mother had given birth without knowing who the father was. But now Ryuji was confessing that it was him.

"Takanori, I also need you to accept this truth. The other four Sadakos, Niimura's victims, all resembled each other closely. Akane, however, only looked a little like them. The reason is the difference in how they were born. The four others were born through asexual reproduction as a result of the virus. But Akane, you were the outcome of true love, between Masako and me. Please believe me when I say that there was affection involved in how you got here.

"Akane, you were born via sexual reproduction, and you're a perfect woman. Your immune system is fine, and so is the rest of your body. But Masako, who was born by asexual reproduction, had something wrong with her immune system, so she died young. Even if the four girls hadn't been killed by Niimura, they might not have led long lives. But you'll be fine. You don't have any problems.

"I didn't try to adopt you and live together after you'd been left all alone, Akane. I didn't deserve to do that. Even before that, I didn't deserve to love Masako.

"I don't belong to your world. Originally, I didn't intend to stay here for long. There was another world that I had to go to, and I've tarried longer than I should have. Soon, I'll have to say goodbye to the two-dimensional one I'm in now. I'll become just a piece of information and travel to yet another dimension. Do you understand? The place I'll go after this is the one-dimensional world. In short, I'll just be a string. Our genetic information is coded in two intertwined strings in a language that uses only four letters—ATGC. You can think of it as a long string with the letters lined up and going on and on. A string wriggling in the shape of an S...

"You see, in the one-dimensional world, compressed information is all that exists. In that world, the other dimensions are scraped off, whittled away, until all that's left is a pure informational existence. Call them the seeds of life. Only after I've become a seed of life can I go to a higher dimension. That's how terrestrial life came to be, too, in fact. It sprouted as information compressed into a single string—with the intervention of light. Without becoming a string of information, you can't ride the light.

"Cruising beyond dimensions is all that I desire. To satisfy my drive to understand the universe, I need to give up everything else.

"If you think about God, it's easy to understand. God is almighty only because He exists in a higher dimension. I suppose you might find me arrogant, but it's the best way to describe it, for convenience's sake.

"I said God is almighty, but there is one thing He can't do. Do you know what it is? He's not able to love a human being and make a child. When I say love, I'm not talking about Agape. I mean Eros, that love. Why can't God love a human being and have a child? Because there's a strong attachment to the child—it would mean not treating others equally. A being who's fated to journey forever beyond dimensions shouldn't immerse himself in the raw love that Eros entails. The moment of separation inevitably comes. If I lived with Akane and that kind of attachment arose, it would sap my courage to embark on the journey. I was afraid of that.

"But Takanori, you're a human being, not God. You can love her with all your heart. You can be consumed by a fierce, jealous devotion to her, and if some enemy appears before you and cruelly tries to take away your loved ones, be bold enough to be able to kill.

"Righteous talk isn't worth shit. Actually, it just makes people unhappy. Human beings have no other way to live but to writhe in the mud. That's how humans are supposed to be. That's why they're lovable, and that's why they deserve to be blessed.

"I have to go now. Takanori, please take care of Akane. Because you're qualified to love her."

With those last words, Ryuji crossed straight down the screen, fell clean under the frame, and was gone.

8

Takanori awoke thoroughly refreshed, feeling as if a fog was gradually clearing. As he lay down on bed, he kept looking at the ceiling, and the world reflected in his eyes looked different from before.

Why was this morning so different? He didn't need to wonder why or how he felt differently from yesterday and the day before that. For the first time in a long time, he'd managed to sleep well through the night. He'd slept all the way until morning without waking up even once for the first time in several days.

The only reason he could think of for such a pleasant night's sleep was the message from Ryuji. Now, Takanori didn't fully understand *everything* Ryuji had tried to convey. His talk about a journey beyond dimensions sounded like Greek to Takanori, who felt like it had nothing to do with himself. The only thing he cared about was reality. Ryuji's words had validated man's behavior in this world, all the anguish and writhing in the mud. He was relieved to know that it was fine for him to be that way. Ryuji had assured him that he could stay as he was.

Akane seemed to have been awake for quite some time already and was preparing breakfast, and he could hear the clanking of dishes from the kitchen.

The clock indicated that it was half past six. Akane had gotten up thirty minutes earlier than usual. Takanori hadn't even heard the alarm going off right next to him.

After passing through the living room, he entered the kitchen,

226

where Akane held out a glass of vegetable juice that she'd just finished making. It was her special recipe, a smooth blend of tomatoes, carrots, apples, and other ingredients.

He gulped the whole thing down, and it felt like all the cells in his body had awoken instantly.

Takanori put the empty glass on the table, sat down, and followed Akane with his eyes as she walked around from the living room to the kitchen to the bathroom.

She was still wearing her pajamas. Standing in front of the mirror, she applied some light makeup and prepared to go to work as usual.

The previous night, before going to bed, Takanori had asked her not to the next day. Akane had laughed for no real reason and told him, "I'm gonna be fine."

He'd appealed to her that he'd be a nervous wreck until she walked through the door again. Checking to see where she was until she was safely on her way home, he'd get absolutely no work done.

She'd simply replied, "Thanks for worrying about me. I'm happy to hear that." His appeal had amounted to nothing, failing to make the slightest impression on her.

He espied her from the living-room table as she put on her makeup in front of the mirror.

I need to take her to buy a dresser this weekend.

There was no furniture akin to a dresser in Takanori's apartment since he'd been living a bachelor's life.

Akane never asked him to buy anything, no matter how much she needed it. Whenever he offered to, she always demurred, saying, "No, it's fine."

Still, he couldn't let a lady stand while she did her makeup. Takanori made up his mind to take her to a furniture store that weekend even if he had to drag her there.

After finishing her makeup, Akane went to the bedroom and started changing her clothes.

That was when Takanori noticed the tablet that had been left on the table, with the news still onscreen. The first thing Akane did after waking up was to read the news on the device. It seemed that she'd held to her routine that morning, too.

As Takanori scrolled through, a certain piece of news caught his eyes. It was the headline that drew his attention.

Fatal Accident at Shinagawa Station Last Night

Takanori enlarged the article.

"Last night, at approximately 6:46 p.m., Mr. Hiroyuki Niimura (31), a resident of South Shinagawa in Shinagawa Ward, fell from the platform at Shinagawa station and was fatally struck by an approaching train. It is unknown whether it was a suicide or an accident. The incident caused massive delays for commuters on all Keihin Express lines."

Niimura's dead?

It took some time for the news to sink in. He read the article once more, and then looked up.

Is he really gone?

Though Takanori felt like shouting for joy, he told himself to calm down and put a lid on it.

Niimura, his greatest threat, was now gone from this world. Nothing could have made Takanori happier. Yet, for some reason, something other than joy crossed his mind.

Just the day before, Takanori had abhorred Niimura enough to want to kill him. And his wish had been fulfilled, just like that.

The timing was too perfect to simply brush it off as a coincidence.

He needed more detailed information. He turned on his computer and searched for articles about Niimura's suicide or accidental death.

A video of his final moments before falling from the platform had been uploaded. Apparently, somebody who'd happened to be standing on the same platform had his cell phone switched to shooting mode and been focusing on Niimura, who was acting strangely, thus managing to catch the rare moment.

Having filmed the precise instant when Niimura fell to his death, the person had then uploaded the video to a site.

Takanori accessed it right away and played the scene.

This was Shinagawa station in the evening, so the platform was especially crowded. Yet somehow there was an open space around one person, a circle about three feet in radius. It seemed as if everyone around him had sensed something odd and moved away. The person in the center of the circle appeared to be Niimura.

With no one left around him, Niimura was free to walk forward without anyone getting in his way. He took one step, and then another, walking straight ahead until he stood at the edge of the platform. Then he raised his leg again, as if to climb another step, and just fell off. Run over by the incoming train, he disappeared.

Takanori replayed the video to examine it in detail. The second playback revealed a pale spotlight coming from above forming a circle around Niimura. The light was very faint and indistinct enough to be undetectable unless you knew it was there.

Synchronizing with the movement of the spotlight on him, Niimura was led to the edge of the platform and off it.

Playing the video a third time, Takanori focused on Niimura's profile. Just before falling, Niimura held his hands in front of him, seemingly pleading or asking for something. The expression on his cheek was not one of desperation, but sorrow. With his mouth half open, it looked like he was about to say something. As he stepped forward, he seemed to be trying to speak to somebody.

Takanori didn't have to play it a fourth time. It was enough. He was certain that a demon named Hiroyuki Niimura had disappeared from this world.

It's like he was being guided as he walked forward and jumped off the platform edge.

But guided by whom?

The time was stamped on the video, so anyone could tell the very minute that Niimura had died. It was 6:46 p.m. Using the GPS tracking app, Takanori had confirmed that Akane had been on the platform at Shinagawa station at that time last night. Of course, she couldn't have known who the victim was, but surely she must have witnessed the accident.

Nevertheless, she hadn't said a word about it after coming home last night.

Whenever she witnessed some kind of accident, Akane usually went on and on about everything she saw. "Hey, listen, listen!" she'd call to Takanori excitedly.

Furthermore, 6:46 p.m. fell within the time period that her cell phone had been turned off—for about five minutes from 6:44.

Why did she turn off her phone? Was it to make sure that it didn't ring at a bad time and break her concentration?

Was Niimura being guided by Sadako, whom only he could see? Did he stretch himself up from the edge because he wanted to play with her?

Takanori couldn't help but wonder. After all, Akane had that power.

Having finished changing her clothes, she was standing in front of the mirror at the entrance, checking her appearance just before heading to work.

"Hey, do I look okay? Does this match?"

It was almost past seven, so there was no time to change. She knew that, but she was still asking just to be told, "You look great."

"You look great, honey," Takanori said.

"Thank you. Okay then, I have to go. I might be able to come home earlier tonight."

"All right. Take care."

As Akane opened the entrance door and was about to leave, Takanori reached out towards her.

"What's wrong?" she asked, turning around with her hand still on the knob.

"Uh, nothing."

It would have been thoughtless to ask what had really happened the previous evening. There were things in this world that were better left unknown, if you could do without knowing them.

Is there any need to reveal everything?

"Okay, Tak, I'm going. It made me so glad to see you there next to me when I woke up. I want it to be like that forever, without anyone getting in the way."

Akane let go of the door, and it shut with a click. She had disappeared beyond the dark-gray door.

Takanori remained standing there at the entryway.

Though Akane must have been walking down the hallway to the elevators, the flawless soundproofing rendered her footsteps inaudible. All he could do was to imagine her lovely figure as she walked on, carrying that little life inside her.

Over the past few days, the fear that he might lose Akane had tortured him. A black hand had sprung from the virtual realm and manifested in reality to take her away, and it had very nearly succeeded. Niimura's true intentions were still unknown, and it was unlikely that they'd ever be uncovered.

In any case, it was all over now. He'd been cut in half by the train and killed instantly, and nothing could change that fact. They were no longer at risk of being stalked and murdered. From tomorrow onwards, they would awake every morning feeling secure.

The only lingering concern was that Niimura—having met a violent end—would have been examined by the police and photographed repeatedly after the incident.

The fact that his death had been publicly confirmed gave Takanori a bad feeling somehow.

Ryuji Takayama's return from the dead had felt like a divine advent. Yet in Niimura's case, his resurrection would seem downright diabolic.

No matter how hard Takanori tried to dispel them, the dark clouds looming over the future refused to clear.

He had no choice but to come to terms with this reality somehow and to advance amid a vague anxiety.

He might slip in the muck and the mire, but he knew that if he took one little step, he'd find his footing.

He'd been protected before, but now he was becoming a protector. All he needed was the courage to take that step.

Living with Akane, he felt, would foster that courage in him.

Epilogue

Although September was already half over, the days were still hot.

On the way to the school gate after getting off at the bus stop, Akane found herself being overtaken by many of the students.

"Good morning, Mrs. Arato."

Every time the students passed her by, they greeted her energetically. By the time Akane turned to smile at them, they were already brushing past her and walking up ahead.

She was more than five months into her pregnancy and in her stable period, but her walking speed hadn't gotten any faster. She moved carefully, placing her hands on her belly at times, taking things at her own pace.

"She's so cute!" some students said, giggling at the way an expecting woman walked as they passed her by.

Although September was already half over, the days were still hot.

On the way to the school gate after getting off at the bus stop, Akane found herself being overtaken by many of the students.

"Good morning, Mrs. Ando."

Every time the students passed her by, they greeted her energetically. By the time Akane turned to smile at them, they were already brushing past her and walking up ahead.

She was more than five months into her pregnancy and in her stable period, but her walking speed hadn't gotten any faster. She moved carefully, placing her hands on her belly at times, taking things at her own pace.

"She's so cute!" some students said, giggling at the way an expecting woman walked as they passed her by.

Everyone at the school knew that Akane was five months pregnant. Just before summer vacation, she and Takanori had gotten married, and at the end of break they'd held a small wedding party, with relatives and friends in attendance. Since they'd also invited people from the school, Akane's marriage and pregnancy was now officially acknowledged.

In fact, had they not invited anyone from the school, scarcely anyone would have attended on Akane's side, and she wouldn't have had enough guests to balance out Takanori's.

Most of the friends who'd come to celebrate were about their own age, but some older men could also be seen here and there. The nonfiction author Kihara had been one of them.

After being greeted by Akane, Kihara had been unable to conceal his wonderment at first. Eventually, he'd opened up enough to divulge his future writing plans.

Kihara had felt that they shouldn't publicly reveal that the true culprit behind the serial abduction and murder was Niimura and not Kashiwada. Despite having gone to great lengths to gather materials, Kihara had no intention of turning his research into a nonfiction title. The impact on society would be too great if people learned that the real killer not only had been found after an execution was carried out, but that he had then taken his own life. Plus, all the events that occurred twenty-five years earlier relating to *Ring* would have to be revealed. Reopening that can of worms would merely prompt needless fear, and nothing good would come of it.

"Instead," Kihara had prefaced his intention to try his hand at something new, "I'm thinking of this as a chance to start writing a novel. I've wanted to for a long time."

Originally having aspired to become a novelist, Kihara believed that taking the fiction route would solve the problem. He'd shown real enthusiasm for tackling a new form.

He had even told them of his idea to make it into a trilogy, with Takanori and Niimura serving as models for the first and second volumes.

There were still many mysteries surrounding Hiroyuki Niimura. He had died without offering up whatever his real purpose was in abducting and killing the girls.

Now Kihara was researching how Niimura had grown up, interviewing his friends and acquaintances.

For his own part, Takanori had drawn up plans to make a cheerful, fantastical musical-style film featuring an abundance of CG technology. He was working out the scenario now.

Everybody was moving forward in his or her own way.

It was just fifty yards to the school gate. Almost all of the students were running because the chime signaling the start of classes was about to go off. Nevertheless, there were students right behind Akane who were taking their time and chatting. The voices of two girls sounded so near that they seemed to cling to Akane's back.

She didn't recognize their voices, but they were surely students at the school.

They seemed to be having fun discussing some sort of rumor.

"Don't you think it's weird?"

"What is?"

"I mean, it doesn't sound scary."

"No way! Of course it's scary."

"Okay, so let's take a look."

"No, don't. I'm sure you'll regret it."

"Regret it? How come? It's just a video, right?"

"Like I said, there's a creepy rumor."

"If it's not a brutal scene or anything, it'll be all right."

"That's exactly the trap. You know, like how people say that every rose has its thorn."

"What's that? You just made me want to watch it even more."

"Okay, but don't blame me after you watch it."

"I'm not gonna bother you, so just tell me how to watch it."

"Just enter 'S' and search for videos. You'll see a lot of them."

"Then we can play together forever, right?"

"Yeah, we're not gonna get bored for a good while."

The two girls sounded so joyful somehow.

Stopping in front of the gate, Akane took advantage of the chance to turn left and looked around. The girls had seemed to be right behind her, but they were nowhere to be seen.

Flanked by trees, the road for the bus route stretched straight ahead. The girls' vigorous laughter shook the leaves and glided over the trunks and rolled away toward the train running on the elevated tracks.

From past where their laughter receded came the subtle scent of autumn.

S

Passing through the gate as if nothing had happened, Akane walked along the flowerbed toward the classroom where her students were waiting.

ABOUT THE AUTHOR

Koji Suzuki was born in 1957 in Hamamatsu, southwest of Tokyo. He attended Keio University where he majored in French. After graduating he held numerous odd jobs including teaching college-prep courses. A self-described jock, he holds a first-class yachting license and has also made a motorbike trip across the U.S. from Key West to Los Angeles. The father of two daughters, he has written a number of books on childrearing, having become quite the expert in his days as a struggling writer and househusband.

In 1990, his first full-length work, *Paradise*, won the Japanese Fantasy Novel Award and launched his career as a fiction writer. *Ring*, written with a baby on his lap, catapulted him to notoriety, and its multimillion-selling sequels *Spiral* and *Loop* cemented his reputation as a world-class talent. Often called the "Stephen King of Japan," Suzuki has played a crucial role in establishing mainstream credentials for horror novels in his country. *S: Es* was his tenth work to appear in English.